Both Sides of

There's more than one path to paradise.

Tim Toterhi

Book Design by Stephannie Beman of Ruis Publishing, stephanniebeman.com
Cover photos courtesy of Ben Goode and G00b dreamstime.com
Broken Glass Font Type courtesy of JLH Fonts

Pop – Thanks for being the kind of man I long to become.

Both Sides of

BROKEN

CHAPTER 1

The CD player in Jonathan's leased Volvo skipped as he hit another rain-filled pothole. He cursed the car, the hole, and then himself for ever agreeing to meet his younger brothers.

What a pair they were. Lazy. Stupid. And as useless as his old man wasting away in that luxury geezer motel. He could almost smell his inheritance burning. "Miserable bastard," he muttered. "Can't even croak on time."

He gunned the engine and blew through a stop sign, deciding that the only people who would be driving in this neighborhood, at this hour, would be in stolen cars or selling crack. He had insurance. "Screw them if they can't take a joke."

The engine lurched, then gasped as Jonathan downshifted

mercilessly from fourth to second in an attempt to avoid the speed bump at the entrance to his brothers' garage. He failed, and the car popped from the ground and skidded sideways to a stop.

Disgusted, he left the smoking vehicle and walked up the drive towards the office. He glanced at the faded sign clanking in the night air. It had once read "Sam & Windy's Gas & Garage." He almost laughed. The twins hadn't fixed anything of value in weeks, and the only gas came from the overconsumption of beer and Mexican takeout. It seemed the sign had sensed the change and faded accordingly. It now read "Sam & Windy's rage."

Jonathan pulled back a flimsy screen door and entered the office. He surveyed piles of dusty folders and crumpled food containers.

"Nice. You two ever heard of a broom?"

Sam looked up from his racing form, nodded hello, and returned to his reading. Windy flashed a mustard-yellow grin and motioned for Jonathan to sit down. "Want a drink?" he asked through a thick cough.

Jonathan shook his head and watched his brother's trembling hand pour three fingers of scotch into a dirty coffee mug. He looked worse than usual: weak, thin, so gray it appeared as though his blood had been sucked out and replaced with formaldehyde. He'd been sick for years but the last few months had been particularly harsh. "Off the wagon?"

Windy looked puzzled. "Hell, I ain't never been on."

"What about you, Sam?" asked Jonathan. "I thought you gave up the ponies when Mom died. Can't even give her that much, huh?"

Sam dropped the paper to his lap and grinned. "Like you're perfect, slick. I hear you fucked up things down at Brustman & Harding's pretty good."

"So you read the papers now? Surprise, surprise. At least I had a job to lose. What do you have? A family you never see, and a business you and this jag-off here ran into the ground. Every parent's dream."

"You're behind the times. She's an ex-wife, Jonny. Filed the papers Friday."

The news surprised Jonathan. Norah had threatened divorce constantly. She had even called him for both personal and legal advice on occasion, but he never thought she would actually see it through. Norah was an Irish Catholic with immigrant parents and a nun for a sister. If the guilt didn't kill her, the family would.

When she had first phoned him, Jonathan relished the idea of dragging his brother through court. She had been his lifelong friend and Sam had all but abused her physically. But now, faced with the reality of the situation, he couldn't help but pity his brother. He'd been through the mill recently and the taste of the split still soured his expression.

"Sorry," said Jonathan, trying his best to mean it.

"Like hell you are. You couldn't care less if you tried." Sam tossed the form towards a rusted metal desk. It toppled a pile of unopened bills. "Pour me some of that scotch, Windy."

The two men toasted his divorce and quickly refilled their glasses. Jonathan got the feeling that Windy knew less about Sam's marital problems than he did, but any excuse to drink was welcome. The only thing that amazed Jonathan more than Windy's callousness was the fact that he continued to breathe.

His drinking should have killed him long ago. Jonathan drifted. He remembered sneaking into his father's liquor cabinet. The brothers took turns nipping at various bottles, while their friend Tommy kept watch. By the third sip Jonathan and Sam were green and fighting for the bathroom, but the taste never bothered Windy. He just called them babies as they puked. Then he took another slug just to prove he wasn't faking. A natural at twelve.

"Look, boys," Jonathan said, "much as I love these get-togethers, I'm afraid I have to take off. I'm an out-of-work lawyer now, with a lousy rep and no friends. The pavement is calling and I've gotta fight the crowd."

"Good luck," said Sam.

"What's that crack about?"

"Face it," said Windy. "You're screwed. That kid you defended raped and butchered seven girls—college girls who lived in that little city. What kind of a coldhearted bastard could argue for someone like him?"

"I get paid to be a bastard. Just like Dad did."

"Not anymore," said Sam. "They dumped your ass as soon as the case made the national press. Gotta love that loyalty, huh, Jonny-boy?"

"Dad would have never taken the case," said Windy.

"Oh yeah, he was a real saint," said Jonathan.

"Well, he wouldn't have bashed the victim's parents like you did. What the hell kinda defense strategy was that?"

"The only one we had. He pleaded not guilty and I had to go with his word. My job was to get the kid off by any means necessary. I hung the jury. Dad would have been proud."

"Of course. Especially when that news reporter made your

client cry. She got in four minutes what none of you retards could get in four months. He spilled it on CNN and made you look like a royal screw-up. Dad woulda puked."

He knew Windy was wrong in assuming too much from too little, but he wasn't in a fighting mood. He tried to turn the argument into a game he and Windy played during his law school days.

"Objection. Counsel is speculating," said Jonathan.

"Overruled."

Jonathan half-smiled despite himself. "You can't overrule me. You're opposing counsel."

Windy took another nip of scotch and slammed the cup to the desk. "Fine, I'll get Judge Sam to do it."

"Overruled," said Sam.

"Why?" asked Jonathan.

"Those were the facts as they would have happened."

"Oh, I see. Practicing a little psychic law, are you Windy?"

"He confessed, for Christ's sake. They should have his head on a platter."

"No dice. The confession was inadmissible. The verdict was reached, the case adjourned, and double jeopardy trumps your cries of foul play."

"That's bullshit."

"That's the law."

"Same thing. Dad was never that way."

Jonathan waved a hand in the air. "Oh, get over it already. The guy was a scumbag. He hit us, ignored Mom, and dismissed anyone who suggested he was an addict. The only thing he lived for was Jack Daniels, cash, and the courtroom. He would have tried the case in a heartbeat, only he would have won and kept the kid from the cameras. He wasn't much of a man, but he was a damn good lawyer. I'll give him that. Why can't you see him for what he was?"

"You mean is," said Windy.

Sam smiled broadly. "Just look at us. Are we his kids or what? Three pricks in a pod."

"I didn't come here to argue," said Jonathan "Happy drinking, boys. Throw one back for me."

"Wait, Jon," said Windy, hopping from the desk with surprising agility. "We've got problems."

Jonathan pushed toward his younger brother, driving a finger into his sunken chest. "*We* don't have shit," he said. "There is no *we*. Not anymore. Isn't that right, Sam?"

Sam glanced at the floor, then the clock. "I'm not talking to this smug asshole."

"The hell you're not. Tell 'im Sam. Tell 'im what you told me."

"Forget it. Go. Get the hell out of here." Sam brushed Jonathan away like lint from a suit and rose to refill his glass. "I'm fine."

"And I'm the one in denial? You gotta talk to him, Jon."

"What's so urgent that you call me here at two o'clock in the friggin' morning?"

Sam sighed and rubbed his eyes. He hated having to crawl, especially to his older brother. It would never be forgiven, never forgotten."I'm in a bit of a bind."

"How much?" asked Jonathan.

"Seventy-five."

"Hundred?"

"Thousand."

"What? How the hell could a nothing like you run up that much of a tab? Nice joke, boys, but I'm not in the mood."

Jonathan turned to leave but Windy was already there. "Listen to him, Jon. Things are bad all around. We have to stick together."

"Like you stuck by me during the trial?"

The twins fell silent. There was no arguing that point. Neither of them had offered so much as a phone call after things turned ugly. His first big case had gone sour with the turn of a phrase. He was too green to handle what it became, but that didn't shield him when the shit began to fall. They left him alone—everyone did. Jonathan would take that to the bank, and the grave.

Moments past as the three men fixated on the clanking door. What a waste it was to live such lives, to be such men. How did they get this way? Three brothers, inseparable in youth, now filled with disgust for each other and contempt for a father they once admired. It was as if they were all lying in that hospital bed with him, just waiting to die. Or perhaps more accurately, failing to live.

Escape. It was all they had left, all they desired. But they wanted to escape themselves, and that, as many discover, is impossible.

"It wasn't my money," said Sam at last.

"I'm listening."

"I was running numbers for Franky out of the restaurant. You'd be surprised how much cash he takes in. I was skimming from the top here and there as usual, nothing too much. I suspected he knew and let it slide. In his line everyone steals. I was just another expense."

"And then?"

"Then I started borrowing big time. Sometimes I took from the back office, now and then I hit the registers, but mostly I lifted from the numbers and the bookie cash. The tips I got from the boys down on Union Avenue usually paid off. I replaced what I took from my winnings. And if I lost, I covered it by borrowing from Donato."

"Donato knew what you were up to and still lent you money?"

"He didn't actually know for sure know, but the guy's smart. He suspected. Anyway, it wasn't that much at first. Besides, you know him. If ever the day came that I couldn't pay, he'd cover his ass by ratting me out to Franky. Then he'd score some real points by offering to whack me as a personal favor. He's a real prince."

"So what happened?" asked Jonathan.

"I took the spread on the Steelers game. Who knew they could suck so much after last year. Lost to an expansion team, for Christ's sake. The fuckers. I lost it all this morning."

"The whole seventy-five today?"

"Yeah. Ah, you know, plus my usual five."

"Eighty? You're into him for eighty? Are you nuts?"

"Apparently so," said Sam with a smile.

"Yeah, this is real funny, jag-off," said Windy, throwing his hands up to a God he had long since forgotten.

"And now what?"

"I need money, Jonny. Big time. Sunday's a big day for Franky. The only good thing is that he doesn't know yet. He won't find out until tomorrow morning, when they tally the receipts."

"Talk to him. Talk to him now. It's the only way."

"Get real. The action on the game was hot. He's expecting a good take. You gotta understand, Jonny, I'm not just responsible for the eighty. I took that money from bets made against mine. Franky is gonna have to cover their winnings out of his own pocket. That's intense cash."

"How much?"

"Can't say for sure, but based on what I collected alone, I think we're talking like two-fifty. Maybe three."

Jonathan sank into his chair. There was no way he could raise that kind of money. Sure he had the condo, but he was already upside-down and two mortgages deep. He almost laughed. It had never occurred to him before how little he was worth. All these years of patting himself on the back. College. Law school. Private pilot's license. Even the old man was impressed with that one. But here and now his accomplishments didn't mean squat. His net worth was donut, and he still owed about a buck forty in student loans.

"Sammy, I can't swing that much. Not by a long shot."

"Dad can," said Sam.

"With the hospital meter ticking away? Be serious. I'd be surprised if he even had that much to begin with. Not that he would ever give it to you."

"He might," said Windy, ducking from the icy glances that followed his comment. "I'm serious. Maybe if we wait a little longer. Who knows? Anything is better than . . . than."

"Than what?" asked Jonathan.

"You know," said Sam, taking a slug of scotch.

"Funny."

"Jonny, Franky is gonna kill me when he finds out. There is

no question about that. If I don't come up with the cash in a hurry I'm dead."

"So you'd kill Pop?"

"Not me . . . us. I need you guys to help me pull it off."

"No fucking way."

"Jonny, it's me or him. Not a wonderful choice I know, but that's all I have, man."

"You see this?" asked Windy. "You hear this craziness? This is why I called you. He's lost it. He wants us to kill our own father."

"He's already dead," Sam said. "He just lies there like a piece a wood."

"A coma is not dead," said Windy.

"It is for him and you know it. Christ, it's been like two years. What, you think you're gonna drink him well? He's not waking up and he's not getting any worse. He's just existing out of spite. He should have died with Mom in the plane. Him and his stupid planes. God, it's just like him. Stubborn bastard. Why didn't he just *die*?"

Sam covered his eyes for a moment and then cleared his throat heavily. "I never liked him. I'm not gonna stand here and lie to you guys about that. But even he doesn't deserve to live this way. He wouldn't have wanted it."

"It's convenient for you to think of his welfare now," said Jonathan.

"We've been talking about it for months, big shot. Right, Windy?"

Windy stroked his three-day stubble and raised his glass. He took a sip and refused to swallow, as if the action would excuse him from having to speak. It didn't. His Adam's apple chased the liquor to his belly and it landed with a resounding thud. Slowly, his answer wrestled itself from his tongue.

"Yeah," he said.

"And you didn't tell me? Thanks again, boys."

"Oh, get off it. You're never even here. You don't see, you don't hear, and you don't know a goddamn thing about the situation. You'd get your share and be happy with the getting. We all know what's in the will: twenty-five percent each, with the rest going to old man Grayson."

"Who?"

"Pop's first flight instructor. But don't worry. The guy's in his early seventies at best and may not even remember the will. The good news is that if he kicks before Dad, we all get a third."

"Charming to the last," said Windy.

"How much is there?" asked Jonathan.

"I figure we'd clear a good three to four hundred apiece after taxes. You gotta take out legal fees and burial costs, but it's still a nice chunk a change. Franky would wait for the processing if you explain things to him. I'd even throw in an extra fifty grand to cover the hassle factor."

"That's big of you."

"Well, I'm that kinda guy."

"Of course, that would leave you with nothing?"

"Better than being dead."

"I guess. And you're sure about the numbers?"

"Searched his office myself."

"You went in there?"

"Christ, Jonny. We ain't kids no more. I can go where I wanna go. Besides, the will was just sitting there in the drawer by his .45. No lock, no foul. Right?"

"I guess."

"Guess nothing. The old man had more than we ever imagined. Way over a million, mostly in cash, and we lived like friggin' bums. Miserable bastard. The money is real, Jonny, and it's going to waste supporting a life nobody wants anymore."

"Jesus Christ," said Windy. "He's our father."

Sam leapt from his chair. "What? You want play martyr? You want to sugarcoat things? Well, fuck you, buddy. We're all screwed in our own way. Each of us would benefit if the old man died. So let him. Let's do this thing while there's something left to spend. Good riddance."

Jonathan reached for the bottle. He swirled the liquid and held it to his nose. He cleaned the top with his shirt cuff, licked his upper lip, and swallowed the remainder in a single gulp. Replacing the bottle on the desk, he looked toward Sam.

"You're not talking euthanasia, are you?"

"Takes too long and cost too much. Lawyers and liberals saw to that. There's no way we could get a plug-pulling in time to save my ass. We have to do it ourselves."

"That's murder," said Windy.

"Yeah. You can rationalize it down to mercy killing if you want, but we have too much to gain for it to be anything else. We'd be offing our father for money. It's that simple."

"What do you mean we?" asked Windy. "I have no reason to take part in this nonsense."

A tall, robust man in a dark tailored suit emerged from the shadows. Jonathan guessed sixty. A wicked scar mapped a trail down the jaw line from his left ear into his gray beard. He was tanned, polished, and remarkably relaxed for someone who had just overheard a murderous plot.

"I beg to differ, Mr. Holiday," said the stranger.

Suddenly, Jonathan was trembling. What if he's a friend of Pop's? What if he's a cop? He pushed the thoughts aside and stepped toward the man.

"What do you mean?" asked Windy, more concerned with the stranger's challenge than his appearance.

"You have more to lose than anyone, even your dear brother Samuel over there."

"What is he talking about?" asked Jonathan.

"Tell them, Jacob. That is your real name, is it not?"

"How did you . . . ?"

"Well I hardly think your parents would have named you Windy. So tell them, Jacob, about the status of your liver, your kidneys. Talk with them about the cost of transplants and dialysis, and the fact that without care you'd be lucky to last half a year. It should prove quite interesting."

"Is he for real?" asked Sam.

"In a manner of speaking," said the stranger.

He raised his ivory walking stick and admired the countless nicks and dents along its length. His smile made it clear that the instrument's purpose was not to help him amble about. He flipped it from end to end, spun it through his fingers, and halted it with a heel.

"You all have reasons for wanting your father dead. And you all will gain remarkably from his passing. Money, yes. But that is the least of what you seek. Freedom from addiction, a chance to live, a new career. In short, new lives and beginnings for you all. But to have them, you must allow the unthinkable to happen."

Sam bolted from his chair and darted towards the old man. He hated people to begin with, but those who got in his business without invitation were simply asking for trouble. He threw a punch—Jonathan was sure of it—but the only thing that landed was Sam's ass on the floor. "Who are you?" asked Jonathan.

"The name's MacLoughlin. I'm here to help you fellows."

"Sammy-boy would argue that point."

"Drunken men are best left to their chairs," said MacLoughlin. "Gentleman, it would be impossible for any of you to be directly involved with your father's demise. Even if only one does the killing, you would all run a tremendous risk. Given your record of loyalty, if one was captured, all would fall. No, you will need alibis, and I have the best one possible."

"And that is?" asked Sam, wiping blood from his mouth.

"Simply, my good fellow, that you were never there."

"So who's gonna kill him. You?"

"Look, whoever you are, we're not killing my father," Windy interjected.

"That's admirable given your condition, Jacob, but it's hardly truthful. Lie to yourself if you wish, but you are only one vote of three. In the end, you brothers must stick together. Ironic: only in the planning of your father's death do you bring him the happiness he sought all his life. His sons together. What a simple request."

"Nothing's ever simple, buddy," said Sam with a sneer.

MacLoughlin ignored the comment. He turned to Jonathan. "I assume you are the leader?"

Jonathan gave a cautious nod.

"Good. So with Samuel at yes and Jacob no, it's up to you to cast the deciding vote. Shall I kill the old boy or not? Tell me quick, as time grows short for your siblings."

Jonathan sat in silence. It was easier to accept the stranger's existence and uncanny ability to know things that should not have been known than to admit to himself that the next word he uttered would decide the fate of the man he called Dad.

"Tough, isn't it?" said MacLoughlin. "It's all on you, Jonathan. But it doesn't have to be."

Jonathan's expression turned curious.

"I propose a game of chance. That way, your father's fate will not rest with you, but with the cards."

He unbuttoned his jacket and removed an unopened deck. Ripping off the cellophane, he shuffled and laid the cards, face-down, on the desk.

"I'm a sporting gent, so here's my proposal. I'll play a game of high card with Jonathan. If I win, I'll dispose of your problem and collect one hundred thousand dollars for the trouble. If Jonathan wins, I'll pay off that Mr. Franky and see about getting Jacob to a qualified physician."

"And what does Jonny get out of it?" asked Sam.

"Either way he gets his dream, his freedom. You don't think he ever really wanted to be a lawyer, do you?"

The twins looked at Jonathan with surprise.

"Jon?" asked Windy.

"Never mind, Jacob," the man said. "You know what I mean, don't you, Jonathan? Here's your chance to live the dream. Just pick a card."

Jonathan offered a glance that told all in the room that his personal desires would not be discussed. What he chose, he chose. It was his business, his fault, his fate. And until he could figure a way to live otherwise, he'd rather play the part of the Bronx kid who made good; than not. He would never speak of regret. He couldn't. He was thinking now, trying to decide. He had always hoped that if ever faced with a moral decision, he would do the admirable thing. The trouble is, he wasn't an admirable man. He realized his true nature the moment he drew the card.

CHAPTER 2

Jonathan's eyes reddened as he piloted his Volvo through the remains of a subsiding storm. The cool October rain, now barely misting the windshield, was too slow to warrant the pounding wipers and with each pass a sharp grating sound pierced his brain. He clicked them to a halt and watched helplessly as tiny dots landed, splintering the glow of passing streetlights. His eyes, already squinting into the dawn, watered further.

He'd been driving for over an hour. Nowhere in particular. Just moving about the neighborhood in endless circles. He tried to focus, but his thoughts fled to the dash, through the vents, and into an air less troubled by sins past.

His straining, bloated veins pulsated rhythmically along the back of his hands only to be turned away by white knuckles dotting the top of the steering wheel. His fingers began to ache, but he held firm, wanting to feel the pain, to feel anything at all. But he was numb.

"A six," he said to himself. "Of all the cards to choose." MacLoughlin had picked a seven.

His father would soon die. The crippled life of a man he detested would be cut short by a ruthless, charismatic stranger, and it was his doing. All at once the weight of responsibility descended upon him like a hammer on an ant. It was almost too large to feel. Almost.

He screamed and pounded the steering wheel, but there was no one to hear, to care, to help, to notice. The game was a mistake and somehow he would have to break the deal. No matter the cost to himself or his brothers, he could not allow MacLoughlin to carry out the sentence.

Jonathan whipped the car around giving little thought to the lone pedestrian he sent scurrying back to the curb. The man cursed as his packages flew, but Jonathan was already rehearsing his speech. His discourse shattered when the fleshy pink of his fingertips alternated in time with the pulsing blue of a patrolman's lights.

"Goddamn it!"

He thought about stopping, unpacking his tale to the officer, but he couldn't. It was too wild and he'd been drinking; not a lot, but enough to divest himself of all credibility, if not warrant his detainment. The only certainty was that MacLoughlin would succeed while he wasted the night away in jail.

"It would make for a great alibi," Jonathan whispered to

himself. "No. It ends here."

Jonathan tore down the street, ignoring the officer's loudspeaker. Sirens roared. The two cars bolted past residential streets towards a deserted service road. Jonathan knew the layout well and was sure that if he could make it to I-95, he could take advantage of what appeared to be an old cruiser. Once he got to the Hutch, any exit he could reach would surely disorient a city cop.

He shifted from fourth to fifth and beamed as the officer faded into the recesses of the rearview mirror. When his eyes returned to the road, he saw an approaching semi.

Jonathan slammed the brakes to the floor, teeth grinding, tires smoking, arms straining to turn the wheel farther than the manufacturers had intended. Too little, too late. The Volvo spun helplessly into, under, and almost completely through the undercarriage of the truck. So much for the world's safest automobile.

The officer approached, and heroically helped the truck driver get out of the burning wreckage. The two men looked towards the Volvo's flaming carcass for any sign of the driver. There was nothing left.

CHAPTER 3

Jonathan massaged the sleep from his lids as he slowly began to regain consciousness. He blinked rapidly, trying to focus, and nearly stumbled into a pudgy bald fellow standing directly in front of him.

"Where am I?" he asked.

The bald man regarded Jonathan curiously, and shrugged. "Not sure. Where did you wish to go?"

Suddenly Jonathan remembered the accident. The truck, the fire, even the pungent smell of his burning flesh. A shiver danced across his spine as he relived the agony.

"Am I dead?"

"Do you wish to be?" asked the man.

He tapped a young woman standing next to him and

smirked in Jonathan's direction. She rolled her eyes and twirled an index finger about her temple. At this moment Jonathan couldn't decide if she meant him, the bald man, or the conversation itself.

"Where am I?" Jonathan repeated, as much to himself as anyone else.

He looked around the room. The space was gigantic, dwarfing any sporting arena he had ever visited. The walls appeared blank, though from this distance, he could not be certain. There were no clocks, no exits, and no readily apparent reason for him being there. He searched the room for signs or instructions, but his efforts were less helpful than the plump fellow who now ignored him completely.

"This is insane."

Leaving his place in line, he began walking towards the northernmost wall. He figured that since all these morons were facing that direction, there must be something or someone to see. *Nobody waits for nothing*, he thought.

His walk became a trot, then a full-out sprint. Still nothing. Breathless, panting, he turned back to the line and noticed the bald man still watching him.

"Monotonous, isn't it?" he asked.

Jonathan nodded, smiled, then punched the man square in the mouth.

"Knocked him on his ass, huh? Not the best way to make friends, you know."

"Friends?" asked Jonathan, turning to identify yet another strange voice. He had no intention of staying long enough to get acquainted with anyone.

"Sure. We all need 'em now and then. But not like him.

Never liked the guy. Pompous jerk."

The stranger stood, wiping the grease from a tool. His coveralls, which were ruffled like an accordion about the circumference of his work boots, failed to conceal a grimy undershirt. Jonathan found himself wishing it did.

"I tell ya, someone gave that guy a fancy degree and told him he could rule the world with a power tie and some snappy shoes. And he believed it! Moron. Probably a doctor, or worse yet, a law jockey."

"Umm. I'm, ah . . . I mean, I was an attorney."

"Wait a minute. You're not Sam Flannel?"

"No."

He removed a crumpled wad of paper from his pants pocket, smoothed it along the base of his chest, and read silently.

"Says here you're that deli clerk from Newark. You know, cuttin' provolone, yakkin' away with the old lady in apartment 3B. Ring a bell?"

"Not at all. I'm Jonathan, Jonathan Holiday."

"Well, don't I feel like a horse's ass. Sorry, partner. It figures. The front office ain't what it was, let me tell ya."

"You don't say."

"Besides, I'm just trying to relate to the customers. You understand? But what am I apologizing for? We're gonna be fast friends, you and me. The name's Grimis."

He held out a pasty white hand. Clumps of coarse blond hair sprouted haphazardly like crab grass in a Floridian's front yard from his wrist to shoulder, giving way here and there to an occasional scar and a menacing tattoo just above his elbow.

"Where did you pick that up?"

"The screamin' eagle? The war. Got it in the war. All the boys got 'em over there. Hell of a time. She's a beauty, ain't she?"

"Look buddy," Jonathan said. "I need to get out of here."

"No problem, Jonny boy. Just as soon as you settle up with the clerk. Hey, I gotta run see the Boss. I'll be back before you finish here. We got business, you and me."

Grimis smiled as handsomely as an ugly man could and trotted towards the back of the room.

"Where am I?" Jonathan called after him.

"You sure you wanna know?"

Jonathan nodded eagerly, and watched as a devilish smile pole-vaulted to Grimis' face. He pointed upward and to the left, then melted into the crowd.

Jonathan recognized the three bold letters, but for some reason his brain wouldn't accept the answer it provided. There had been nothing on the wall a moment before, and now this, of all things. How could he have missed it? How could he be here?

Denial failed him sooner than he hoped it would. A moment later, his mind confirmed what his eyes saw.

"The South Side Department of Motor Vehicles?" Jonathan asked aloud.

He fainted straight away and a fat man with a bruised lip giggled cautiously.

CHAPTER 4

Sam looked over the rows of empty chairs laid out before his brother's closed casket. He knew the wake wouldn't attract much of a crowd, but he had expected more people than flowers—most of which were plastic and on loan from the funeral home.

He'd be the first to admit that Jonathan was a quick-tempered, stubborn pain in the ass. But this was frightening. He tried to picture his own death. How would it happen? When would it happen? Would anyone even notice his passing? A shiver sliced down his lower back.

If this was all Jonny got, he thought, *Windy would be best advised to save the cash and just toss me off a bridge wrapped in a garbage bag.*

Both Sides of Broken

The brothers had reluctantly agreed to a one-day service. They simply could not afford to spring for the traditional three-day, five-session affair. Windy protested as always, but after seeing the morning crowd his guilt subsided. The way things were shaping up the longer session would have been too painful and embarrassing for anyone to bear.So instead of the deluxe package that Mr. Feathermore described, the twins opted for the base model deal, something just above being tossed over a rowboat in a wooden crate.

Sam stood solemnly in the back of the room. The last visitor had left an hour ago. He hated wakes. People lie to you all your life and when you die, they bullshit you some more. Gaudy flowers, dim lighting, the painfully rehearsed condolences of the director and staff. What a load of crap. He couldn't take another stupid question from another stupid bitch who couldn't have given two shits about the guy when he was alive.

An old woman entered the room with labored steps. "Are you one of the brothers?" she asked.

"Who you looking for?"

The old lady pointed to a whiteboard with Jonathan's name printed in black marker and underlined in red. He'd been there all day and hadn't noticed. How incredibly tacky.

"No," lied Sam. "Just a friend."

"Oh, I'm sorry. It's just that I was hoping to meet them."

"They should be back in a few. Just went over to the store. You can stay a while if you want."

"Can't. I'm on layover en route to London. My first time, you know. I had a direct flight, but when I heard the news I decided to change planes."

"Where from?"

"Fresno."

"That's a bit outta the way, huh? Must have cost a bundle to make the change. "

"Yes, but worth it I think."

"Why? I mean . . ."

"I know what you mean. I was a teacher of Jonathan's. Oh, I think it was sixth, no eighth, yes, eighth grade. I'm sure of it now. He was such a good boy. Always smiling, talking up a storm. Full of dreams, that one."

"Jonathan Holiday? Lady, you sure you got the right room?"

"Yes," she said, smiling away his surprise. "I was hoping to hear what became of him. Grade-school teachers are lucky if we find out whether our students went to college. Once in a while it's nice to see if you made a difference. You understand?"

"I guess," said Sam with a smirk. "Go to many funerals, do ya?"

Her smiled faltered, but she recovered quickly and scolded him with a glance.

"Sorry," said Sam.

"Don't be. It must be tough."

"What?"

"Losing a brother."

"Lady, I told you I'm just a friend."

"Son, my walk has slowed, not my noodle. You must be little Sammy. I had a brother named Sammy. Oh, he was such a talker."

"I go by Sam now. How do you know me, anyhow? Who

are you?"

"Relax, Sammy," she said through a giggle. "You act as if you've seen a ghost. Norah Ann called me. She was such a dear. Sent me Christmas cards every year."

"Wonderful. I bet they're just great."

"I'm sorry I wasn't being completely truthful when I said I needed to find out about his life. But you should treat old ladies with more respect. You deserved a little scare. And despite what you think, my smirky fellow, I *was* Jonathan's teacher. I'm Miss Madison."

She pulled a faded yellow paper from her purse and handed it to Sam.

"What's this?"

"Did Jonathan ever tell you he had detention? I couldn't believe it when he failed to turn in his poetry assignment. He was such a good student. In fact, I almost let him get away with it, but he just wouldn't admit he had forgotten. You should have seen him. He swore to high heaven that he had brought the paper to school. So I decided to punish him. And gave him a week of detention."

"Pretty stiff."

"I'm feisty."

"I bet."

"But I'm not always right. The next morning, while I was sweeping out the coatroom, I found his paper. This paper. I was so ashamed, first for not believing him, but also for failing to apologize when I found out I was wrong. I tossed it in my desk and never said a word. The poor boy suffered all the while in silence."

"Tragic."

"I see you've never had my detention."

"So why is this so important now? Why did you come all this way?"

"I'm not here for him. I came because of what the poem says. I know about your problems, Sammy. About Jonathan's and Jacob's. I took a shine to that boy. The way he handled the punishment, so much like a man, when still such a boy. I watched him grow up, grow old, and, though it pained me, I watched him fall apart. I know it seems strange—some crazy old woman coming here like this, nothing better to do. But it's not that way at all. I just wanted someone to have this."

"So what am I supposed to do with the thing?"

"Read it. Read it when you're ready."

"Yeah. Sure, sure," said Sam, stuffing the paper into his slacks. "I'll do that. You have a nice trip."

She frowned and walked towards the door. Windy and Norah entered and graciously held it open for her. She paused and turned to Sam.

"Promise me," she said.

Sam nodded and brushed her away.

"Who was that?" asked Windy, who seemed sober for once.

"Just some old lady who went to the wrong wake. Forget her. I already did."

"True to form," said Norah.

"You had to bring the bitch back with ya, huh?" Sam asked. "What, the morning show wasn't enough for ya?"

"We met in the parking lot, for Christ's sake. She took the day off for Jon. You know that. Tell 'im, Norah."

"Look, Sam, we promised to be civil," said Norah. "When

28

it's over we can get divorced and hate each other's guts, but for right now I would appreciate you leaving me the hell alone."

She bumped past Sam, walked to Jonathan's coffin, and knelt in prayer.

"Give her a break," said Windy. "She's taking this harder than anyone. No offense, but it's like they were the ones who were married. By the way, did his ex ever show?"

"Julie? Yeah. She stopped by for a full five minutes while you and miss 'take half of what I've ever owned' over there were off goofing around. It turns out she had some kinda meeting in the city this morning. Convenient, huh? She popped in, dropped off those flowers, and then it was right back to Boston and that asshole doctor of hers. She didn't even kneel at the coffin. What a trooper she turned out to be, huh? Jonny can really pick 'em.

"Hey, did I tell you how much I hate being cooped up in this place?"

"You made the rules," said Windy. "I took care of the paperwork and you played host. That was the deal."

"Yeah, well, this little party is costing us big bucks, right?"

"Not more than three, maybe a little less if we go cheap on the service at the site. But I wouldn't worry about the money."

"What, are you crazy? I knew you couldn't go the day without taking a slug. What's the matter with you?"

"Nothing. I'm serious. Norah said she'd cover it. She's even gonna do the eulogy if that's all right with us."

Sam looked at Norah, still crouched over the coffin. He had always been jealous of the friendship Jonathan had with his wife. They were the same age, went to school together, and even dated once, or so he suspected. There was a history between them, one that he could never hope to duplicate. And while he may have succeeded in stealing her attention, her body, her hand, he never managed to reach her soul. She had given that to Jonathan years before.

"There's no way I'm letting her pay."

"We don't really have much of a choice."

"I thought we could cover it."

"The flowers, maybe. We just don't have the cash we figured."

"How?"

"What do you mean how? We haven't even seen a car in two weeks. A job came in this morning, but I had to tell him to come back Thursday."

"Thursday? Are you nuts? We need every dime. You should have done the work."

"Sam?"

"Forget it. Forget it. What's the word on the street?"

"Franky knows, but we figured he would by now. I'm surprised he hasn't paid you a visit yet."

"That's not his style. He's probably heard about Jonathan. He won't come here. Jonathan did him too many favors to have me whacked at his wake."

"True."

"What about Pop?"

"Well that's what I wanted to tell ya."

The twins fell silent as Norah approached.

"What about your father? Has anything changed?"

"No, no," said Windy. "We were just thinking we should pay him a visit, right, Sam?

"Yeah."

"That's nice."

Her eyes were puffed as if she'd been stung a dozen times.

Windy handed her a box of tissues that some thoughtful attendant had placed by the nearly empty guest book.

"Look, we're just about done here," Windy said. "Sam and I can take care of things. Why don't you go home and rest a while? We'll see you at the funeral."

Sam looked at her. "About the money," he said.

"Forget it. I told Windy I was taking care of things and I will."

Sam nearly argued out of habit, but stifled the urge. "I just wanted to say thank you."

She looked at him in surprise. Mouthing a soft "you're welcome," she hugged Windy and left.

"Wow. That was nice of ya."

"Forget it," said Sam. "We got bigger problems to deal with than who pays for Jonny's box. Now, you were gonna tell me about Dad."

The funeral staff noticed the empty room and, with a quick nod from Sam, began clearing the arrangements from the tables. Two men. One trip. Except for the body, they were ready for the next contestant. There wasn't much to clean.

Windy snatched the guest book and a handful of mints from the side table, and walked with Sam to the front exit.

"Five signatures. That's all he got. He lived thirty-three years and all he got was five signatures. Wait. You never signed. That's six, but still."

"Pop, Windy. We were talking about Pop."

"Oh yeah. Well, there's not much to tell."

"What do you mean? Is it done or not?"

"Well, there was nothing in the paper or on the local news. I checked the messages at the garage three times. Nothing. I didn't want to go to the hospital—too spooky, you know? Maybe this guy MacLoughlin was full of crap."

"Could be," said Sam, "but I don't think so. Something must have happened."

"So where to? You can't exactly go home the way things are."

"If Franky wanted me, he'd have me by now. No. Something is going on. I just wish I knew the full damage. With any luck, it's not as bad as I thought."

"If it's any of *our* luck you'll owe him twice as much as we figured."

They walked into the evening, past a row of barren parking spaces marked reserved, to Sam's 1998 Honda. It was uncharacteristically warm for October and every weatherperson in the Northeast was singing the praises of El Niño.

"Shit. I can't believe someone gave me a ticket."

"Huh?" asked Windy, looking up from the street.

"A ticket. I can't friggin' believe it. My brother dies. My wife, who probably never loved me, is filing for divorce after almost ten years. I owe a quarter million to a wannabe Mafia asshole. Paid professionals are without a doubt looking to bury a few slugs in my head. And to top it off, I get a fucking parking ticket."

"I don't think it's a ticket," said Windy as he approached the car. "It looks more like a note."

CHAPTER 5

Jonathan had lost track of the bald man. He assumed the sniffling fool was somewhere near the front of the line by now, but it was difficult to estimate the exact position because he had no idea how long he'd been unconscious or when exactly he had awakened. In this place, it seemed, things ran together. It was difficult to keep focused on anything or anyone for very long.

He was part of a line, a thing. His existence, once destructively independent, entwined itself now with thousands of others. Every so often he tried to remember what a person was, a singular being. He wondered what it was like to be distinct, different, to have meaning of one's own. But there was no meaning in the line. Everyone stood perfectly still, surrounded by featureless walls brushed lazily in a mellow tan. There was not a face to be seen from his position, just the backs of a multitude of unidentified heads, which quickly filtered down to the one directly in front of him. He wondered what kind of person it belonged to back on Earth. Then he didn't.

He could have lessened his suffering in an instant. Simply turning around would have produced a million faces to view and dream about, but it was pointless. They all wore the same blank expression. They were one with the suffering, and so was he. He couldn't figure out exactly when or why he had given up.

With the bald man gone, he found himself standing behind a tiny head covered carelessly with short blonde hair. He assumed it was another man, but it might just as easily have been a woman.

Jonathan sighed. He immediately felt guilty for the lapse and began breathing in time with the others. Inhale. Hold. Exhale. Millions at once, breathing endlessly. To an outsider, the sound would have been deafening, but to those who contributed to its existence, it went unheard.At one time, ages ago or so it seemed, Jonathan had prayed for a clock. It never came. He reduced his request to a calendar, then a church bell, anything to keep him sane, to assure him that, despite his lot, at least somewhere, for someone, time was happening. But there was no time here in the line, at least none to be counted.

Shortly after he had given up on estimating the moments invested, there appeared a large stack of numbered posters hanging on the left wall. At first it was a blessing, something to see. Jonathan rejoiced and longed to thank someone. He tried to remember the name of the God his Sunday school teacher had talked about, but couldn't. It was just as well, for he soon discovered the cruel reality of the gift.

The first sign was labeled "one." It stood for a while, then fell to the ground, revealing another poster labeled "two." Counting in his head, Jonathan tried desperately to assign some measurement to them, but soon discovered they fell at random. Some plopped off in seconds while others, he guessed, took weeks to fall. Soon the posters themselves turned to tan and faded from view. If he concentrated long enough he could still make them out. The current count was 7,347, not that it mattered much.

At one point he considered suicide, but there were no means by which he could accomplish this goal. His pockets were as barren as the room. Then it occurred to him: he was already dead. He raised his head. What he saw almost caused him to faint a second time. He was next. He was actually next in line! He began beaming like a maniac, and wanted to kiss someone.

The head of short blonde hair standing in front of Jonathan, it turned out, belonged to a rather attractive young woman. She turned from the window carrying a stack of forms and folders. Jonathan considered fulfilling his urge with her, but was too eager to meet with the clerk. Finally he would have some answers.

"Hey, how are you?" Jonathan joyously asked the portly woman in a dark green uniform. She reminded him of a pool table, only rounder, with fewer pockets and more teeth.

"I have to say, I've never been happier to see a woman in my life. You got a hell of a line back there."

She peered sternly over the top of her thick black-rimmed bifocals. It became clear to him that she wasn't one of those jolly fat people you read about in Christmas stories. He noticed the bars lining the window of her cubicle. Was there really something to steal in there?

"And you are?" she asked.

"Jonathan. Jonathan Holiday."

"Well, Mr. Holiday, do you see that line there?" she asked, pointing to the floor behind him.

Jonathan scanned the red tape laid haphazardly about the tile. He sensed her anger increasing. The conversation wasn't going as planned. Not at all.

"Yeah," he said.

"Well then, perhaps you can tell me what are you doing on my side of the tape?"

Jonathan fought back a stutter and quickly shut up.

"Step back, mister, or there'll be trouble and plenty of it."

He stepped hurriedly back over the line and stood with shoulders back and eyes forward like a freshmen military cadet trying to impress a senior.

"Better," she said. "You don't move until I say 'next.' That's your cue to step over my line. Got it? Oh, and another thing, you ever pull that 'nice to meet ya' nonsense with me again and I'll have you brought up on sexual harassment charges, buddy. This is a one-man woman you're looking at and I don't appreciate being courted. Try it again and I'll sic my Marvin on ya. Understand me, bucko?"

"Marvin?"

"My significant other," she said. A schoolgirl's smile retreated behind her chiseled features.

Both Sides of Broken

Jonathan's confusion turned to amusement at the thought anyone engaging in sexual relations with this large-lipped, cellulite beast. His fake coughing trick didn't work and soon he was laughing like a maniac, right in her face.

The clerk realized she was the butt of his joke and retaliated. Jonathan's heart almost stopped when a metal panel guarding her window came crashing down. She was gone. A sign affixed to the outside read "out to lunch," but in this place, lunch could take years. He almost sobbed.

* * *

The gate rose eventually, of course, but not before Jonathan had time to develop a new strategy for handling the woman. He would be polite, but professional. And he wouldn't look at her for more than two seconds at a time. Assuming such a subservient posture made his skin crawl, but he'd do anything to get off the line. Well, almost anything.

"Next."

Jonathan steadied himself and crossed the line. The fact that he didn't know why he'd been waiting all this time didn't seem to matter anymore.

"Name?"

Jonathan swallowed his disgust.

"Name?" she asked again.

"Jonathan Holiday."

He proceeded to supply the teller with a list of earthly information, including his social security number, birth date, and political affiliation. He even answered the optional questions concerning food and music preferences, but it did little to strengthen his relationship with the woman.

"Purpose?"

The question sounded simple enough, but it stumped Jonathan. He'd been on a roll, answering questions skillfully, quickly. Not once had he stuttered or disturbed the robotic ticking motion of her pencil as it moved down her form. She had to pause to erase a misplaced checkmark, but a broken pencil could hardly be blamed on him. No. This was a deliberate trick, a surprise essay on a multiple-choice exam. Jonathan was flustered, but quickly reverted to his old law-school tricks. He began to bullshit.

"My purpose here is no different from the purpose of any other man or woman in this line. I seek only to provide you, the teller, with my personal information and obscure consumer preferences so that your forms may appear complete and tidy, but without any hint of anal retentiveness. Yes, my purpose is a simple one, but one that—"

"Yes, yes, Mr. Holiday. I think I see the problem here."

"Really? So you know what I have to do to get out of here? Not that it isn't a lovely place to work, mind you."

"Yes I do," she said, coldly feeding his stack of completed documents into a shredder. "You need to try a teller in a line over there to the right."

"What? Why the hell didn't anyone tell me where I was supposed to stand when I got here? I don't even know why I'm here, for Christ's sake."

"I'm not qualified to help you with your philosophical uncertainties, Mr. Holiday. The administration has determined, through a series of laboratory tests and analyses, that people are the best judges of which processing line they should frequent. Any predetermination regarding order or class would infringe heavily on the individual's right to choose his or her own purpose and outcome. That is something we simply do not do at the South Side Department of Motor Vehicles."

"That's insane. What the hell kinda of system is that?"

"Mr. Holiday, you're obviously a Republican driver. Your mock attempt at political correctness made that perfectly clear. If you had claimed to be a politically independent motorist, for example, I might have been able to let your attitude slide, but we simply cannot process your application on the far left line. Many of our major contributors would be outraged. You belong somewhere in the middle over there, if not on the far right."

"Can't you at least be more specific?"

"That's not in my job description. If you're already a registered driver and your license is free of warrants and violations—other than parking tickets, of course—you can schedule an appointment with one of our political driving consultants. They can advise you as to the most appropriate position, but it'll cost you. Between you and me, I think they don't know more than the average Joe. My advice is to start at the far right and try lines until one clicks for you."

"Until one clicks for me? There's gotta be a hundred lines here."

"Oh there's plenty more than that."

Jonathan released a primal shriek and reached through the bars. He longed to snap her flabby neck, if only to stifle her smugness. She leaned back in her chair and watched in amusement as his straining fingers danced inches from her throat.

"You can't reach through the gate, Mr. Holiday. Skinnier ones have tried and failed. Besides, harming me just means another few dozen forms and that won't get you out of here any sooner, now will it?"

"She's right, Jonathan," said a concerned-looking Grimis. "I think it's time you and I had a little talk."

"Grimis? Just let me kill her first."

"Ah, she's dead, Jonathan. Remember?"

He had forgotten again.

"Let's go."

Grimis passed his bleached arm through the air and the two men vanished. The teller shook her head in disgust and slammed down the gate. A frown formed on the face of the redheaded woman who had been standing behind Jonathan. This time the sign read, "In therapy. Back when cured."

CHAPTER 6

Sam yanked the note from Windy's hand and quickly devoured its contents.

"Son of a bitch!"

"What? What's the matter?"

Sam dropped the paper and mashed it into the dirt with his shoe. He was almost shaking with hostility. Windy had seen him like this before. It usually involved some wise-ass customer who figured he could get off without paying. They always figured wrong. Sam didn't look like much, but rub him wrong and he'd make damn sure you walked away with a bruise or two, even if he got the worst of things.

But there was something different about this look. It took Windy a moment, but he soon realized that his brother was

41

more frightened than angered. Things scared Sam like they scared everyone else, but he had a good way of hiding it. Windy hadn't seen that face since they were kids and the old man called them down for beatings.

"He called it off."

"The hit?"

"Yeah."

"Why?"

"Said it was too risky for us with Jonathan having just died. The cops would be all over the place. He'll wait a week or so for things to slow down, then he'll take care of him. Until then, it's up to us to handle Franky."

"He's not gonna wait a week."

"No shit."

"What are we gonna do?"

"Nothing we can do but take separate cars."

"What?"

"If Franky is half as pissed as I think, then I'm a dead man walking. I'd bet five to one I don't even make it home. If you're with me, they'll whack you for bonus points."

"Sam."

"Hang here for an hour, then take a cab to the garage. Act like you don't know shit about shampoo. It shouldn't be too hard. Who knows, maybe you can talk Mr. Feathermore into a two-for-one special."

Sam climbed into his Honda and started the motor.

"You got money for the cab?"

Windy didn't respond.

"Figures."

Sam removed a ten from his wallet and handed it through

the crack in the window. Windy reached for it, but he snapped it back.

"What am I doing? Here, take the fifty. It's not like I'm gonna need it."

"Thanks."

"Just remember to invent yourself an alibi for when MacLoughlin finally does the deed. And make sure someone can swear you were with them at the time. We don't want old man Grayson to wind up with all the loot."

Sam spun the tires on a patch of loose asphalt and made the quick right to the street without stopping. Windy watched him leave, wondering if it would be the last time he'd ever see his brother alive. He looked at the funeral home, then at the little bearded fellow staring back at him from the bill. He wondered why none of the faces on American currency wore a smile. Then he walked across the street to the liquor store. Health and sobriety were highly overrated.

CHAPTER 7

A large-breasted waitress filled their wineglasses for the third time. From his angle, Grimis could see the young coed had forgotten her bra again. Silly girls, how he loved them. His tongue, now only inches from her loosely buttoned blouse, dangled grotesquely over what remained of his linguine. He danced his eyebrows to gain Jonathan's attention and then dropped his fork on the floor. He winked knowingly and nodded towards her bottom. As she bent to retrieve the utensil, Grimis let out an embarrassingly orgasmic sigh. Jonathan wanted to call a cop.

Apparently unaware of having been victimized, the waitress smiled innocently and offered Grimis a clean fork. He declined, electing instead to wipe the old one on his sauce-covered overalls.

"Good as new," he said.

Seemingly impressed with his crude resourcefulness, she giggled like the moron she appeared and left for the kitchen.

"Ah, Ginger," said Grimis. "What a body!" He clamped another load of pasta between his soiled fork and soupspoon, raised it towards the heavens, then paused. "Buddy, you can travel high and low, far and wide, but of all the sights you'll see and all the things you'll do, nothing can ever compare or compete with a nice big set of jugs. Am I right or what?"

He tilted his head back and quickly jerked his hands to the far sides of his body, allowing the mound of food to fall the six inches to his face. His mouth was large enough to capture most of the pasta, but spillage ran down the sides of each cheek and stained the carpet below. He grabbed his wineglass and emptied it with a glug.

"Not hungry, Jonathan? I figured with the wait and all, you'd be starving by now. Personally, I'm always in the mood for a little food. It's like sex for your stomach. What the hell took you so long, anyway? I mean, three decades? I'll check with the Boss, but that's gotta be the longest on record."

Jonathan looked at him in disbelief. "Are you saying I was in that line for thirty years?"

"Give or take a few."

"Oh my God."

Jonathan crumpled in his seat. How could it have been so long? He felt his face frantically. He was sixty-three. Christ, he didn't feel that old, but who knows? Maybe it was gone. Half his life just gone, lost in a blink.

There was nothing left for him now. His father was dead, if

not by MacLoughlin's hand, then surely from old age. He had failed before he'd even begun. What's more, he'd never get to say he was sorry. And he was terribly sorry now. The line had made him realize so much about so many things.

"That's not the best saying to use around here."

"What?"

"You know, the 'G-word.' We try to avoid it as much as possible. The Boss, well, you can imagine how he feels about it."

"You mean I'm . . . I'm living . . ."

"On the South Side of town."

"So that's what they call it now?"

"Always have. But hey, look on the bright side. Time don't mean a damn thing here. You just gotta learn the ropes, kid. If you keep going on like you are, every time you go to the dry cleaners it will take a hundred years."

"So time hasn't passed?"

"Passed, forward, sideways. Who gives a flying fart? You're due south, kid. You can forget about that stuff now."

"But how? Why?"

"How's tricky. Haven't figured that one out myself yet. But *why* is a piece a cake. Things are like you want them to be. Understand me, boy? You want it to be thirty seconds instead of thirty years? Just think it so and it's done."

"You're crazy."

"Hey, I've been here a lot longer than most. I know a few things."

"So then technically I could go back to Earth and it will still be the day I left?"

"Hold on now. Inter-dimensional time travel isn't like

hopping a Greyhound for Ohio. You can't even pick up your processing forms from Marge without causing a scene."

"You know that troll?"

"Yup, for a few centuries now. She's not the prettiest thing, I know, but she makes a mean plate of fried calamari."

"Bullshit."

Jonathan folded his arms and slouched.

"Gonna pout? I'm serious. Me and Marge go way back. I even knock a few balls around with her boyfriend."

"Marvin?"

"Oh, you know him? Dumb as a stump, but the best golfer I've ever seen. I'd lay five to one against anyone from the Sticks or the North End, and twenty to one against any of those Earthly boneheads. No offense. Though you should really stop considering yourself one of them."

"But I have to get back there."

"Impossible."

"For me?"

"For anyone at your level. You can't even control your most basic surroundings. Maybe in a few thousand years, but by then the urge will have past. Always does. Nope. It's just not done. Relax, Jonathan. Try to enjoy yourself. Want an eclair?"

Grimis snapped his hairy fingers and a sterling silver dessert cart appeared. It was overflowing with pastries and chocolates that would make any high school cheerleader willingly develop bulimia. A brunette waitress, as wonderfully constructed as Ginger, accompanied the cart and began unloading piles of snacks onto Grimis' plate.

"Thank you, Candy my dear."

Besides the name and hair color, the only noticeable difference between Ginger and the new server was that Candy's skirt was considerably shorter. Jonathan had been in the line a long time, and though part of him wanted to forcibly screw her right there on the pastry cart, the other wanted to give Grimis a stiff punch in the mouth. She was nineteen, if a day.

"Jonathan, you gotta try these," said Grimis. He smacked Candy on the ass and sent her scurrying to the kitchen.

"How did you do that?"

Grimis flattened his palm and swung it back and forth at the elbow. "Well, it's a skill like anything else."

"The cart, Grimis."

"Oh. It was nothing. Wanna try?"

"I can't do that."

"Then I guess you won't."

"What, are you gonna send me a self-help videotape and a bill for $19.95? Sorry, but I left my wallet in the other life."

Grimis swallowed a chunk of raspberry tart and licked the cream from his lip. He studied Jonathan for a moment, then turned his attention to his coat. He removed a wad of crumpled paper and began smoothing it out.

"You know what I need?" said Grimis. "A clipboard. That would make my record-keeping a hell of a lot easier. You think you can rustle me up a clipboard, Jonathan?"

"Sure. I'll just run down to the stationery store. No problem. Or maybe I could just yank one right out of my ass."

Grimis was clearly disappointed. He looked to his notes and began reading quietly. "Suffers from low self-esteem. Holds little dear and less to be of value or importance. Never forgives. Runs from the arms of what he wants to the clutches of that which he loathes. Remains proudly angry at things he can't control and is sad when there is no real reason to be."

"What's that?" asked Jonathan.

"Just some notes I was keeping on a guest. I thought I'd go over them, since you're so set against learning anything."

"What? How to find clipboards? Forget it. I need to get back to Earth. You don't understand a goddamn thing. Oops. Sorry."

"Forget it. The Boss allows it in certain contexts."

"I see."

"Jonathan, you must realize that I do understand. I understand all too well, my friend."

A tone sounded and Grimis reached for his beeper. He took a last sip of wine, gathered his things, and stood. He started to leave, then turned back. He tapped the table and a clipboard fell to his hand. He held it up for Jonathan, then tossed it in the trash.

"But I thought you needed one," said Jonathan.

"I need the one *you'll* give me, when you finally believe you can."

Then he was gone. The waitress returned and asked Jonathan if he wanted more wine or coffee, but, for now at least, his cup was full.

CHAPTER 8

The night came and went without the expected fatality. As the twins listened to Norah describe her lost childhood companion, Windy began to wonder if Sam actually regretted not being in a grave next to his brother.

Sam's life sucked, always had. Sure, Windy was a worthless drunk with no real family, friends, or future; but at least he enjoyed his drinking. Sam didn't enjoy anything. He wouldn't let himself.

Windy turned his back to the grave for a moment and took a quick nip from a pocket flask. The burning liquid massaged his throat and slowly warmed his stomach. Sam was eyeing him as he turned back towards the casket, but Windy simply shrugged his look away.

To Windy, drinking was almost a religion, a deity who commanded his daily attention. Though demanding, the god was often kind and offered more in return for his devotion than any father he had ever known. So many people kill themselves paying homage to things they detest. Shit jobs, bad marriages, phony friends, none of them worth the ulcers they create. But not him. He wasn't exactly thrilled with his existence, but he came close to contentment, which was more than most could say. Screw people if they didn't understand.

Norah finished her eulogy and quietly walked away from the grave. She was crying again and for a moment Sam hated his brother for making her weep. He saw her suddenly as the girl Jonathan knew and realized she'd been a bitch to him out of self-defense. The way he acted, he left her little choice.

She wiped her eyes and, to Sam's surprise, hugged them both. It was their most intimate moment in months. She declined Windy's offer of coffee and climbed into her car. He made her promise to call if she needed anything. She nodded and disappeared down the dirt trail.

Half a dozen people who the twins had never met piled into their cars. Probably former coworkers of Jonathan's looking for an excuse to take the afternoon off. Bastards, they didn't even acknowledge the brothers.

Standing alone by the Honda, the twins watched as the casket was lowered into the earth. The groundskeepers wasted no time in filling in the hole. A rush job to the end.

"So sudden," said Windy.

"What?"

"I was just thinking. It goes so fast. Hours separating life from a box in the ground. Makes you think."

"About what?"

"Forget it, Sam. Forget it. You wanna go for that coffee now?"

"Why not?"

As they walked to their Honda, a lanky olive-skinned man in a casual outfit of loose-fitting cotton emerged from behind a nearby tree. He began cracking his bony fingers.

"God, I love funerals," he said. "So beautiful, what with the flowers and all. In fact, the only thing I like better than attending funerals is causing 'em."

"Hello Tony," said Sam.

"You know what I'm here for, I gather?"

"Wow, Franky sent you? Jeez, times must really be tough. Or did you just get some big gangster promotion I didn't hear about? Tell me, Tony, does the new job come with a health plan?"

Tony cut through a row of plots sharing a single stone marked "Finelle" and stood just inches from Sam. He was tall, nearly six-six, but built more like Gumby than a contract killer.

"Don't get smart. Otherwise . . ."

"Otherwise what?"

"Otherwise your brother here might get a little of your brains splattered on that nice suit of his. Where did ya get that bad boy, Windy, K-Mart or Sears?"

Windy thought seriously about cracking him over the head with his flask. He was close enough, but he hit like a girl and lacked the bravado to make himself believe otherwise. He backed off without a word.

"Fuck you, Tony. Leave him out of this."

Both Sides of Broken

Sam had known Tony since they were kids in the old neighborhood. They ran scams down on Arthur's Avenue, worked the lookout spot for Franky's shake-down men, and even fought together against rival gangs. But they were never really friends and the association stopped before high school ended. The Holiday boys escaped to Westchester when their father started making the big money. Tony's family accomplished nothing and stayed in the Bronx, as did most of the people with whom the twins kept company.

"Still the same Sam, trying too much too fast."

"Not my fault you're a fag. You could never handle things."

"And what those balls get you, big shot? Two years in a reformatory for boosting a fucking Toyota Corolla of all things. 'Oh what a feeling' Sammy boy. Man, if your Pop wasn't a law jockey, you'd be an ass puppet on Rikers Island by now."

"Funny."

"But that's not the best one. Windy, remember when we were kids and this asshole brother of yours got six months' community service for trying to steal the bingo money from that old folks home down on East Tremont? Talk about your moron capers. The thing was sponsored by the local PBA, for Christ's sake."

"I was nine. What did I know? I figured it would be an easy score, something to impress the boys with."

"Yeah, I'll say."

Tony closed his eyes for a moment. "I can still see it," he said. "Sammy here is working the concession stand with a couple of nuns when he decides to drop his muffins, grab a two-dollar cap gun, and yell 'Freeze!' About twenty cops, all of whom somehow managed to escape his sharp criminal eye, broke out laughing. They thought he was kidding."

"We know the story," said Sam.

"Oh, but it gets better," said Tony. "Some dumb rookie went over to give him a talkin' to and little Sammy asks in surprise, 'What's this? You guys are cops?' One of the older blues couldn't help himself. He yelled out, 'Bingo!' The friggin' room roared.

"I'll give you this, Sam, you sure talked yourself out of a beating that day. I thought your Pop was gonna kill you. I guess, looking back, the six months of afterschool labor wasn't so bad. They figured it would straighten you out, but you managed to screw them on that too, huh?"

"At least I did something," said Sam. "You talked all kinds of shit about how tough you were and how you were whacking people for your uncle Frank, when all you were really whacking was your pecker in the boys' room. Still got that picture of Annette Funichello in your bedroom closet? Call *me* fucked up? At least I don't get a rise out of a Mouseketeer."

Tony raised a fist and took a step towards Sam. Sam laughed at him and started dancing around like an idiot.

"Come on. Come on," said Sam, trying to imitate an old Saturday-morning cartoon character. "Put up your dukes. Put up your dukes."

Windy watched in amazement as his brother threw a couple a feigned punches at a smiling Tony. You had to love Sam. What a set of balls. Here he was about to get shot in the back of the head by a childhood friend and he was egging him on, almost daring him to pull the trigger.

Both Sides of Broken

"What the hell is going on?" asked Windy.

"Just your brother being an asshole. Nothing out of the ordinary."

Sam flattened his hands, put them on the sides of his head, and started waving back and forth like Dumbo trying to take off. He cleared his throat and began to sing.

"M-I-C-K-E-Y, why? Because we like you. M-O-U-S-E. You know Tony, as much as I bust 'em on you about the Mickey situation I do have to admit, she had a nice set of tits. Who knows, if I was a pervert like you and into old school teenage girls I might have thought about taking a crack at her myself."

"Sam. The guy's got a gun. A big one. Would you give it a rest?"

"Relax, Windy. He's not gonna pop me. Are you, you little mouse-mounter?"

Tony tensed, but he stayed silent. He raised his hand and motioned for another man to start the car.

"You see," said Sam, "we gotta go see Franky. Nothing is gonna happen to me until I explain what the hell happened to all that money. Then he'll kill me in what I imagine will be an entirely painful and most likely humiliating display of torture and mayhem. That's how these things work, right, Tony?"

Tony shook his head in disbelief.

"You were always nuts, but now you're completely gone. Airmail to the fucking loony bin. Checked out of hotel reality, never to return. You know, I really don't care what Franky does to you. I just hope he lets me watch, you arrogant son-of-bitch. What, you wanna show me what a tough guy you are?"

"No. I just don't wanna give a do-nothing asshole like you

the satisfaction."

"We'll see."

Sam started to walk towards the car. He paused for a second to look at Jonathan's grave. He shook his head. Jonathan got to do everything first. And knowing Franky's lack of originality, his death would probably be more creative. What an end to a lifetime of losing.

"See ya around, Windy."

"Oh no," said Tony. "The drunk is coming with us."

Windy looked up in fear. He thought about running, but his legs had turned to bags of sand. He tried to lift them, but suddenly felt woozy.

"He's not involved with this thing," said Sam. "He doesn't know anything about anything and you know he wouldn't say shit if he did. Not that anyone would listen to him. Let him go."

"Can't do that, my friend. Franky said to bring the brother."

Tony grabbed Windy's collar and pulled a .38 from his coat. He pressed the gun to Windy's neck and cocked back the hammer. Sam rushed towards his brother, but the thug by car heard the commotion and had already reached the scene. His gun, a Glock special, was drawn and pointed at Sam's back. Unable to speak, Windy signaled his arrival to Sam, but he knew. Tony never did anything without back up.

"So," said Tony, "you kids wanna go nice-nice, or should we blow a few holes in your legs? Franky didn't say nothing about wounding them, did he Jeff?"

"Jeff?" asked Sam. "Your uncle hired a hit-man named *Jeffrey*? What's your last name buddy, Rubenstein? Don't tell me, you became a hit man when you couldn't get pre-med at

Harvard. Am I right, Jeffrey, old boy? Or was it when your takeover of the film industry was halted by a guy named Joel Wisenheimer?"

Jeff strode up to Sam, raised his gun, and cracked him across the temple. Sam dropped like the bass in a rap song.

"Amusing fellow," said Jeff. "It's a bit of a ride back to the Bronx. If this one talks as much as the other clown I suggest you put him to sleep as well. I'm not in the mood for chatter today, Tony. I was up all night with the kids again."

Windy's eyes widened as he gulped down a mouthful of fear.

"I . . . ah . . . could be very quiet, you know. See? Look, I'm not saying a word. I mean, I am now because I'm telling you how I'm not gonna talk later, you know in the car and all, but I could shut up right now. See? I—"

The two killers were grinning despite themselves.

"Close your eyes," said Tony.

He did. And then there was black.

CHAPTER 9

Jonathan sat at the table for a long time. In the life before, he would have been up and gone before the coffee came. There was always a client meeting to attend or a paper to file. Certain as sunrise, someone, somewhere had an emergency that required legal assistance and he'd be the first vulture on the scene. Now there was only time, and from what Grimis said, even that was not of the essence anymore.

Ginger had long since returned with the check. The dinner rush was over and Jonathan watched as she and Candy moved from table to table refilling the saltshakers and adjusting the flower arrangements. He placed his Visa in the bill case and motioned for her to retrieve it. He left a generous cash tip on the table. He wasn't sure if people paid taxes on the South

Side, but he figured it was a safe bet.

He walked to the door, a little curious as to what was on the other side. It was the first time since his arrival that he traveled of his own free will. It was almost awkward, as if he didn't deserve the privilege.

Outside, he found himself on a boardwalk. He looked cautiously towards the railing, half-expecting a river of lava to rise up and engulf him, but the crisp ocean air filled his nostrils. His legs twisted themselves through the bottom bar and before he realized it, he was sitting with his arms wrapped about the cool metal railing. What a calming joy it was to watch the sea.

"Is this seat taken?"

Jonathan turned. It was a woman. She was tiny, no more than five-two, with shoulder-length blonde curls and eyes that rivaled the color of the water. He spotted a hint of crow's feet and guessed forty, but her stature and smile reminded him more of a Catholic schoolgirl than an older sister. She was innocent, beautiful, with the kind of unrehearsed elegance only sincerity could foster.

"Help yourself."

"Thank you. I'm Amber."

Jonathan took the hand she offered. It was pale and soft. He thought about kissing it, but it was difficult for someone from the Bronx to do that without seeming like a complete idiot. He let it go, and immediately wished he hadn't. What a fool he was for never falling in love. There weren't many opportunities for him on Earth, but there were a few, and he regretted ignoring them.

"That was quite a trick you pulled, Jonathan," she said.

"What do you mean?"

"The restaurant."

"I don't follow you."

"Show me your credit card."

Jonathan thought the request strange, but felt eager to please the woman. He reached into his back pocket, but there was no wallet to pull out. He panicked, quickly scanned the boardwalk, and began sifting through the pockets of his jacket.

"It's not there, is it?" asked Amber.

"I don't understand. I just had it. Maybe I left it inside. Excuse me for a second."

He stood and walked toward the restaurant.

Her voice stopped him. "It's not there either," she said.

"Well, I have to find it."

"Why?"

"Come on. Why do you think?"

Amber stood and quickly walked over to him. "Think, Jonathan. Where are you?"

He stared at her. Then he walked to a nearby bench and sat quietly with his eyes closed. He thought himself strange. For a man who all but muddled through a miserable Earthly existence he was certainly reluctant to leave it behind. Part of him wanted to pack it all in a case to be tossed over the railing, but he knew nothing of this new place and he wasn't learning anything. Besides, even if he somehow learned to enjoy it, he couldn't stay. His heart was filled with home and things left undone.

Amber met him at the bench and began rubbing his shoulders. She kissed him gently on the top of his head and sat beside him.

"It is a little strange, isn't it?" she asked. "That's the trouble with the South Side."

"What is?"

"Well, you're dead, so you can do anything you want. But they don't give you any instructions. No one ever says a thing."

"What do you mean you can do anything?"

"Consider your meal."

"Yeah?"

"Where do you think that credit card came from?"

Jonathan thought for a moment, then shrugged hopelessly.

"You made it," she said. "Scooped it right out of the air."

"No way."

"Then explain how it got there. And what about the cash for the tip?"

Jonathan lost himself in possibilities, but none fit. His pockets had been empty when he entered the restaurant. They had been empty when he thought about killing himself in the line. There was no explanation, but he couldn't accept that he was suddenly Presto-the-Magnificent.

"Don't feel bad, Jonathan. It takes people forever to accept that they can learn anything and even longer before they begin to understand the rules of responsibility that come with an After-Earth existence."

"See, this is what I don't get. I'm in the South Side, right?"

"Yes."

"Then how come I supposedly have all this freedom to learn and stuff."

"Your address is nothing compared to your outlook."

"Pretty, but I don't buy it. I mean, I landed in the DMV, of all places. What's with that?"

"You made it. You tell me."

Jonathan stood and began to pace. He spun abruptly on his heels.

"You're saying I made that entire room? All those people? That witch of a clerk? The fat obnoxious guy in line? I made it all and then put myself in the back of the wrong line and waited pointlessly for thirty years?"

"Well, almost. You didn't create the people. I don't really know how they came about."

"So who were they?"

"Regular folk who had roughly the same idea of death as you. You're not very creative, I'm guessing."

"So you're telling me that when people die they put themselves wherever, whenever, and in whatever situation they want?"

"Not exactly. You got the *what* part right, and you're about fifty-fifty on *where,* but there is no *when.* I thought Grimis explained that to you."

"You know him?"

Amber blushed. She looked at the ground and began pecking at the wooden planks with her shoe.

"No. You and Grimis?"

She straightened. "We're just friends," she said. "I mean, more like acquaintances. Friendly acquaintances, I guess. There's nothing going on."

"Oh, that's obvious."

Jonathan saw the topic was becoming unbearably difficult for her. Perhaps she was a jilted lover, still carrying a torch. It was hard to be sure of anything anymore and people were never his favorite sport.

"So you were saying about the *where*," said Jonathan. "I got it half right?"

"Yes. That's right. The *where* part. You can go anywhere on the South Side you want, but that's it."

"No Earth?"

"Of course not. But I was talking about the North End and the Sticks."

"The Sticks?"

"Forget it, Jonathan."

"Hey ho! Hey ho!"

They turned to see Grimis walking along the railing with arms outstretched. He quickened his pace, lost his balance, and began flailing from side to side. His knees buckled, and he toppled headfirst into the sea. Jonathan and Amber ran to the ledge, but Grimis was already climbing out, soaked to the bone and laughing like a fool.

"Dry," said Grimis, and in a moment he was.

Jonathan looked at Amber in amazement. She shrugged and mouthed "Showoff."

"Amber, you know you're not supposed to give the new arrivals any details about the After-Earth. If the Boss finds out, he's gonna be pretty pissed."

"Looks who's talking. You've stirred up more trouble around here than anyone in a thousand years. Should I tell Jonathan about your toga party?"

"Hey, people were bored. I've got a lot a folks to look after and every now and then you have to consider their mental health. It was a smash."

"Sure," said Amber. "The Boss was thrilled."

"He doesn't like parties?"

"Nope. Stiff as a board."

"Bite your tongue, mister. He's just a little upset about the incident."

"What incident?" asked Jonathan.

"Oh, get over it. That happened when, at the beginning of time? Some say it was for the best. You think those people in the North are any better off?"

"What incident?"

"Forget it, Jonathan. We have to go."

"Wait a minute. I want to know what's going on. Tell me what these places are and why I can't go home."

"Later. I promise."

Grimis put his hand on Amber's shoulder and walked her a few feet down the pier. Her knees buckled at his touch.

"See what you did? He's one of the most reluctantly deceased since Elvis. I finally start making some progress with the guy and you go and mention the North End."

"He has a right to know where he is and why he put himself here."

"And he will in time, but not now. Don't you understand? This guy won't shut up about going back to Earth."

"They all do that at first."

"He's different. Frankly, I think he may try to escape."

Amber laughed and daringly put her arm about his waist. "This isn't a cheesy prison-break movie. It's impossible."

"No it's not. He can do anything he wants, even leave. Granted, I haven't seen it done in a while, but it can happen."

"You're overreacting."

"Am I? He's already produced a physical object. That

usually takes people centuries."

"True, but you planted the seed. It's unlike you to take a shine to someone that way. I find it . . . I mean . . . ah, I think it's nice."

Grimis noticed his arm around her shoulder and quickly removed it. She wilted instantly.

"No," said Grimis. "There's something different with him. I feel it. He'll be flying within a month and teleporting in two."

"So let him meet the Boss," said Amber.

"Why would I wanna do that?"

"Because you know how he gets when someone wants to leave. He'll do his damnedest to prove that the South Side is a wonderful place to spend eternity."

"Are we talking about the same guy?"

"Of course. He'll send him on a wild quest through our world. By the time he returns, he'll have learned and done so much that his Earthly problems will have faded from view."

Grimis looked at Jonathan, trying to understand what such a bitter man could be so determined to do. Jonathan was watching the sea. A pelican appeared off the horizon. It flew towards the shore, scanning for food. It swooped to the waves, snatched up its prey, and flew off.

"Whatever we do, we should do it quick."

"Why?" asked Amber.

"Because he's better than I thought."

"You didn't make that bird?"

"Nope."

"Then you're right. It's time to start treating our friend here like the man he's becoming."

"Yup," said Grimis, still watching the bird. "And I think I'll pay a little more attention to him. At the rate he's going, I want to be on his good side when he gets there."

The two walked back toward Jonathan, proud of the talent they discovered.

"You want answers?" asked Grimis. "Then it's time I introduced you to someone."

He winked at Amber, took Jonathan by the arm, and disappeared. Amber stood alone on the pier. The pelican was gone, but she missed Grimis more. She closed her eyes and savored the wink. What a child she was to feel this way. Excited, frightened, thrilled at the possibility of no longer being alone. Perhaps she could gather the courage to tell him how she felt. The thought of a lover's touch brought a shiver to her neck.

CHAPTER 10

"Oh, you're going to college, buddy. There's no two ways about it."

"But I don't want to, Pop," said Sam.

"Since when?"

"Since forever. I told you a hundred times, but you don't listen."

"Angela, can you please explain to me what the hell your stupid son is talking about?"

"Thomas."

"Don't Thomas me. He knows we've have been planning and saving for this since before we were married. But does he care? Does he give a moment's thought to what is best for the family, his future, anything but what looks easiest now? Of course not. Do you have any idea what I'm talking about, Sammy?"

Seventeen-year-old Sam nodded across the dinner table to his father, but the look didn't register. The old man was deep within himself, searching for a single weekend not lost to work. None came to mind. He had spent a lifetime trying to get his family into a decent home, a safe neighborhood, and one by one his sons disappointed him. It was like their bodies had left the Bronx, but their minds and souls remained.

Mr. Holiday smashed his fist on the table, sending the spaghetti bowls flying. Angela jumped from her seat before the sauce even reached the tablecloth.

"Leave it," said Mr. Holiday.

"I just wanna get a quick sponge on there before it stains, or maybe some club soda."

"I said leave it."

Mr. Holiday pushed his half-empty plate away and began tapping the table with a clenched fist. He looked with disgust at the two unused places set for Jonathan and Windy. Dinner was the only time the family had together and there would be hell to pay for them missing the meal. The thought of two boys late made the lines about his eyes crinkle further. In the Holiday house, even studying was not an acceptable excuse. The tapping turned to light pounding. He noticed the noise and the look of concern on his wife's face, and held fast.

For a while now he had been losing his boys. He wasn't sure when it had started, or why. Maybe it had something to do with the hours he kept. Whatever the reason, he liked them less and less as the years passed. It scared him. His family was beginning to turn his stomach.

"You have no idea what I went through to get us here, do you, son?"

"I know exactly what you did. You and Mom worked like crazy to give us things. But you're never here to see them. I don't want that kinda life. Why can't you understand? You're okay with Windy not going to school. How come it's so different for me?"

"Because somewhere in that thick head of yours is a brain. But who knows, maybe I was wrong. Maybe you're a do-nothing like your brother."

"Honey, you know Jacob has dyslexia."

"My son? I don't think so. There's nothing wrong with him a good kick in the ass won't fix. I don't care what those doctors say."

"I don't want the money, not for school. Use it for yourself, or maybe to help out Jonathan."

"He gets nothing. He knows how I feel. Not a penny comes from this house as long as he's dating that Jew girl."

"What's wrong with her?" asked Sam.

"You know exactly what's wrong with her. Cheap bastards. They own everything. It was Jews who worked your grandfather to death in the butcher shop. And no son of mine is gonna bring a Jew into this house. Let them pay for his education."

Angela gathered a handful of dishes and disappeared to the kitchen.

"Whatever, Dad. Look, I want my own business. I hate working for other people. Besides, I got it figured. Franky said he'd let me work at the restaurant until I could start the garage. I make decent bucks there, enough to see it through. I mean,

I'm almost managing the place now, and that's good experience for when I go into business. It shouldn't take more than two years to save enough to buy out Mr. Ronaldi. He'll be looking to retire by then anyway. It's perfect."

"According to who? Franky?"

"And me."

"Well, that's just great then. Go ahead. Hang out with the criminals. Waste your life away in some grease pit down on Morris Park. What do I know about anything? I just bust my ass twelve hours a day to put food on the table."

"I know, Pop. You tell us all the time."

Mr. Holiday reached across the table and cracked Sam in the mouth. "Is that how you treat me after all I've done?"

A thin trail of blood trickled from his lip, but Sam never cried, never said a word. His father seized his shirt collar and shook him from the chair. He smacked him again with the back of his open hand.

"Answer me, boy. Is that how you treat me?"

Sam knew what he wanted to hear, but he wasn't going to give in. Not anymore. If Jonathan had the balls to go against the old man, then he sure as hell did.

Smack! Smack! Sam could hear his mother sobbing in the kitchen. There was a time when she would have challenged her husband, but that was before the pressures of the mortgage and the influence of the booze removed his inhibitions. Try it now and she'd wind up with a crack in the mouth herself. Judge Holiday had ruled long ago that a wrong word meant a beating, and no one was above the law.

Sam cursed his father as he carried out the sentence. But he never answered him and that just made the lashing last longer.

Both Sides of Broken

* * *

"Leave him alone," said Windy. "He can't even hear you, for Christ's sake."

"Yeah he can."

Tony's next blow shook Sam from the dream. He was almost happy to find himself bound to a chair in the basement of the restaurant. The pain was more vivid, but at least in this reality his father was old, helpless, and less of a man than he. The thought made him smile.

"Happy, Sam?" asked Tony.

Sam strained to open puffy eyes. Tony was standing over him, fist clenched, lust in his eyes. He hated happy people."Fuck you, you ugly bastard," said Sam, spitting blood-soaked saliva. His arms were stretched to the back of the chair and bound at the wrists with a nylon cord. He struggled to free himself but the restraint pierced his skin and sent a slice of hell dancing towards his shoulder. As he winced, Tony giggled.

"Feels good, huh, asshole?" asked Tony.

"Oh yeah. Like fucking your mom. Hey, how is that fat bitch? Still pulling lunchroom duty down at the school?"

Tony shook his head in amazement and looked at Jeffrey.

"Does this guy have some set of balls or what? I'll give you that, Sam. You sure are a stubborn son of a bitch. Pain just doesn't seem to bother you."

"Perhaps we'd get a rise out of him if we tortured his brother," Jeffrey said.

The blood in Windy's face dropped to his shoes. So far he

had been treated well. He wasn't tied and had been woken from his slumber by a bucket of ice water. But all good things die in the end, or so he assumed. He sank in his chair, trembling. Jeffrey pulled a knife from his belt and moved towards him.

"I think it's about time this one had a shave."

The blade inched towards Windy's scruffy cheek. He looked at Sam, knowing full well not a word would be uttered. Sam would let him die rather than lose face. His stony stare made that perfectly clear.

Windy could have fought back, but, as always, he froze. He closed his eyes and awaited his fate.

"Behave yourself, Jeffrey," said Franky from the top of the stairs.

Windy almost sobbed in delight.

"Put that away," Franky told Jeffrey. "He's not the reason we're here."

Windy squirmed as Jeffrey playfully tapped the blade against his chin. He stepped to the shadows, loving his life and savoring the taste of fear he aroused. Windy's eyelids were so taut they hurt. He began to fear he might never get them open.

"I see you boys had some fun," said Franky, admiring the abrasions on Sam's face and neck.

The two men grinned. It was clear they had picked the perfect profession.

Sam wondered what guys like Tony and Donato would do if there were no organized crime. What skills did they have? What could they contribute? He wasn't judging them. Even after their assault, his thoughts weren't clouded with anger. Sam understood their nature and accepted their ways. He was simply questioning their ability to survive in a peaceful environment. He doubted they could.

Luckily, that wasn't an issue. Loan sharks, hit men, pimps, hustlers, dealers, and hookers all came about as a result of consumer demand. There is a large segment of the population that is not only willing to pay exorbitant prices for these services, but is also willing to risk legal entanglements to acquire them. Can you imagine going through all that for a haircut or a loaf of bread? Sam didn't blame them. He blamed the world for making them a necessity, a coveted natural resource.

"All right," said Franky. "You two take the drunk upstairs and keep an eye on him. I want to have a word or two with my buddy here."

"Franky?" said Tony, a bit plaintively. If he wasn't going to perform the execution himself, he at least wanted to watch.

"I said go."

The two men gathered Windy and disappeared up the stairs. Franky paced the floor for a few moments as though uncertain what he had come to do. Sam had seen him work before. All his life he had been around Franky, but nothing had ever taken this long. He moved quickly for a fat man and made decisions even faster. Something was wrong, and for the first time Sam allowed a twinge of fear to creep under his skin.

Franky stopped suddenly, his back to Sam. He had yet to look him in the eye. He walked to the far wall and took a rusted saw from a metal clip. He turned, still looking at the floor, and walked towards Sam.

"You and I have a few problems to work out, correct?"

CHAPTER 11

Jonathan flicked through the pages of his sports magazine for the third time. They had been waiting well over forty minutes and had yet to draw the attention of the receptionist. It was maddening.

Grimis was snoring like a busted chainsaw in a chair at the opposite end of the waiting room. His posture took on that of a college student funneling a keg of beer at a frat party. Mouth opened, neck outstretched, head tilted so far Jonathan feared it might snap off. How could he be so relaxed? Was this not the Devil's waiting room?

Another twenty minutes passed. Jonathan longed for company. He called to Grimis, but the rumbling in his nose continued. Frustrated, Jonathan tore several pages from the magazine, crumpled them into balls, and began hurling them at his friend. A few bounced off his belly and chest, but didn't rouse the slob until a direct hit filled Grimis' mouth with an advertisement for a miracle fishing lure. Grimis began to gag like an asthmatic Darth Vader. He swallowed the ball in a labored gulp and shot into an upright position, eyes wider than a 747.

"What? What's happening?" asked Grimis.

"Nothing. That's the problem. We've been sitting here for over an hour, and I don't even think he knows we're here yet."

"Jonathan, you have to get a handle on this time thing."

Grimis snapped his fingers and the previously comatose receptionist sprang to life. She made a quick call, retrieved a document from her printer, and returned to her desk.

"Mr. Grimis and company?" she called to the all-but-empty room.

Jonathan rose joyfully. "Yes?"

"The Boss will see you now."

Grimis shrugged and spread his hands. "It's easy as pie."

"Then why can't I do it? Why do I have so much trouble with the simplest things?"

"Because you expect to fail. You expect to be kept waiting for hours. You expect situations to be difficult. But most of all, you expect people to be incompetent or completely obnoxious. I wish you would believe me and learn to believe in them."

"Maybe you're right," said Jonathan with a sigh. "But why do I think that way?"

"I can't answer that for you. Maybe it's because you think that's what you deserve. But I'm no shrink, buddy. All I know is that in this place nothing is impossible. If you expect something to happen, it does. Just don't expect crappy things. Hey, look, why don't you go on in ahead of me? I want to chat it up with Mrs. Big Boobs over there."

"Grimis?"

"Come on. Just five minutes. I'll see if she has a sister."

"I'm not going in there alone."

"Why?"

"Because it's the Devil, for Pete's sake."

"Oh, I almost forgot. Keep off the religion thing as best you can. And I wouldn't call him the Devil if I were you. He gets all offended. Thinks he got a bad rap. And stay away from anything cute like Toby or the Prince of Darkness. That really pisses him off. Just call him Boss. He loves that. Understand? Oh yeah, and if you wanna get on his good side mention the Buffalo Bills. He loves 'em. I'll see you in five."

"Grimis."

"I promise. Now scat."

Grimis snapped his fingers and Jonathan was teleported inside.

The dimly lit room was not at all what he had expected. It reminded him of a home office, or a war room in one of those trendy art companies down in the village. There was lots of space, but it was randomly employed. One corner was completely bare, another a disaster. It was as if certain areas were designated for thinking and others for doing.

Jonathan stood at the edge of the doing zone. A computer hummed on a littered desk. Surrounding it were bookshelves stuffed with legal reference guides and intergalactic business texts.

He surveyed the remaining two walls and briefly critiqued the artwork. To the right sat an outrageously fake Picasso so laughable in construction, it offended even his untrained eye. But the work bought him a reluctant smile for it seemed to somehow warm the room with a certain cozy reality only a cheap knock-off could provide. It was as predictable as an Elvis head lampshade in a red neck's trailer, but it belonged. Finally, in this insane place, something looked lived-in.

A toilet flushed. A door creaked open and footsteps followed, tapping on the hardwood floor. Jonathan kept his head lowered.

"You like that?" asked The Boss.

Jonathan froze, still staring at the Picasso. He suddenly remembered every hell story told to him by the nuns in Sunday school. Would rays come out of his eyes? Would he chew on his bones? Why wasn't he already burning in the eternal fires of brimstone and so forth?

"Hello?" said the Boss. "It's all right, you know. I'm not gonna bite your head off."

Jonathan hadn't considered that one. He closed his eyes and tried to think of something pleasant. Nothing came.

"The kid's in a daze," said the Boss to himself. "Let's stir things up a bit."

He clapped his hands. Jonathan levitated and began to spin. His speed increased with each rotation and he was soon hurtling about in a tight spiral. His tennis shoes, dangling an inch from the carpet, were a blur of white and blue. The laces came untied and began to trim the shag from the carpet.

"Excellent!" shouted the Boss. "I was getting tired of that look."

He levitated the furniture from the floor and began to move Jonathan around the room like a giant weed-whacker. To his surprise, Jonathan felt no pain. He was certain his brains were beginning to leak out his ears, but he refused to worry. He had never used drugs as a teenager, so he figured he had some cells to spare. For once he would just go with the flow.

When the carpet was properly trimmed, Jonathan began to slow. At first he didn't notice the reduction in speed, and when he finally stopped, he found himself running uncontrollably about the floor in the same direction. This worried him. It wasn't the monotony, but the fact that his cardiovascular conditioning wasn't what it used to be. If the movement didn't cease soon, he'd have a heart attack and die again. He really wasn't up for that this week.

"Um . . . excuse me, Mr. Boss, could you ah, you know—" Jonathan said.

The Boss politely suppressed his laughter and nodded in understanding. He whipped Jonathan about in the opposite direction until he felt the effects had been neutralized. This time, when the motion stopped, Jonathan projectile vomited on the Picasso and passed out. It wasn't pretty, not in the least.

Grimis entered, reveling in his apparent success with the receptionist. He looked at Jonathan, then to the wall.

"Nice painting."

"Hysterical as always," said the Boss.

"What happened?"

"Never mind. Why did you bring this one to me? You know I'm a busy man."

"Sure, things have really been hoppin' around here."

"Grimis."

"Relax. I'm only kidding. Jesus, buy a sense of humor, will ya? Now, about Jonathan here, we need to talk. Got any of that Swiss mocha around?"

"What about him?"

"Let him lie. He could use the rest. Man, for someone so talented he sure is high strung. You fart and he faints."

The two men walked towards a door that hadn't been there a moment before. It led through a brief hallway, which opened to a marvelously modern kitchen decked with the finest names in home appliances. The Boss refolded a half-read newspaper and pushed it to the side of his place setting. He walked to the stove and began heating the water. Grimis loved the way he still did the simple things by hand. The Boss had learned so much since his passing. His knowledge was as startling as his reputation was inaccurate. The gentleman whom so many had come to fear could instantly form valleys of greatness with rivers of thought. Yet, despite the talent, he had the patience to allow a simple kettle to do its job.

"Quite a set-up," said Grimis, motioning to the room.

"Designed it myself."

"And you're busy?"

The Boss sighed and nodded. The South Side hadn't been busy since the blood lust of the Crusades. Occupancy was down. Guests were constantly complaining about the outdated facilities. And many new arrivals were trying their damnedest to escape. What he needed was an old-fashioned moral crisis, complete with false idol worship and maybe a cult or two. He'd take anything if it would convince people that they deserved to go to the South Side. Once there, he could show them the truth. A little evil now for a lot of good later. He hated the reality of the lie, but there was no other way.

"I don't know what to do, Grimis. The bills are piling up. I haven't turned a profit in centuries. It's looking pretty bleak."

"I figured something was up. You haven't been this depressed since the 1970s."

"Don't remind me. What a decade. There was so much nothing going on, I'm surprised people had the decency to die at all."

"Yes those were the wimpy years. But you got through them. Even then, when the worst thing people did was invent disco, you had a plan to attract guests. You're a creative guy. Give yourself some credit."

"Bell bottoms, Grimis. I tried to convince people that bell bottoms and John Travolta were my way of saying boogie your butt on down to eternal damnation."

"It was a strategy."

"It was stupid. Inadvertently trying to damn an entire branch of the U.S. military? Come on. Even I can admit when I go overboard . . . ew, sorry about the pun."

"So you forgot about sailor's pants. So what?"

"I got one murderous gang and two Christian kids who felt terrible after accepting a joint at a party. Nine people a decade does not a business make."

"We need a new plan."

"No shit, Sherlock. Think it up."

The kettle whistled and the Boss rose to fetch a pair of mugs. He prepared the mocha and brought it to the table. It was deeply stained picnic-style oak with long benches and an intricately carved base. Grimis began sipping his drink, thinking more of his uncle's health than the problem at hand.

He seemed to be aging. In a place where people could look, live, and feel as they pleased, this man was wet burlap, molding in the icy dew of a fall shower. Like the car keys of the inattentive, his hope had been misplaced.

Despite the recent aging, however, the Boss was still a handsome man. He dressed like a bond trader in the eighties. His suit was a gorgeous double-breasted number. His shoes were shined to a mirror gloss that caused Grimis to wonder whether they would allow the wearer to see up the dresses of his coworkers. But even the wardrobe couldn't hide his defeated expression. For the first time, Grimis noticed the awful red in his eyes.

How must it be for him to watch the world he had created shatter before his eyes? Alcoholics know, but not like this, not when the place provides shelter for so many. His failed venture would pain a great number of people. Rumors aside, that wasn't why he went into business. The guilt was overcoming him.

"Well, I suppose you want me to let him go," said the Boss.

"Jonathan?"

"Yes. That's why you're here?"

"Well . . ."

"Save it." The Boss pulled a pen and paper from his jacket and laid it flat on the table. "I've got a transfer form right here. There's no use fighting it any more. We lost. I guess the Big Guy was right. You can't have three eternal life spots."

"Bite your tongue. This is your dream you're talking about. Remember why you started it in the first place?"

The Boss shrugged. "It's an idea whose time has come and gone. Now, should I make the transfer out to the North End or the Sticks?"

"He wants to go back to Earth."

"Earth! Are you mad?"

"He says he has some unfinished business there."

"They all have unfinished business. The only way they wouldn't is if they instituted an age limit on mortal life and threw each other deathday parties. I can't authorize an Earth pass. It's just not done."

"Come on, you've signed them before."

"Yeah, but that was when business was booming and I had some clout. I do it now and the Big Guy will chew me a new one. If he hates it here so much, I'll let him go, but I can't send him home. If he wants Earth he'll have to talk to the Big Guy."

"So let him."

"Why not? But I tell ya, I really think he'll be happier here, and that's no sales pitch. The North End isn't what it's cracked up to be."

"That's it!" cried Grimis, jumping from his chair.

"What?"

"I've got a plan that will save the business."

"Well?"

"Well, the answer is right there on the table."

"The paper? You know we can't afford advertising anymore."

"No. I'm talking the kind of press you can't buy. I say we let Jonathan go everywhere. The hot spots here. The North End. Even the Sticks. And when he finishes his quest we make him write a review for the *After-Earth Tribune*."

"That's brilliant. He could compare the three like they do

new cars in those automotive magazines."

"Exactly."

"But wait. What if he doesn't like us best?"

"Doesn't matter. The exposure alone will get people talking. Studies show that the thoughts of the dead directly affect the thoughts of the living. We change the attitudes of people here and we'll draw crowds from our competition. Then we can tackle the Earth's recently deceased."

"Right. Right. We have to make people think about the South Side again. Goddamned atheists, they're killing business for everyone. When did the common man get so much balls as to not believe in anything?"

"Who knows? Things are tough down there."

"True, but then they always were. Get moving on that article idea."

Grimis stood and headed for the door.

"But wait," said the Boss. "Jonathan's one of us. Nobody would think him impartial."

"They would if we published his dated transfer form with the story."

"Right. And if he comes back to us, we've got it made. That's a hell of an idea, Grimis. Just one question. Why would he agree to do it?"

"Simple. We cut him a deal. He does this for us and we'll see about getting him an Earth pass. It's a square deal."

"But we can't swing that. It's lying."

"And that's a problem for you?"

"Grimis."

"Sorry. That was a cheap shot. Look, I like the guy. He's a real learner with excellent potential. But he's only got thirty-five years of After-Earth experience, most of which was spent on line at the DMV. He couldn't possibly understand the importance of what we are trying to do. I say we take care of him and feed him information as we think he can handle it. Boss, he's really cooking, already created two objects. It won't be long before we can fill him in on the plan. Don't worry about it."

Grimis threw the rest of the mocha down his throat. He rubbed the back of his hand across his mouth, ignoring the cloth napkin laid out beside the cup.

"I'll go wake Jonathan and tell him the good news."

"You better pack a bag first."

"Why?"

"Cause you're going with him."

"But Boss, I got a date on Friday. Saturday and Sunday too, but Friday's a big one: the Nardoni twins."

"Cancel."

"But—"

"This was your idea. I want you to take care of Jonathan. We may not be able to give him what he wants directly, but maybe we can open a few doors for him. Either way, we may end up owing him more than either one of us realizes."

"How do you mean?"

"I'm not certain yet. But I think you're right. There's something about him that stands out. I just can't put my finger on it."

Grimis again found the door that hadn't been there a moment before and reached for the knob. He thought it strange that it never appeared in the same location twice. He blamed it on his uncle's eccentricity. But who could fault him? Perhaps once you've designed an eternal After-Earth complex capable of housing an infinite number of people, you return to enjoying the little things. Maybe that was why he did his own cooking. Whatever the reason, he thought it charming. And Grimis was a man who was not easily charmed.

"Wait a sec," called the Boss.

Grimis turned from the door to find his uncle neatly drying the mugs with a dishtowel.

"What is it that has Jonathan so intent on returning to Earth?"

"Never asked. But I get the feeling he wouldn't tell me if I did."

"Probably not. Good luck."

The door snapped shut behind Grimis. The Boss sat at the table and dropped his head to his hands. Then he slept.

CHAPTER 12

The coolest thing about believing in multiple lifetimes is that it enables you to handle your demise. If the faith is true, one's death is met with little fear and, in some cases, a certain eager anticipation as to what lies ahead. Believers often equate their pre-death feelings to the emotions experienced during the time between high school graduation and life in the college dorms. In both cases rumors provide a general sense as to how life will be once you leave the familiar, but you never know for certain until you arrive.

Sam wasn't sure when he had become a believer. He tried every now and again, but couldn't remember reading about such ideas or seeing them on television. Lord knows he wasn't taught to think freely in Sunday school. He just always had a sense that the philosophy was true. Progressing though an eternal existence, lifetime after lifetime seemed to make sense. You kept at the chore of living until you fixed all the mistakes, and then, when everything appeared perfect, you discovered new problems to be solved. It seemed peaceful in a time when so little was. And such an idea was more appealing to a man with his sins than the final judgment and damnation he was assured of under his father's faith. Perhaps that's why he never flinched when threatened. Maybe it explained his ability to look Franky in the eye now, even as he felt the rusted saw upon his neck.

"Why?" asked Franky.

Sam stayed silent, sensing the question was more for Franky than himself.

"How could you take so much from me? Me, the person who had given you things your entire life?"

The pressure from the blade tormented Sam's skin, but not nearly as much as the monologue. Franky never talked in these situations. He was a capable but reluctant killer. He rarely did jobs himself and when circumstances forced such a task upon him, he liked to get it over as quickly as possible. Murder is a tricky business. In the movies you can be creative, give speeches, reveal your plans for world domination, but in the real life of local Mafia, hits are simple, systematic, and rare. The fact that he was talking meant this one was none of the above.

"Who was your father? That lawyer in New Rochelle? I don't think so. It's me. The man who raised you in this restaurant, brought you up in the business, and paid for your wedding."

Franky dropped the saw and turned his back to Sam. He sighed at the weight of the loss. The money was part of it, but only a small part. Most of what he felt concerned the stinging sensation you receive when a trusted friend cracks you across the cheek. The sting is not from the knuckles, but from shock and the simple disappointment of having misjudged someone's character.

"Franky," said Sam in the most sensitive voice he could muster.

"We're so much alike, you and me," said Franky. "But I raised you, so I guess I shouldn't be too surprised. Hell, it's almost funny."

Sam looked inquisitively at Franky. His head was bowed, his shoulders rounded, and his breathing was shallow. Franky was lost to the world, dancing a solitary waltz. The music, the partner, the dusty old ballroom deep in the heart of the Catskill Mountains were just memories now. Faded ones that would soon be lost altogether. Age was a bigger villain than he, Franky was certain of that. Christ, barely sixty-five and already he was losing bits of his most treasured years.

His eyes strained, attempting to finish the dance, but his eighteenth year had been long ago. Nothing remained of that peaceful time. His brothers lost to war, his father lost to scotch, and his mother, that tiny giant whose reputation became his inspiration, lost to cancer before he even learned to speak. They were all gone. He lived the lonely life of a single fat man who pretended all he was and lost all he could have been.

"Franky?" said Sam again.

Some spirit in Franky's world lifted the needle and the

music stopped. He aged forty years in the moment it took to raise his head. He missed the thin happy boy he had been, and God, how he missed the dance.

"I can't fault you for what you did," said Franky.

"No?"

"No."

Franky untied Sam and invited him to sit at a flimsy card table. Franky set up two glasses, flipped the top off a wooden crate, and pulled out a bottle of red.

"A drink?"

"Sure." Sam would ask no questions, at least not right away.

Franky poured the wine and toasted the old times. Sam winced as the acid stung his bruised lip.

"Sorry about the pummeling. Tony gets out of hand. But, I couldn't have it out that I let people get away with fucking me outta two million."

"*How* much?"

"Relax, it's not all your fault. Don't get me wrong, your stunt didn't help matters much, but I can't blame you for something I did myself."

"You took the spread on the game too?"

"Yup. You believe that? Same game. Same bet. They say great minds think alike. Well, I guess that works for assholes too. I'm responsible for at least half that number, probably more. And believe me, the people who will be knocking on my door will make Tony look like a nun."

"So what now?"

"Shit if I know. Got any cash?"

"Are you kidding?"

"Well, then I guess we're all dead. Me, you, anyone we know. Lucky we're both single. Norah's out of the picture, right?"

"Yeah."

"Good. You never brought her around so she should be safe. Windy and Tony, on the other hand, better watch their asses. Two million is a lot of money in this town."

"Franky, I'm sorry. I really am."

"Save it. You fucked up. Royally, but it was just a fuck-up. You were never into the money, never wild. Sure, you dabbled in the ponies, but it wasn't like they said. I know you, son. You evaluated risk and took the shot, just like I taught you."

"But we lost."

"That we did, and now we gotta pay."

Franky removed a crumpled paper from his pants pocket and handed it to Sam. The note was clear. The unidentified party wanted the money in twenty-four hours or people would start to die. They had specific folks in mind and Franky's nephew would be the first to go.

"They don't know about you yet, but it won't take them long to find out. They got money so everyone is singing. I'd love to be able to shield you from this thing, but I can't take the heat alone. It's gonna have to rain on you too."

"I know."

"I figured you'd step up sooner or later. Sorry I can't play martyr, but those are the rules. You play, you pay."

"So what's the plan?"

Franky topped up their glasses. "I can raise about five hundred grand in the time required. Maybe that will buy us a week."

Both Sides of Broken

"Then what?"

"Then it's up to you. I might be able to come up with another hundred or so if I call in a few favors, but that's about it. What's the chances of you coming up with a million five?"

Sam laughed out loud. They were dead men talking. That's why Franky didn't kill Sam right off, that's why he was allowing him to live now. It wasn't their mock father-son relationship, the years of doing business together, or even a new stirring of morality in Franky. It was loneliness, pure and simple. Franky was a condemned man now and he didn't want to die alone.

He raised his glass and motioned for Sam to do the same. He wasn't certain, but it seemed as though this giant of a man, one feared by all in the local community, was actually troubled. He wanted to live. His flushed cheeks and glassy eyes revealed an emotion he would never convey with words. It wasn't fear, but sadness. Simple sadness and a weak remorse, not for the deed, but for the consequences it entailed.

How curious, thought Sam, for a man with his life not to be thrilled by the inevitability of its passing. Sam's own was not nearly as troubling and he viewed death as the ultimate aspirin before bedtime. A magic pill that relieved the pain of a trying day and allowed the consumer to begin anew. How he longed for that dawn in this, the darkest of his hours.

"To Mr. Holiday," said Franky, clicking his glass against Sam's. "A man wise enough to leave people like us behind."

The words hit a nerve with Sam and he replaced his glass without drinking. Everyone admired Thomas Holiday, even the people he had stepped on to get to the top. It was disgusting. He used his local charm to con the voters into

91

believing he was one of them and all the while he was mucking it up at the golf course with those Westchester assholes.

God, what a simple man he was, talking trash about those who loved him to gain the admiration of those who thought he was a low-class piece of city trash. He got in the door, but he never got in the club. In the end he was burdened with the life he created, a lonely lifeless body, surrounded by scandal and devoid of well-wishers from either side. No wonder he retired his judgeship and returned to private practice. Believe it or not, he was too much of a scumbag to make it as a politician.

"Sam? You okay?"

"Yeah."

"It's a lot to absorb, I know."

"What is?"

"Your own death."

"I wouldn't go making any funeral arrangements just yet."

"Why?"

"Can you really buy us a week with that five hundred?"

"I think so. They should want the money more than they want us dead."

"Good. You do that. It's time I own up to things."

"What are you thinking, Sam? I can see the smoke, for Christ's sake."

"Have Tony send Windy home. Make sure he waits for me there. I gotta check on a few things, shouldn't be more than an hour. I'll leave a message telling him what to do, and I'll meet up with him afterwards. I'm gonna need his help with this thing. I'll get back to you in a day or so."

"What's going on?"

"I've got an idea. Something that may at least let some of us walk away from this thing. I'm gonna need a few days. Who are we dealing with here?"

"Sam?"

"I need to know who they are to understand how they play. If they kill you, game's over. I don't want that on my head, not after all you've done."

"The Campanella family."

"Good. They've got more greed than brains. A deal might work with them."

"But what's the plan?"

"Can't say now. Gotta work it out in my head first. Just get me that week."

Sam patted Franky on the shoulder and took off through the cellar exit.

CHAPTER 13

Grimis' arms trembled under the weight of his luggage. For a man who could create things out of air, he was certainly a heavy packer. Forehead resting squarely against a musty duffel bag, he danced a cautious toe along the porch, hoping to find the step that his eyes could not. He managed the three with his usual dexterity, but misjudged the walkway and toppled head over feet, dirty laundry flying about the Astroturf.

Jonathan watched him gather the items, thoroughly convinced the packing was taking far too long. He considered assisting, then didn't. He was much better at not doing things. No need to start jostling around his personality now.

"Goddamn it," said Grimis, as gathered up a sock. "I hate

this. I hate this whole damn thing. Get me? You and your Earth-loving ideas got me packing instead of pumping. Do you have any idea what the Nardoni twins like to do in bed?"

Jonathan shrugged.

"Things that would kill a normal man."

Grimis kicked open the trunk of his 1970 GTO convertible. The car was impressively red, but in need of a wash and some minor bodywork. Jonathan had always wanted a muscle car, a man's classic that got six miles to the gallon and barked back at the dogs. But the game he played made that impossible. No lawyer could drive one and keep his clients.

Grimis stuffed the bags in, grabbed the trunk with both hands, and slammed it down, but the lid never made the latch. It bounced off a poorly packed box and shot upwards, catching Grimis in the forehead. The poor slob landed ass-first on the ground. Like most New Yorkers, Jonathan found another's pain priceless, and burst into laughter. Grimis failed to see the humor. He felt the swelling above his eye, adjusted the box, and employed the mass of his beer belly to secure the lid. Task complete, he walked to the door, tapping affectionately along the metal quarter panel. He paused and looked at Jonathan.

"You comin' or what?"

Jonathan could appreciate a good piece of ass, and thus understood the attitude. He wanted to say something, but when a man expects sex and gets a road trip instead, no words will do. It's kinda of like winning a lifetime's supply of toothpaste on a quiz show. He would have to let Grimis mellow himself for a while.

"Well?"

Grimis leaped over the door like no plump man could and

landed confidently in the driver's seat. Three-hundred-plus horses began bucking wildly in anticipation of their master's command. A quick rev of the motor convinced Jonathan that demons lived under the hood. He was shamefully frightened and the car sensed the fear. It reared up on him as he approached, forcing him to back away. Grimis laughed, then patted the dash to settle the beast.

"Come on. She's just a little testy in the morning. Hop in."

* * *

Jonathan thought it odd that he could not remember the trip. They had been in the car for more than an hour, he was almost certain of it, but he couldn't recall a single sight, smell, or sound. It was as if there was nothing but the Nothingness itself between the Boss' chambers and the golf course. Roadways, signs, and the soothing motion of linear transport were illusions in this world. Meaningless. Only the destinations seemed to matter.

Such facts should have felt comforting. Point "A" to point "C" without the distractions of the unsought in between was a concept ahead of its time. Yet Jonathan felt cheated. Maybe the blur of the white lines was important. Maybe even the most mundane moments of one's life are hidden treasures, appreciated only when they are stolen. Or maybe he had fallen asleep in the car and was just over-thinking things again. He was too ashamed to ask and forced himself not to care anymore. His growing apathy began to concern him. Then it didn't. Apathy is a tricky fellow.

Grimis stood, driver in hand, about to lead the trio into the third hole. What a week it had been. The last thing Jonathan expected from Hell was a round of golf. He had things to do, cosmic laws to break. There was no time for leisure. Besides, he'd never been more than a caddie and was losing terribly now. Jonathan hated to lose.

"Three forty-seven!" yelled Grimis, driving a solid shot down the middle of the fairway to the edge of the green. He was excellent. Marvin, of course, was godlike, but Grimis could have handed that Tiger guy his ass ten times over.

Jonathan turned to Marvin. "What's with him and three forty-seven?"

"Ah, the old fool. That be the exact time him there came to the South. It was 3:47 in the morning, more years ago than I can count."

"Sentimental, huh?"

Marvin shrugged off the question and took his turn at the tee. He was poetry to watch, even for someone who knew nothing of the sport. Two strokes, maybe three at most, but generally two and the hole was complete. This fool, who could not string together a simple declarative sentence, had the ability to will the ball into the hole. Grimis could do some impressive willing of his own if he employed his After-Earth powers, but such actions were frowned upon by serious competitors. Marvin was working strictly from Earthly talent and thousands of years of practice. It was a pleasure to see hard work pick up the check for once.

They finished the game and decided that Jonathan, the overwhelming loser, should buy the group burgers and beer before heading out. A rumble in his belly stifled Jonathan's inclination to protest and a moment later they were sitting around a table at a rustic bar and grill miles from the course.

"How did we get here?" asked Jonathan.

His tongue tickled with the crispness of fresh brew, but couldn't remember the drinking. The big picture issues - his father, Sam, the terrible wager were all in tact, but he couldn't summon the most mundane aspects of his recent past.

"What do you mean?"

"When? Exactly when did we sit down here?"

"Dat boy is skippin' without a rope," said Marvin. "Maybe my doc should check him out right quick."

"Are you serious?"

"I remember talking about getting food. I remember being hungry. I just don't remember driving anywhere, walking in here, or ordering this beer."

"Are you still hungry?"

Jonathan thought about it a second. The rumbling was gone, but at times one's belly monster has a tendency to hibernate. He closed his eyes and concentrated on his stomach. Grimis watched him frown. The answer was obvious.

"Why? How am I not hungry?"

Marvin pointed a stringy finger towards the table and Jonathan caught sight of a napkin-lined basket housing three curly fries sitting in a pile of ketchup.

"We ate?"

Grimis laughed out loud. "Of course we did, boy. You gotta get your shit together or you're gonna wind up in the nut house with my buddy here. No offense, Marvin."

"Hell, I like the nut house. Got good towels there."

Jonathan was clearly upset, but the two were immersed in booze and tall tales of fish caught and women lost. Grimis was as animated as Marvin was country-mouse quiet and their respective styles kept people watching. There was no room for philosophical conversations at this table. Jonathan's questions would have to simmer. So he joined the parade of onlookers, delighting in the eccentric antics of the drunken duo.

Jonathan was beginning to notice that one was never truly alone with the man. For better or worse, people were drawn to this amusingly glib caricature of the paste-eating nerd you tormented in high school. This time around, however, the swarms of onlookers devoted more energy towards inquisitive dialogue than bantering and spitballs. It was refreshing to find such acceptance. As the beer turned to scotch, night turned to morning. No one left. No one got tired. Somewhere around four a jukebox appeared.

Games, Grimis, wine, women. They didn't make aspirins big enough for what Jonathan would have to deal with the next day. He almost felt sorry for them, but not quite.

CHAPTER 14

It was early evening when Sam pulled into the hospital parking lot. He clicked off New York's only country music station, retracted the headlights, and pushed in an emergency brake that hadn't worked in months. A cool breeze passed over his cheek as he stepped from the car. He closed his eyes and inhaled deeply, trying to steal a bit of summer from an autumn night.

He murmured his intentions to a preoccupied desk nurse, signed the register, and walked towards the elevator. She grabbed a ringing phone, told the party to hold, and advised Sam that visiting hours were over in ten minutes. Sam nodded, but she was already deep in conversation.

Sam hated hospitals. Not the way most people hate them,

because of the inconvenience, the aggravation, the way they take the weight of your mortality and drop it on your face like a cold sack of shit. No. He despised their utter existence. Hospitals, doctors, anything or anyone that tried to cheat nature out of its due. Sure, broken bones could be set. Cuts could be stitched. A Band-Aid or two for the kid who thought himself better than the tree he climbed. But pity the poor fool who believed himself stronger than an airplane's twisted metal carcass. To hell with those who attempt to battle cancer or AIDS. They are just masks for the Reaper. He always wins in the end, and none of the dances we do can ever stop him.

Healthy living. Preventive care. What jokes they are. Being in shape just slows the rate at which you die. Sam felt dead most of the time, as if his call had come and he'd put the hereafter on hold. It wasn't his intention to subject his maker to nifty jazz Muzak, but the beep of call waiting was too tempting to resist. Now he was stuck listening to life yap away again, and he was tired of it. Funny that, for a man who had nothing, Sam had a written will. It specified that if ever he suffered a fate like his father's, the plug should be pulled as soon as legally allowable. He didn't want to make the same mistake twice.

He pushed open the door to his father's room and suddenly felt a hint of hatred towards his brother. He was still jealous of the way Jonathan died.

"What are you doing here?" asked Sam.

Norah put down the mystery she'd been reading aloud and flipped her long blonde hair over her shoulder. She was tired. Old makeup, red eyes, blackened bags, all trying their damnedest to make her seem less appealing. They failed.

"How long have you been here?"

"Not long."

"Yeah, right. When was the last time you slept?"

She looked down at her book and began rubbing the pages between her thumb and forefinger.

"Have you eaten?"

"Dinner or lunch?"

"You're amazing. Windy tells me you're here every night, for Christ's sake. He's not even your father. Why do you care so much?"

She laid the book flat on her lap and patted it smooth with the palm of her hand. "I don't know, Sam. Why does anyone care about anything?"

She tried to leave it at that, but his stare pressed her for a deeper answer. She sighed gently. He wanted to breathe her in, to know her again.

"Maybe because I was part of the family. Maybe out of grief over Jonathan's death. Or maybe because I never got to do this for my father. Who knows? Does there really have to be a reason to love?"

Sam completely forgot about the circumstances surrounding her old man's death. She was just a kid then. It shouldn't have happened. Not to her.

"You wanna get a bite?" asked Sam.

"I don't think we should."

"Come on. Don't you at least want to talk? We used to talk, remember?"

Norah was surprised to find herself smiling. It had been a long time since Sam had made her feel anything but sadness.

"Yes. I remember."

"So let's go then. There's a cafeteria right downstairs."

"It's closing, Sam. And visiting hours are up. We'll talk. I promise we will. Just not right now, okay? Not with all this running through my head."

Sam clasped his hands together and began tapping them against his lips. He could feel his breath burning his lungs. Why was he such an idiot? It was better to live alone for eternity than to feel this way for a single day. A lifetime without a word, a touch, a kiss would be better than having those things stolen away from you. Who ever said, "It's better to have loved and lost than to have never loved at all," was a fucking moron.

"Is everything okay?" she asked.

"Yeah. Sure."

She was halfway out the door already, purse bouncing against a thigh that was no stranger to Pilates class. He examined her eyes, her cheek, the curve of her waist, and the elegance of her hand. It's amazing how a man can miss every part of a woman.

"It's just that you looked . . ."

"Forget it. You seen Windy?"

"Haven't spoken to him all day. Have you checked the garage?"

"Yeah. No dice. He was supposed to meet me at the house over two hours ago. Never showed up."

"Strange."

"You're telling me. For a drunk, he's as punctual as they come."

"So where is he? You're not in any trouble, are you? If you need money or anything you could always . . ."

"No, no. I saw him this morning. Probably off goofing around. He'll turn up. It's not like he has that much to do."

"You know, Sam, maybe if you tried to help him a little he would start to help himself. He idolizes you, you know."

Sam stuffed his hands in his pockets and tapped a toe uneasily. The look in his eye told Norah that the man he had become could not accept being anyone's hero. She knew the look and knew the problem. For all their talents, there was not a scrap of self-confidence in the Holiday boys.

"When was the last time you had a decent thought about yourself, Sam?"

"What?"

"Forget me. Forget Jonathan, your father, and this mess of a life you've made for yourself. Forget all that nonsense and just think of yourself, the person you are at this moment. When was the last time you looked in the mirror and thought something besides, 'I'm a complete piece of shit'?"

She began to leave again, paused, and turned back to Sam.

"You're not, you know, a piece of shit."

She walked out the door and Sam's heart sank. The most caring, supportive, intelligent woman he would ever meet still spoke to him as a friend, after all he'd done to her. What a fool he had been to let her go. What a fool.

Sam walked over to his father and sat by the bed. He was thin—thinner than he had ever been. It disgusted Sam. The thinness, the hospital—the whole situation ate away at him.

"You stupid fuck," said Sam, almost to himself. "Why are you living? Why you, when people like Mom burn in the ashes you create?"

He punched the bed-frame and rose to his feet.

"Can you answer me that? Huh, Dad? Didn't think so. Son of a bitch. Don't worry, I'll take care of you like you took care of us."

There was a knock at the door.

"Visiting hours are over, sir," said an overweight orderly.

"Sure. Just a minute."

"That your old man?"

"Yeah."

"Quite a fighter, huh? Must have been a helluva guy."

"Brother, you don't know the half of it."

"Well, at least he had some good people in his life. Things are pretty quiet up here. Not often I gotta chase out visitors, especially after a guest has been here a while. But not him. He got that blonde number in here all the time, and that scruffy-looking guy."

"Windy."

"Yeah"

"He comes here a lot?"

"At least twice a week since day one. Tuesdays and Fridays like clockwork, sometimes Wednesdays. Never pull weekend shifts, so I couldn't tell you about them."

"What time usually?"

"What? You a cop or something?"

"Do I look like a cop?"

The orderly smiled as if to apologize for the insult.

"Always right before closing. Helluva guy. Brings me the papers, and some good coffee now and then. Starbucks. Gotta love it. A shame he hits the sauce the way he does. But hey, who's perfect?"

"Sure ain't me. Listen. He been here today?"

"Naw."

"I thought you said he came in every Tuesday?

"Man. It *is* Tuesday, isn't it? I'm getting old. Mind's turning to mush. I don't know where the boy is. Maybe the drink's got the better of him tonight."

"Doubt it. Not his style. Thanks for the info."

"Anytime, friend. But if you really wanna thank me, how about a little donation to the kids' college fund?"

"Your kids?"

"Grandkids actually, but a man's gotta take care of his own. Don't want all the Washingtons except George scrubbin' up hospital floors."

"I hear ya. You know that's funny, but now that you mention it, I can't think of another white guy named Washington."

"Just proves that old George had some good taste in women."

Sam pulled a five from his wallet and laid it in the orderly's outstretched palm.

"You're a true gentleman, my brother."

"Friend, your lies are good, but you don't know the first thing about spotting gentleman."

Sam bumped past the old man and headed for the elevators. He spotted a phone in the lobby and checked his pockets for change. Quarters in hand, he lifted the receiver and placed a call to old man Grayson.

"Put him on," said Sam. "What do you mean he isn't there? I left him a note at his apartment. He was supposed to go to your place as soon as Franky let him go. Of course he let him go. I called to check. What, you think I'm a fucking idiot? I wouldn't take chances like that with my dear sweet brother. It's not safe out there. Whatever old man. Just make sure he calls me as soon as he gets in. Understand?"

Sam slammed the phone down and burst into the parking lot.

* * *

He sat in his car, tapping the steering wheel. How could Windy be missing? The guy went to four places at most, one of which was the liquor store across the street from the garage. Maybe he was restocking his supplies when Sam checked the place. It made sense: Sam's fifty was burning a hole in Windy's pocket. No. He would have seen the rusted Ford in the driveway.

Sam turned the key and the car made a sound like a cat caught in a blender. It was already running.

"Damn," said Sam.

He closed his eyes and rubbed his temples, hoping to clear the sound from his head. An image of MacLoughlin appeared in his mind's eye. Suddenly, he knew what had happened: Windy had gone to find MacLoughlin. But how? And why would he look for that mad man now? There could only be two reasons. To stop him from killing the old man, or to hurry the job along. Sam doubted the latter and sped from the hospital parking lot.

CHAPTER 15

Hangovers are fun when they're someone else's. They make you appreciate the little things. Focused vision, clarity of thought, bearable breath. Ah, the wonders we take for granted.

Jonathan woke in a strange living room. It was barely nine, still early by weekend standards. Insanely early for a drunken weekend. He couldn't sleep. Thoughts spun in his brain. He longed for aspirin, and was surprised to find a bottle sitting on the kitchen table. He shrugged off the miracle, gulped down four without water, and began to search for some coffee.

"Third cabinet to your right."

"Amber?"

Jonathan turned to find the tiny angel dressed in a tasteful white nightgown. Even the morning couldn't make her look her age.

"What are you doing here?"

"My house."

"You mean you and Grimis . . . ah . . ."

"Certainly not. He and Marvin are still passed out in the guestroom. Drunken fools, smelling like a bar, sleeping in their clothes. The usual."

"How did we get here?"

"I came and found you. Seems I've been doing that a lot lately. What's wrong with him? Can you imagine acting like a teenager at his age? You think you'd get tired of it. You think he'd want something more in his life by now."

"You love him, don't you?"

The question shocked her and she had to catch her breath. It's amazing how we can feel something so strong for so long and never have the courage to let our hearts tell our minds what's going on.

"Is it that obvious?"

"Apparently not to him."

She shrugged in agreement and began to make the coffee. Jonathan sat at the table and watched her.

"It's okay," she said.

"What is?"

"Thinking of me as your mother."

"How did you . . . ? You can read minds too?"

"No. Not exactly. That would be worse than breaking and entering. But I can pick up on things you send out. Like that compliment. You wanted me to know and so I did."

"You don't mind?"

"Jonathan, I may appear thirty-nine, just as you appear

thirty-three, but I've been around a lot longer. Even you have had thirty-odd years to think things over. Time passes here, like everywhere else. It just doesn't affect a person as much. In the After-Earth, regardless of one's address, people can control time. People can do so many wonderful things here if they just believe."

She placed a cup and saucer on the table.

"Sugar? Milk?"

"No. No thank you."

"How about an omelet?"

Amber set up the stove and pulled the ingredients from the refrigerator.

"Why don't I cook for you?" Jonathan said. He rose, took another sip of coffee, and traded places with Amber. How could Grimis not see what he had here? Why do people need to be hit by a bus before they learn to stop and look around every now and again?

He fried up a mean fare and dotted her plate with parsley before serving.

"I'm impressed."

"Well, I was a bachelor for a time. Had to keep Mom on speed dial. Besides, Julie wasn't much of a wife and I ended up doing most of the domestic work."

"I'm guessing she was a mistake?"

"You're not guessing and yes, she was."

"So why did you marry her? If you don't mind me asking."

"No. It's fine. I guess I just needed someone and she was there. Well, actually she wasn't really there, but it's still nice to curl up with something besides a body pillow at night."

"Bitter?"

Both Sides of Broken

"I was. If you'd mentioned her name when I first came here I would have gone berserk. But not anymore. I feel so much of me has changed."

"You haven't changed at all, just grown a little."

"Maybe."

Jonathan joined her at the table and sampled his creation. He smiled as he chewed. Life is lived moment to moment and this was one of the happy moments he'd lock away and pull out during the next trip to the dentist.

There was a rumbling in the guestroom and then voices.

"Get your foot out of my face," said Grimis from behind the door.

"What? Me?"

"Oh, my head."

There was a thud as if someone had fallen out of the bed. Grimis' laughter indicated it wasn't him. Marvin groaned, gathered himself, and followed Grimis through the door.

"You look like shit. Oh, ah . . . sorry Amber."

"Hey, call 'em as you see 'em."

The two stumbled to the table and planted their butts on the padded chairs. Marvin plopped his head on the table and began to sleep again.

"Poor boy, can't take his liquor. It's a shame when a grown man can't handle a night on the town. Me, I always have my wits about me."

"You sure?" asked Amber, motioning to his forearm.

Grimis rolled up his sleeve and turned slightly red.

"Well I'll be damned. How'd you know?"

"You spent half the night moaning about how much it hurt. Really, Grimis, it's not like it's your first tattoo."

"True, but there's only one I like."

"The eagle?" asked Jonathan.

"You got it. But to tell you the truth, this ain't half bad. What you think?"

Jonathan took Grimis by the wrist and pulled his arm across the table. It was a fire dragon, red as they come. A perfect match for the eagle on his left. The coloration was superb, as was the detail in the face. So lifelike that Jonathan half expected the creature to fly off the pasty canvas and wreak havoc on the drapes.

"As much as I hate tattoos, I have to admit I kinda like it."

"Then I'll keep it."

"Like there's a choice."

"There's always a choice, boy."

Grimis rubbed a flat palm across the beast and it was gone. He smiled knowingly at Amber, repeated the process, and the dragon returned.

"Gotta love being dead. Here, give me your arm."

"What?"

"Your arm, give it here."

Grimis took him by the wrist and copied the tattoo onto Jonathan's forearm. He wanted to scream in disgust, but didn't and in a moment he didn't want to scream at all.

"A perfect match."

"Great," said Amber. "Now I've got two of you."

"Three," corrected Grimis.

He lifted Marvin's pant leg and revealed a teddy bear.

"Marge is gonna kill him when she finds out. What would possess him to do a crazy thing like that? Oh, wait. Don't tell me. I'm looking at him."

Grimis smirked like a schoolboy and patted Jonathan on the back.

"So you like?"

"Yeah, Grimis. I don't know why, but I like it a lot."

"Fantastic. Then let's get movin'. Amber, could you fix us up some of them finger sandwiches? You know, the ones with the crust cut off."

"Grimis I—"

"Oh come on, pretty please."

Amber blushed and darted off to the kitchen.

"Women. You gotta know how to handle 'em."

"Ever think they want more from a guy than being handled?"

"What's eating you?"

"Nothing."

Grimis stood, stretched his arms out as far as they could go, and began to shake himself like a wet dog. Belly bouncing, cheeks flapping, saliva flying from his lips. He willed himself dressed and headache-free, and packed. He thought about waking Marvin and helping him through the consequences of his intoxication, but had yet to figure out a way to tell him about the tattoo. Marvin was a kept man if ever there was and he'd catch hell for staying out all night. In death you can cheat Father Time, Mother Nature, and most everyone in between; but in no life, after or otherwise, can a man effectively cheat on his woman. You can try like hell, but the end is always the same.

Amber returned just as the boys finished packing the GTO. Marvin began to snore obnoxiously and Jonathan had to plead with Grimis not to stick the poor fool in the trunk.

"Thanks, doll," said Grimis, taking the basket of food. "We'll see ya in a while."

"Oh, you'll see me before that."

"Huh?"

"I'm coming with you."

"No, no, no," said Grimis. "This is a manly adventure for men. We can't have a chick tagging along, slowing us down. This ain't no walk in the park. We've got three After-Earth dimensions to see and I wanna be back before the weekend is over."

Amber willed herself into jeans, hiking boots, and a sweatshirt. She drew her blonde locks into a ponytail, and began staring at Grimis. He accepted the challenge and stared back. The contest was over in less than five minutes. Grimis lost, blaming his blink on some unidentified dust particle. She laughed off his protest and snatched the keys from his hands. He looked up in shock.

"I'm driving," she said. "Hop in, boys!"

They blasted down the road. Jonathan leaned against the passenger door. He looked at Grimis sulking in the back seat, and wondered why it was so easy to spot the mistakes others made in their relationships, while being a blind to his own. He thought briefly of girlfriends past. Each ended in a different way, for different reasons: the wrong time, place, person. Maybe. But, if asked in an honest moment, most if not all were because of him.

Marvin stirred as Jonathan snoozed. He blinked slowly, noticed Grimis in the back seat, figured he was dreaming, and faded off again. Grimis muttered something to himself, crossed his arms and began to pout again. He caught Amber looking at him through the rear view mirror, and though they tried, neither could hide their smiles.

"Get some sleep," said Amber.

He curled up like the child he was and faded off.

CHAPTER 16

The harvest sun had long since drifted behind the uninspiring New Rochelle skyline. It was a dark, quiet evening, the kind loneliness likes. Sam found himself in his car again. He caught a glimpse of his worn face in the mirror and winced. He hadn't changed, showered, or shaved since the morning before. He felt dirty, used, older than he should. His stomach rumbled painfully, reminding him that he hadn't eaten much either.

It was a stupid idea to come to his pop's old neighborhood. Windy hated the Westchester scene as much as Sam did. It was a long shot at best, but there he was pulling into his father's driveway, half expecting to see Windy's Ford nestled under the open garage. It wasn't. No one had stayed in that house for more than a minute since Mr. Holiday's plane went down. Neither of the boys had performed the ritual walk-through in a while and he debated whether it was worth checking the house now.

"Screw it," said Sam.

What his father had wasn't worth stealing and his mother—well, his mother's belongings had been separated and donated about a week after her death.

He started the car and turned his thoughts back to Windy. He couldn't believe it. Since leaving the hospital he had rechecked his apartment and the garage, and had even called Norah to see if he had turned up there. Nothing. Sam was at a loss. If he hadn't gone to Grayson's where could he be? Windy wasn't a normal person with hobbies and friends and places to go. He went to work, drank, and then went to sleep. There was no Thursday bowling night, no softball team, no evening pottery class to fill up his existence. There was nothing but the work and whatever scraps of socializing his brothers threw him.

Poor bastard, thought Sam. He wondered if Windy had had a friend since high school.

He pulled from the drive and drove a block through the college to an all-night convenience store. A few coeds were loitering in the parking lot, smoking cigarettes, talking trash. They were cute, firm, and legal enough, or so he imagined. But they dressed like whores and Sam never got off on that. Like most men, he enjoyed looking at the trashy ones, but never took them seriously. They were fine to fuck and flash around, but often weren't worth the cab fare.

Age had taught him that a woman with respect for herself

will always be the better lover. Trust, communication, understanding. That's where foreplay starts. You get a woman like that, one who knows you deeply, and she'll do all the things the others will, and she won't fake it. She won't have to.

"Hey mister," said one of the younger girls. "How's about hookin' us up?"

Sam felt weird being called mister. At thirty-one it wasn't inconceivable that he could date a college girl, even an eighteen-year-old. Hell, the stars do it all the time. But he wasn't a star. His look and smell made that apparent to the gum-cracking females before him.

"We got cash. Look. Just see if they got Aftershock. If not, then get us some Bud . . . no—Coors Light."

She jammed the money into his hand before he could say a word. The girls circled him and offered pleading looks. Eight girls, all doable. And all but one was checking him out. Oddly enough, it was the one who wasn't who caught his eye. There was something about her.

"Hey, nice ass," said one playfully, tearing Sam from his thoughts.

"Shut up, slut," said another.

"*You* shut up, bitch."

"Whore."

"Tramp."

"Girls, girls, come on," said a third. "So what do you say, mister? Gonna help us out?"

He hadn't planned on buying for them, but it had been a while since he had received any attention from a woman. A moment later he was in the store, sandwich in one hand, twelve pack in the other. He waited his turn in line behind some drunk buying Lotto tickets. The elderly clerk was diligently running his cards, not doing a damn thing else. The line began to grow.

"Let's go, buddy," said a patron near the back of the five-customer queue. "You ain't got a shot in hell anyway. The whole thing's rigged."

"Shaddup, you," said the ticket-buying man.

"What? You want a piece a this?"

"Relax," said the clerk, motioning to a bat hanging on the wall, "or I knock the crap outta both of ya."

The room chuckled. Problem diffused.

The last stack of tickets spilled from the machine. The clerk took a pile of bills from the slob and sent him on his way. Sam stepped forward and placed the items on the counter.

"Got any, ah . . ."

"Aftershock?" asked the clerk with a look of disgust. "Yeah we got some in the back, but not for them girls. What's with you guys? Get your jollies off trashing up kids? Gonna come back around later and try and pick 'em up?"

"Never thought of that. Does it work?"

"Sicko."

Sam wanted to punch him, but he was angrier at New York. What a shithole it had become. The Bronx was always the Bronx, despite what the politicians would have you believe, but now Pelham, New Rochelle, Mount Vernon, and Tuckahoe were becoming part of it too. He wondered how long before there were hoodlums in Scarsdale.

He looked down at himself. Hell, he fit right in. It wasn't a nigger thing. It wasn't about the dot-heads, the spics, the chinks. He used to think it was their moving in that killed property values and sent the white folks running from their neighborhoods. Not anymore. Now he knew there was good and bad in all people. It's just that in most cases the bad kicked the good's ass.

"Comes to $23.50."

"For this?"

"That's why they call it convenient."

"Fine. Gimme a cup of coffee too. Black."

"That's $24.50."

The clerk handed him the coffee, made his change, and offered a final look of disapproval. Sam turned to leave.

"Those kids better not get wild with my windows again."

"Screw you," said Sam softly, more to the situation than the man.

The girls rushed Sam as he left the store. They thanked him, moaned briefly about the lack of hard liquor, and took off for the other side of the lot. Sam caught the one who had given him the money and returned it to her.

"Tonight's on me darling."

"All right!"

The gesture was more against the clerk than for the girls, but he enjoyed her kiss anyway. He watched her run to her friends, ass shaking the way only muscle can. Oh, the things he had missed by not going to college. Maybe the old man had a point on that one. No. Fuck him too.

Sam turned to find a blonde of about twenty leaning against his car and eyeing him curiously. Fickle creatures—she had all but ignored him moments before.

"Need something?" he asked.

"We all need something. But I'm just looking."

"How long you gonna look?"

"Why, got a date?"

"No, just things to do."

She pushed up against him. "Don't you like me?"

"No. I never had a thing for cops."

She pulled back in a hurry.

"Relax, sister. I won't give you up if you won't bust 'em for the beer thing."

"How'd you know?"

"'Cause I know the case. You're watching for the kid my brother defended. The one he got off. They probably got you here looking for copycats too. Makes sense: some nut hoping to get a piece of his fame. Probably the most action you New Ro cops seen in a while."

"You're related to that asshole?"

"Yup. But don't worry. He's through being an asshole. He's dead."

"I heard. I guess I should say I'm sorry."

"Why lie?"

Her friends began to miss her and called playfully.

"Go girl. You ho. Scheming on the old guy."

"Old guy?" asked Sam softly.

"Shut up and kiss me."

She pushed him up against the car, grabbed the back of his hair, and kissed him deeply. The girls saw the move and hooted their approval.

"Gotta make it look real," she whispered while biting his ear. "Besides, it's a great way to frisk ya."

Sam was stunned, but not enough to prevent him from

kissing her back. Then he yanked a fistful of hair and began sucking her neck.

"Not bad for an old man, but I think they've seen enough."

She pushed him away and smiled.

"So, what now?" asked Sam.

"Give me your number."

"Why?"

"Why do you think?" she asked, motioning to the group of onlookers.

"Do I at least get a name?"

"Samantha."

"You're joking? Or is that your cover?"

"No, it's real. Why?"

"I'm Sam. Sam Holiday. Ain't that a bitch? So how old are you anyway?"

"Twenty-eight. You'd be amazed at what the right lifestyle will do for you. Maybe I could get you on a program. You know—diet, exercise. It could help." She patted his budding beer belly.

"So why are you doing this anyway? The guy's fresh outta jail. He's off. Free. Sure he confessed, but it don't mean squat. You really think he'd be stupid enough to try something in the same place so soon? It would be throwing away a miracle."

"They're all stupid, or haven't you heard? The shrinks say if they're gonna do it again, it's soon, and generally near the same place."

"What a whack job."

"He ain't Peter Pan. I just hope I get him if he does come back. I went here, you know. One of those girls was a friend's baby sister."

"Nothing like a small town in a big-city mask. New Ro is like that, I guess. Anyway, I hope you catch him. Thanks for the kiss."

"You kidding? I've wanted to do that for years."

"What?"

"You really don't remember me?" she asked.

"Should I?"

"Skinny girl. Braces. Had a crush on you in high school your senior year."

"Oh my God. Sammy Lee? You were that freshman?"

"Yeah."

"You grew. In all the right spots, I must say."

She blushed and patted his hand. "Well, see ya round. I trust you'll keep this quiet."

He nodded. "You know, you sure were a strange chick back then. Now too, I'd bet."

"Those are chicks, Sammy. I'm a woman."

"Yeah, I guess you are."

Sam opened the car door.

"Oh and sorry about the performance," she said. "I just had to check you out. You understand?"

She didn't wait for an answer.

He got in the car and drove to his apartment. It started to rain lightly as he passed through Pelham. He thought of the girls dancing drunk in the rain. He wanted to join them, but his chance had passed. He clicked on the country station and let the songs stir his pain. He was a sucker for sad songs, a bull's eye for the blues.

* * *

123

Sam stepped from the shower and lathered up for a shave. He didn't grow much of a beard and didn't need a razor every morning. Most days he showed teenage stubble, removing it only when occasion demanded. There was nothing special tonight. He just wanted to clean up a little. New shirt. Cologne. Dressing up for the hell of it.He looked himself in the eye and gave a shot at a De Niro impersonation. He could have been an actor, maybe not big time, but definitely one of those extras they use when a script calls for a scene by the docks. He cleaned up good, but not so good as to lose his gruffness. Norah's words of encouragement echoed in his mind as he passed a hand over a smooth cheek. For a moment he believed them; believed he could do and be anything in the world. Then he spotted an old racing form on the dresser. Sam felt a twinge of regret. Maybe he was a bum after all.

He buckled his Timex and reached for his dirtied Dockers. His pockets were barren, strike a pair of twenties and crumpled ball of yellowed paper: the poem the old woman had given him.

"Crazy broad," said Sam.

He lifted his arm, aiming the paper at the trash, then paused and lobbed it to his dresser instead. It was half past ten and not a word from Windy. He figured he'd make the rounds again. Not like he had much else to do. If the sap didn't turn up by morning, he'd start to worry.

He walked to the living room and plopped himself on the couch. He wanted a beer, but the refrigerator was bare. Shopping was never his forte. Instinct made him search for the remote. After fruitlessly checking the cushions and coffee table, he began to rummage through piles of discarded clothes that had never quite made the hamper. He lifted a pizza-stained football jersey, surprised to find a blinking answering machine. Sam usually ignored the device, knowing too well the temperament and motivation of his callers. He debated whether he could stand a chorus of idle threats from two-bit bookies. The debate ended with a click of a button. The machine screeched obscenely as it rolled back the tape. A moment later, Windy's voice filled the air.

"I'm here. Ah . . . at Grayson's place. Sorry about being late. I was—" A vicious cough sliced through his speech. "Nothing. Nothing. God, this sucks. My chest is killing me. Anyways, I'll see you when you get here. Hope things go okay. Thanks again, Sam."

The next caller began his message by calling Sam a fucking asshole. Sam unplugged the unit before the learning the reason for the call. He really didn't care. His thoughts were with Windy now. He sounded worse every moment. He'd be dead soon and there was nothing to stop it.

The phone rang as he snagged his keys from the dresser. He let it ring a second time, then lifted the receiver.

"Yeah."

"Tony's dead," said Franky, as though he were ordering a pizza.

Franky had been a father to both of them and good friend to most of the people in the neighborhood. He was a criminal cut and dry, but if you got past the occupation most would call him a warm man. Sure, he put up the tough front during business hours, but get him alone and he'd cry over the Flintstones. Something was afoot.

"You're not alone, are you?"

"No."

"Are you hurt?"

"Bounced around a bit, nothing much."

Franky groaned as one of his assailants laid a bat to his gut. He coughed wildly for a second as if he were about to hack up a lung. When he returned to the line, his voice was hoarse, but otherwise unaltered. Sam knew he was hurting, but Franky would never let on. He knew the rules. You never let them break you. They could tell you they had just gang-raped your mother in the back of a Chevy and the best way for you to get revenge would be to sit there, smile, and maybe if you really wanted to give them a "fuck you," ask if they'd enjoyed the ride.

"Where's Windy? I haven't seen him since I left your place."

Sam knew that, with Tony dead, Windy was the next logical target. He had to play stupid in case someone else was on the line.

"Don't know. I let him go about an hour before they came. I'm sure they'll go after him now that they know about you. You know, make him another Tony. Sorry, pal, but I couldn't stand alone."

"You didn't tell them where I was, did you?"

"Sam?"

"Sorry."

"I had to tell them the truth."

"Which version?"

Franky actually started to laugh, but his sore muscles and bruised ribs put an end to his chuckle. He shrieked in pain, then laughed despite himself at the sound of his voice.

"You're crazy," said Sam. "I guess your five hundred didn't get us the week?"

"I had second thoughts on that myself, so I gave them one. Told them we'd get the rest if they let me go and gave us the time."

"Didn't buy it, huh?"

"I wouldn't be on the line if they did."

"Right."

"What I need—"

One of Franky's captors snatched away the phone. His breath was heavy and rapid, like he had just finished a sprint.

"What I need is for you to get the fucking money you owe us. The hundred is interest. A gift. Got it? Maybe if you come up with the two million by game time Sunday we'll kill that brother of yours quick. A second late and the bunch of you die slow. Get me?"

"I need more time."

"You got four days till kick-off. The money don't mean shit if it's late."

"I need Franky out."

"Right. You're lucky he's still breathing. The stupid fuck."

"I need to talk with him."

"Listen to the balls on you. I need, I need, I need. I don't give a shit what you need."

"Really? Then shoot him, big shot. Go ahead and pull the trigger, you dumb fucking wop. But see if you ever get a dime."

"You crazy?"

"And then some."

"Oh, only you, right?"

"Buddy, I'm the kind of crazy where you just don't give a shit anymore. All this live-and-die stuff. Bite me, okay? Just put him on the phone before I hop a flight with the cash and start sending you postcards from paradise."

Franky was on the phone a second later, trying to stifle his laugh.

"You are nuts. Why you gotta be pissing them off? I'm tied to a chair here, you know."

"Where's here?"

"I don't know. They had me blindfolded. I got a number for you, though, one to call when you get the cash."

Sam jotted the number on his hand. The ink smudged slightly, but he didn't mind. It would take a miracle for him to use it. Franky knew he was just biding time.

"Relax, Franky. They ain't gonna kill you."

"I'm glad you're so sure."

"Think, Frank. They want the money by kick-off. What does that mean?"

"Oh. . . ."

"That's right. That's the beauty of being a cockroach: you're gross, but none of the other roaches mind 'cause they're just as bad or worse. I fuck you, you fuck them, they fuck somebody so dangerous that his voice is cracking like a twelve-year-old's. When was the last time you heard a suit like him lose it on the phone? We're small time, but we caused big trouble. They need the cash 'cause they're gonna bet the cash."

"You think?"

"I know."

"Funny, I always thought them smarter than that."

"Why, 'cause they dress like pimps and have leased BMWs?"

"You're right. If any of us had a brain in our heads we'd be doing the nine-to-five for a shit salary. Instead we're standing in our own graves holding a shovel."

"You think they'd let you go if we had the money?"

"Not willingly, but maybe if we did an exchange. Why, you think you can get the cash on time?"

"I can sure as hell give it a shot. Just do me a favor and never ask how, okay?"

Franky nodded to a dial tone and replaced the receiver. He looked up at his captors and shrugged. The larger of the three smiled slightly, then punched him square in the jaw. It was going to be a long four days.

CHAPTER 17

The rugged hum of the GTO's motor became a mantra for Jonathan. In his mind, the highway's white lines transformed themselves to rippled waves and began dancing along the asphalt. His sleeping body bobbed along obediently as if it thought he were actually at sea. Even now, with the car stopped, Jonathan heard the soothing sound. It was comforting, virtual bliss, the closest thing to peace of mind he had experienced in a long while. He would have liked to remain in the state, but bliss is fleeting.

"Jon. Wake up," said Marvin.

Marvin wore a game-show host's smile and a ridiculous golfer's hat, complete with a fuzzy red pompom. He reminded Jonathan of a cartoon character. Jonathan looked into his big brown dopey eyes. They were wide with a surprise like an infant's, but soft and senseless, incapable of doing harm.

"We there?" asked Jonathan.

"Where's that?"

Jonathan shook his head, amazed at Marvin's half-track mind.

"Where are we?"

"The Quik Mart."

"Huh?"

"Well, they got gas here too, but you'd never know it from the name. The pump kinda gives it away though, so I guess it's all right."

"What are you talking about?"

Marvin stepped from car and pointed to the sign. It looked like a normal convenience store. Nothing fancy. Nothing supernatural. Jonathan became excited. He wondered if he was back on Earth. He jumped from the car and stepped towards the door.

"You're supposed to wait here till Grimis gets back."

"Why?"

"'Cause."

"Well, that explains a lot. Where is Grimis now?"

"He was taking a leak. Now he's in there with Amber paying for the gas and buying beer nuts, I think."

"Well look, Marvin. I gotta take a whiz too. Where's the john?"

"Who?"

"The bathroom, Marvin. The bathroom."

"Out back behind the dumpster, but you should wait for Grimis."

"Why? He gonna help me hold it?"

"I guess if you really needed help he would, but you should know how to do it by now, shouldn't you?"

Jonathan sighed heavily and walked to the restroom. Marvin protested again, but Jonathan threatened to whip it out right there and relieve himself on his shoes. Marvin considerably loved his shoes and didn't look favorably on that option. He let him go without another word.

The restroom looked more like an indoor outhouse. There was only one stall. It was doorless, dirty, and offered no paper. Some poor slob had taken a dump anyway and not bothered to flush. The stench was overwhelming.

A six-foot sink doubled as a urinal. Its rectangular shape reminded Jonathan of something a barn animal would feed from. A tall man in cowboy boots stood a foot from the edge of the basin, holding his huge penis in one hand and a cigar in the other.

Jonathan wasn't terribly small, but he was by no means gifted in that area. His relative size and insecurity made him a stall man. It wasn't too bad usually. Awkward waits for the john, an occasional stare from men who wondered why he would offer an open spot to the guy behind him. Nothing so terrible as to make him relinquish the practice. But it was moments like this, when some drunken fool had pissed all over the floor, seat, and flusher, that made Jonathan wish for more confidence. He held his breath, cursed his fortune, and went about his business.

"What's a matter, son?" asked the cowboy. "Don't like stepping up to the plate?"

"Well, I wouldn't want to make you jealous."

Both Sides of Broken

"Ha ha. Got a little pecker, huh? Well, don't feel too bad about it. We can't all be stretched like a hung man's neck. Know what I mean? Besides, having a ten-spot ain't all it's cracked up to be. A lot of women can't handle that, and the ones who can without complaint been around a little too much to suit my tastes. Hell, I end up screwing fat chicks."

"A shame."

"Telling me. A tool like this going to waste. Ah, but a screw's a screw. Am I right? You need to get yourself a small girl, a skinny little thing about five-three. She'd appreciate that little wonder wand of yours. Yup, it's all about how you pick 'em."

Jonathan shook himself, zippered up, and met the man by the door.

"Hey, mister . . ."

"Name's Red, like redneck, only don't call me that if you wanna keep what little you got."

"Well, ah, Red, where the hell am I?"

"What kinda question is that? You ain't no fag, are you boy?"

"No."

"Crazy? Don't try none of that psycho cannibal shit on me. I'll tear you a new asshole."

"No. No. I'm as normal as they come. Just fell asleep in the car is all."

"Well shit, why didn't you say so? You in Texas, boy, about twenty miles outside of Houston. The greatest place on Earth, in case you didn't know."

"Sure, mister."

"Red."

"Red. Right. Red it is. Thanks a lot, mister."

Jonathan made his way to the store. He met Grimis at the door.

"What the hell is going on?"

"Why aren't you in the car?" asked Grimis.

"'Cause apparently I'm in Texas."

Grimis dropped his smile and the bag of junk food he was carrying. He bent to retrieve it, paused, and looked up at Jonathan.

"Who'd you talk to?"

"Some redneck."

"Did you tell him where you were from?"

"No."

Grimis sighed, smiled, and bounced to his feet.

"Well, then, everything's fine."

He walked to the car, handed the goodies to Amber, and opened the door. Jonathan chased him down with a smile as wide as the location.

"You're damn right everything is fine. We're on Earth, Grimis! Aren't we? Man, I thought you said the dead couldn't go back to Earth. God, I can't believe we're actually here. You're the best. Texas is a little off the map, but it's home.

"All right. Now all we have to do is get to New York. How far is the nearest airport? I'm gonna go ask the guy inside. I'll be back in a second. This is great, just great, Grimis."

Grimis looked to Amber for support. She just shrugged at the inevitable.

"Tell him," she said.

"Tell me what?"

"This ain't your Earth, Jon. Not by a long shot."

"What are you talking about? Look at this place. It's dirty, disgusting, and the people are rude as anything. And look, I'm sweating. I never sweated on the South Side. I never got cold or hot or tired or hungry. I never got anything unless I wanted to. Maybe you guys just forgot what it's like here, but I know Earth and this is it."

Amber left the passenger seat and walked to Jonathan. She put her arms around him and led him back to the car.

"Remember when Grimis mentioned the Sticks?"

Jonathan shrugged.

"Well, this is it."

Jonathan felt cheated. He knew what he knew, but the rules were changing faster than he could track. It wasn't fair at all.

"What kind of After-Earth is this?"

"The most popular kind, I'm afraid," said Grimis.

"Why?"

"I don't know," said Marvin, through a mouthful of candy.

"I wasn't asking you."

"Then I wasn't answering you. So there!"

Marvin crossed his arms, rolled his eyes in defiance, and returned his attention to the candy.

Jonathan felt helpless. It was becoming apparent that the more he lived the less he understood. All he wanted was a moment of clarity.

"Why, Grimis? Why does this place look and feel the way it does?"

"'Cause that's what people want."

"Oh come on. Give me a real answer for once. I'm tired of all this fortune-cookie crap. I wanna know what's going on."

Grimis sent a pleading look to Amber. He was tired of

playing tour guide, tired of breaking bad news to good people, just plain tired. He loved his uncle and was sorry about the slow-up in business. He had enjoyed his job in the early years, but not anymore. Everyone was sad all the time and somber never sat too well with him.

Amber took Jonathan by the hand and walked him a few paces to the front of the car. She offered him a sip of her cherry soda. He declined and leaned against the hood.

"So what's the deal?" he asked.

"It's pretty much the way Grimis explained. People come here because that's what they expect when they pass from the first life."

Jonathan frowned.

"Remember why you landed at the DMV?" she asked.

"I remember, but I still don't know exactly why."

"Take a guess."

Jonathan closed his eyes. It had been so long since he'd been truly honest with himself. He wondered if he could make it through the wall all those years of lying had built. He tried to visualize it crumbling, but it was too thick to handle. He felt like Luke Skywalker trying to lift his X-wing fighter from the mud. It could be done, just not by him. He opened his eyes, half-searching for a little green creature. There was none, but he wasn't exactly alone either. Amber's stare told him that much.

"All right. I guess I landed there because I was going nowhere in my life and I expected death to be about the same."

"And why the South Side?"

"Maybe because I was guilty."

Both Sides of Broken

"Of what?"

Jonathan didn't want to tell her. He had come to love this woman as a friend. He'd never done that before and he didn't want it to end. But for all practical purposes he was indeed a murderer. Someone like her could never forgive someone like him. If he let it out now, he'd lose everything. He'd be alone in a world he didn't understand, with no hope of getting home, and no chance to right the wrong he'd committed.

His lie stuck him like thorns to the brain, but he spoke the words anyway, fearing the deeper hurt the truth would bring.

"I'm guilty of being a terrible son and brother."

"Were you really that bad, to will yourself to what you thought was hell?"

"Yes."

"How can you say that with no hesitation?"

"Well, I couldn't go to heaven, or the North end, or whatever it's called now. I wasn't worthy, not with all the things I'd done. The sins, the lies, the life I lived and the choices I made. Not in a million years."

"So you understand this place, then?"

"What?"

"The Sticks. It's an in-between. The default setting on your home computer. The place you go when you're an average person who gave little thought to the future and not a moment to the *what came next.*"

"Are you saying that this is just another Earth?"

"Yup. And sadly there are thousands of them."

"No way."

"It's true. People are born into worlds like this one, live their entire lives, and never notice anything different. Lifetime

137

after lifetime, world after world, they wallow in normalcy. They get a different face, a different location, even a clean slate to start from, and still they stay the same tired soul."

"Well, how are they supposed to know there's something else?"

"How did you know?"

"I didn't. Not at all. But I get it now. And it sucks."

Jonathan folded his arms and pushed himself off the car with his foot. He walked towards the road, thumb out, hoping to catch a ride, any ride. Amber chased after him.

"Where are you going?"

"Away."

"Why?"

"'Cause I'm tired of the lies. No wonder nobody believes in anything anymore. God, politicians, family, they're all bullshit fantasies. This whole thing is bullshit."

"What are you talking about?"

"Think, Amber. People are stuck living shit life after shit life unless they're pompous enough to will themselves to heaven, or screwed up enough to think themselves to hell. What kind of system is that? No wonder this place is so popular. It's the only normal locale."

"You don't know what you're saying."

"Oh really?"

"Really. These people have given up. It doesn't take a megalomaniac to go North, nor does it take a sociopath to go South. You just have to want something different, something more. They refuse to see that possibility. They never give it a thought. Any one of them could will themselves rich or famous or wonderful if they wanted to, but they don't believe.

They eat, sleep, and watch big-screen televisions, but that's about all.

"Even if we could give them a free ride out of the Sticks, do you think they'd be any different? Awareness is something you have to earn and learn on your own. It can't be given as a birthday present. Do that and you'd be giving them an empty box, nice wrapping for the things they can't see.

"It's a long hard road, Jonathan. You're remarkable but it took even you thirty-odd years on a DMV line to begin to see. They'll get it too, but you must balance concern with patience."

"So they're just stuck here, then?"

"For now, but not forever."

"That sucks."

"No one said death was perfect. At least no one who knew anything."

Jonathan smiled slightly as an image of his parish priest came to mind. He wondered where he'd put himself when he died. His smile faded at the thought of his father. Odds were if the old boy kicked it he'd end up going South. Jonathan's skin crawled as he imagined their initial exchange. How do you apologize to your father for killing him?

"You okay now?" asked Amber.

"No. Better, but not okay."

"I understand. So are you coming with us, or are you going to sink back into an Earthly existence?"

"I'd be lying if I said that part of me didn't want to hide here for a while."

"Nothing wrong with that. It's your soul, and even the best souls need a break now and then. Just look at your friend there."

Grimis was trying to listen to another of Marvin's golf stories, but his mind was far down the road. For the first time, Jonathan saw him wear something besides a smile.

"What's with him?"

"You."

"How do you mean?"

"He's supposed to watch out for you, lead you to what you need."

"So?"

"Grimis has been around a long time. Remember how I knew what you were thinking the other day? Well, he has a deeper sense of perception. Thousands of souls look to him as a sort of After-Earth guidance counselor. He carries their fears and hopes and dreams around in his heart and head. No computer database. No secretary. Nothing but those crumpled bits of yellowed paper to help him sort it all out. He knows the feelings you have inside are too much for you. They're too heavy a load and, whether you know it or not, you've been giving them away for some time."

Jonathan swallowed a lump of fear. He was sweating again and the warm air wasn't the cause.

"Does he know everything?"

"Only what you want him to. You're a troubled soul, Jonathan."

"You could say that."

"What exactly is it?"

"Sadness, I guess. This place sure didn't help any. No, doesn't look like I'll find what I need here. I appreciate the pit stop though and the answers it provided, but I think it's time to move on."

"Time to meet the Big Guy?"

"I'd say so."

"Well, then let's get moving."

Jonathan gave one last look at the outgrown Mini-Mart. He'd never go back there. He'd never need to.

CHAPTER 18

Sam woke early, refreshed from the shower and the decent night's sleep. It had been a while since he'd bothered to take care of himself. He used to run, eat with silverware, think about the future—all the wonderfully simple things normal folk do and never notice, never appreciate. Yet Sam could see the importance of focus and clarity in one's existence. The day began with no booze to cloud the mind, no woman to drain the heart, and no fear to stifle his intentions, for, unlike so many of the day-to-day drones, Sam actually had a plan. He reviewed it again as he sipped his coffee, then picked up the phone.

Norah's secretary answered on the third ring. Normal practice for the Baxter Ad Agency was to grab it by the second, but it was before nine on Wednesday and the floozy was probably filing her nails.

"Ms. O'Conner is in a meeting now. Can I take a message?"

Sam winced slightly at the sound of her name. She'd worn his for almost a decade, and though he was beginning to accept the inevitability of the split, it hurt him to know she'd discarded it so quickly. She'd liked it once, said it fit like her favorite pair of blue jeans. It seemed odd to him that she would replace them now with a forgotten pair of Sergio Velentas. Out of date, out of style, but styles live on, returning to fashion after years of obscurity. He thought of their marriage. Perhaps, he was just her down time. Perhaps she was his.

"Hello?" asked the secretary, trying her best to sound busy. "Message? Can I take one for you, sir?"

"It's kinda urgent. Can I speak with her?"

"May I ask who's calling?"

"Sam. Sam Holiday."

"Oh, the ex. How nice." Her voice ditched the professional tone. "Is she expecting your call?"

"Linda, don't break my balls. Just put her on the phone and go back to your *Cosmo*."

She transferred Sam to the hold music without a word. Three songs later, Norah came to the line.

"I'm in a meeting here, Sam. What's the problem?"

"Well, hello to you too."

"Save it. I've got a client waiting. What is this about?"

"Windy."

"Yes?"

143

"I can't find him."

"Haven't seen him. Sorry. Gotta go."

"What's with you?"

"Look, Sam, I have my own life now. I don't mean to be a bitch, but I've got to start fresh. I'm only thirty-one. I still have a shot at being happy, at having a family, a career, and all the things a woman is supposed to have."

"That's it then? You can walk, just like that?"

"No. It wasn't just like that. That's the problem. It's been years of heartache, months of loneliness, days in therapy, and nights lying awake in bed. You just never noticed. Look, I don't blame you, Sam. It's no one's fault. We were kids and we made the right choices given the situation. I don't regret the time we spent. But we're grown-ups now and our needs have changed. It's time our choices did too. You never left my heart. You never will. I just can't love you anymore. I really have to go."

Sam heard her voice crack under the weight of her last words. She was crying. He pictured her walking into the client meeting with red eyes. She'd hide them as best she could, but the vultures would know, and they'd soon come swooping.

He imagined some young executive putting his arm around her in the cafeteria, telling her to forget about her ex, inviting her to dinner . . . just to talk, of course. He thought of her drinking too much too soon as she listened to the lies he told. He knew she'd want to believe them. He knew her heart would convince her mind it was the right time, the right guy, and, what the hell, she deserved some fun too. He pictured her fucking the good-looking twenty-something and wondered how many of them it would take before she forgot what it was like to be with him that way. Maybe she already had.

She was right, of course. Maybe they could be friends again someday, but not now. Not when his voice made her cry and her dating made him want to buy a machine gun. The rules of breaking up and starting over are as follows: Don't ask. Don't tell. Don't dwell. Don't care. It's the last two that get you, but then again something always does.

"I understand," said Sam. "About everything. And I'm sorry."

"Don't be. I'm not. We were okay once, you know?"

Sam smiled at the phone and held her face in his mind. Oh, the things she'd taught him. He'd gone from boy to man in the time they'd spent, and he'd watched her become a woman. That was something no other man could experience or steal. It was his and hers and they'd never forget. He took some comfort in the thought. Memories—what a consolation prize.

"I'm gonna go to the cops about Windy."

"You think that's necessary?"

"He's pretty sick, Norah. I'm worried. I lost one brother already. I think it's time to start playing it safe."

"They're calling me, Sam. I gotta—"

"I know. I guess I've known now for a while. Good luck, kiddo."

"You too. Let me know if anything happens."

"Will do."

Sam clicked the flash button and dialed the nine of 911. For a long minute his finger hovered over the phone. Then he replaced the receiver and grabbed his keys from the table. Norah wasn't the only one who needed to start over.

Tim Toterhi

* * *

Sam watched a cop watch the scalpers peddle their wares in front of Yankee Stadium. Game six series tickets: Yanks versus Boston. The uniform finished his chili dog, walked to one of the better-dressed perps, and scored himself a pair of bleachers. From where Sam sat it looked as if the cop actually handed over two C-notes. No sting operation, no toss and arrest, just the free-market system at its finest. He wondered what it would cost a regular Joe to procure a decent seat, then shook his head. If the blues were paying, the rate he'd be charged would only depress him further.

An angry horn sounded, telling Sam that the light had long since changed. He turned left under the elevated train and began his quest for a parking space. There was a lot nearby, but he lacked the funds for such an indulgence. Besides, the Honda was not exactly on the car thief's hot list. After ten minutes of searching, he parked questionably close to a hydrant and walked the four blocks to the forty-fourth precinct.

The lobby was as restful as the others Sam visited. Crime drops with the temperature, and is always less during the day. This chilly afternoon brought only a few domestic disputes and robberies. To the credit of the young, gung-ho officers Mayor Giuliani had brought in, the murder rate had dropped off consistently over the past few years, transforming a precinct that once boasted the second-highest rate in the state to one that no longer appeared on the watch list. Even the nights weren't as bad as they used to be.

The desk sergeant was as fat as a desk sergeant is supposed

to be and equally as rude. He sat behind the enormous structure, thumbing through a *Water Sportsman* magazine. He made the people in the line wait until he finished whatever paragraph he was reading. He marked his place with a red pen and, after a sigh, peered at them officially as if they had no business stirring him from his thoughts. Though disgruntled by his lot, he was not without a work ethic. Once engaged, he dutifully listened to their lies, offered an appropriate scowl, and then grumbled whatever advice or instructions were warranted.

He was a sad man, balding, wrinkled, and gray of beard. He had a calendar somewhere, for sure. You could almost see him crossing off his final days on the force. He'd had enough. Soon he'd be fishing in Florida and all these low-life dirtbags could kiss his ass.

"I'm looking for an officer named Sam."

"Sam who? We got a lotta guys named Sam here."

"This one's a girl."

The blue's face took on the look of a father protecting his teenage girl. Sam was a delinquent in the eyes of most, but more so to this old-school Irish boy. If he had a say, Sam would never step to the plate. No one would.

"And who are you?"

"A friend. I have some information for her that could have something to do with a case she's working on."

"Well, let's have it."

The stocky officer pulled a pencil from his ear and tugged a steno pad to his gut. He held the pencil as a barbarian would hold a salad fork.

"Well?"

"I think I should tell her myself."

"Oh, one of those," said the cop as he folded over the pad.

"Look, I'm not trying to be one of anything. She's just a friend that I wanna get in touch with. You know how it is."

"And you don't have her last name? Must be good friends."

Sam shrugged.

"Buddy, you know how many guys see her on the street and then come in here pretending to be her brother or something?"

"So you know her?"

"Well let me see, tall, brunette, rhythmically beautiful, super-intelligent. Of course I know her, ya mook. She's the doll of everyone here and I'm not gonna just hand her off to some whack job."

"Paranoid much?" asked Sam. "Look buddy, the concern is admirable, but I really gotta talk with her. Just get her on the phone and tell her Sam from the other night is here. If she doesn't know me, I'll leave."

The officer put his fist to his chin. He ran his eyes across Sam, decided he posed less of a threat than a warm ice cream sundae, and reached for the phone.

"Thanks, man."

The sergeant grunted and motioned for him to take a seat. Sam watched the officer's expression as he spoke with Samantha. At first he was happy, as if she'd forgotten him. Then his faced dropped. Sam's brightened at the sight.

"Hey," called the sergeant. "She'll be out in a minute."

Sam smiled, but the officer refused to acknowledge any misdoing. Sam was still a bum, as far as he was concerned. No apologies.

Both Sides of Broken

Samantha burst through the double doors guarding the office section of the precinct. She looked older in a suit than in the jeans she'd worn the prior night; nowhere near twenty-eight, but not quite the nineteen she'd been playing. There was a crispness about her as if she knew she had her shit together. She worked in the most testosterone-filled environment on the planet and yet had the confidence to allow her hair to dance about her shoulders.

"Sam Holiday," she said, smiling. "Contribute to the delinquency of any minors lately?"

He started to speak, but nothing came out. He was enchanted. He eyed the perimeter of her gray suit and watched it embrace the curves of her body.

"You know, I have to say I'm hurt that you never called," he said, with a half smile.

"Expected me to?"

"More liked hoped."

"Don't men have the three-day rule?"

"Yeah, I guess so."

"Well, we met last night. Would you ever call a girl the morning after meeting her? Talk about looking desperate."

"Last night, huh?"

"What?"

"Oh, nothing. It's just that it seems a lot longer."

The hint of a blush touched her cheek. "I'm flattered."

"You don't think I'm desperate, do you?" asked Sam sheepishly.

"Are you?"

He laughed, hoping she would join him. She did and it made a world of difference. He wasn't desperate as much as thrilled with the possibility. She knew it, but would let him stir a while.

"I'm kinda out of practice. Haven't had a date in over a decade."

"Wow. Talk about a dry spell. What happened?"

"A wife."

"And now?"

"A divorce."

"I'm sorry."

"Why? You didn't dump me."

She chuckled and told him to wait a second. She disappeared behind the door and returned a minute later with a small black knapsack. She winked at the desk sergeant and took Sam by the arm.

"I'm not under arrest, am I?"

"Tempting, but no. I'm thinking more along the lines of lunch. Italian?"

* * *

Samantha and Sam sat at a cozy table in an Italian sandwich shop. For some reason there were three chairs, but it mattered little to them as they used the third for their jackets and motorcycle helmets.

"How long have you been riding?" asked Sam.

"My father taught me when I was a kid."

"Is he a big man?"

"Yup," she said, smiling. "With a lot of guns. Got brothers, too. Five of them. Big, but not into guns so much as chainsaws. They own a home-repair business."

"Well, nothing like starting off a date in total fear."

"Relax. Dad's a pussycat. They all are. Besides, I'm the one you should watch out for."

"I bet."

The waiter came and refilled their iced-tea glasses.

"Hey, I was meaning to ask you," Samantha said. "How did you track me down? I never gave you an address or number."

"Well . . . I, ah . . ."

"Come on. Spit it out, detective."

"Doubt I'd ever make the cut. I kinda spent the morning driving from precinct to precinct. I mean, I knew you worked in the city and it had to be somewhere near the convenience store. God, these territories are hard to figure. The four-four was the fifth one."

Samantha nearly choked on her tea.

"You went to four other stations! With what? You didn't even remember my last name, right?"

"Yeah, well, I ah . . . kinda described you to them. I hope you're not mad."

"Mad. I'm flattered. Don't get me wrong. I'll probably catch a lot of flack from the guys over this, but still...."

Sam dropped his head and began stroking his chin.

"Well, it was some kiss."

"Yeah, I guess it sure was," she said, smiling. "So what now?"

"I don't know. Like I said, this is new to me. But would you mind if I switched gears for a second? I've gotta ask your advice on something."

"Sure, what's up?"

"My brother's missing."

Samantha's happy expression scampered away. She was a good detective and any mention of business knocked all else from her mind. Sam found himself regretting his choice. He missed her smile already, but it was amazing to see her in her zone.

"How long?"

"A little over a day."

"You know it takes forty-eight hours before a report can be filed, and around here nothing gets touched for at least three days. People disappear all the time. It could be anything, a fight with the wife, bad day at work, anything at all. Unless it's a kid with no run-away record, these cases tend to get lost in the slush pile. I'm being honest here, Sam, and I need you to do the same."

"Sure."

"What kinda guy is he? What I mean by that is, is he prone to taking off?"

Sam knew exactly what she was getting at. She'd followed Jonathan's case for the duration. She knew Jonathan, his work, and his family history. He wouldn't be surprised if she even had a file on him. He couldn't fool her, wouldn't try.

He spent the rest of the meal explaining Windy's condition and the fact that he took in as much scotch as air. Still, he made it clear that Windy wasn't the type to get up and leave. It wasn't because he was wonderful. He just had nowhere to go.

She listened, guided, and comforted him the way a friend should. When the Windy tale was over they switched to small talk. Music, movies, favorite colors. A decade gone and not much had changed about a first date. Sam was relieved to find it so simple, but he credited it to the woman and not the task.

Both Sides of Broken

They never got around to eating and about halfway through the conversation, she asked the waiter to bag up the meal. He noticed her hand on his. He twitched like a schoolboy and she retracted instinctively. His eyes told her all the truth she needed, and by the time the coffee came they were holding hands across the table.

"This feels nice."

She nodded, and Sam sighed through his first real smile in months. She gave him her number and a brief kiss on the sidewalk. They wanted more, wanted to speed through the beginning, but like the saying goes, "You can't grow anything in a hurry."

They planned to meet Friday night, but it quickly changed to lunch the following day. So much for old sayings.

CHAPTER 19

The road North was uphill and longer than any in the GTO had expected. The landscape evolved from level plains to red mountains to the sandy brown of wheat fields that seemed to roll and twist with the summer wind. By lunch, earth tones gave way to the virgin green of untouched grasslands.

Grimis was again piloting the vehicle. The rest had done him good. His wit returned, as did his laughter. Amber zipped through another *New York Times* crossword puzzle. They were child's play for her, and the novelty was beginning to wear thin. She tossed the finished product on the dash and looked back at Jonathan. He was struggling to remove Marvin's arm from his shoulder.

"Marge. My sweet little baby doll," mumbled the

slumbering oaf.

Jonathan could hardly be classified as homophobic, but he wasn't nearly comfortable enough to afford a simple-minded large man the opportunity to grope at his chest, intentional or not. He tilted as far left as space allowed, drew back his free hand, and cracked the poor fool in the head.

"Jonathan!" scolded Amber.

"What?"

"He was sleeping."

"Well he ain't no more."

Marvin rose to reality with a stupefied gaze. "We need to stop, guys," he said.

"Why, Marv?" asked Grimis. "Gotta take a whiz?"

He looked at his member and waited a moment as if he expected the organ to respond for him. He shrugged slightly and gazed at Grimis.

"Guess not."

"So what, then? You hungry?"

He looked at his belly in the same fashion, but Grimis was losing patience fast.

"What? What is it?"

"Marge."

"Marge?"

"Yup. We shoulda brought her. I miss my Margie."

"Great gobs of goose shit, Marvin. We've been through this already. She's home. Home as in real far away home. We can't go back for her now."

Amber patted Grimis' shoulder. He sighed and turned his attention to the road.

"You understand what Grimis is saying, don't ya?" asked

Amber. "We'll be back soon."

"But I have to see her. I was supposed to see her this mornin', but I was sleeping. I hope she doesn't get too mad at me."

"What the hell is he talking about?" asked Jonathan.

"Who knows," said Grimis.

"Well, I could sure use a rest. Let's hit the next exit."

The party followed a dirt trail as it twisted along the bank of a shallow river. Grimis took advantage of the muddied roads and used them to fishtail his eight-cylinder, 350-horse-power demon. They pulled into a service station, turned a few donuts in the barren lot, then settled by a pump that still offered regular gasoline.

Marvin removed his backpack from the trunk as his comrades entered the store. He pulled a comb from an inside compartment, swiped it through what remained of his hair, and stuck it in his back pocket. He clapped his hands and a strange-looking device dropped from the sky. He laid it on the hood of the car and labored through the operating instructions. By the time he concluded the third and final sentence, the gas was pumped and the rest of the party circled him, eyes fixed on the curious machine.

"Marge," said Marvin.

The contraption belched out a chorus of disheveled notes, tried its hand at white noise, then repeated the process. After good three attempts, silence returned, accompanied by a holographic image of Marge. She sat in a recliner eating ice cream and watching some low-budget horror flick.

"Hello, dear."

"You're late."

Both Sides of Broken

"I know. I'm sorry, schnookems. We were on the road and there was this—"

"Save it."

She capped the ice cream and pried herself from the chair. Once erect and balanced, she stood A-frame with arms crossed. Her shaggy robe was the sort of pink sane people see in department stores and make fun of. Jonathan shuddered, hoping to shake the image, but it held fast like a bulldog to a bone.

"I want you home right quick," she said. "And bring some Devil Dogs. We're fresh out. Oh, and we need some light bulbs. The one in the bathroom burnt out."

"Again?"

"That's what I said. I had to put on my makeup in the dark this morning."

"So that explains it," mumbled Jonathan.

"Got an issue, boy?" asked Marge, catching the tone of this comment.

Jonathan shrugged and took an unconscious step backwards. The last place they'd met was on the line. She had ultimate power there and the concept of her as oppressive ruler lingered in his mind.

"I'll get right on it, dear. First thing I do. I promise."

"Good. So when you coming home?"

Marvin crinkled his face the way people do when answers escape them. He looked to Jonathan, but received only a blank stare. Grimis sat in the car, no longer amused by the exchange. He had seen them fight before. Nothing changed. Marge made rambling accusations. Marvin apologized endlessly. Silence hung like a bad painting on a cracked wall. Then they made

157

up. Always the same. To him their relationship was about as interesting as a morning floss. Amber knew the routine as well, but her romantic soul made her watch.

"It's gonna be a few days," she said.

"Was I talking to you? You . . . you . . . *hussy*! I know what's going on here. I see the way you look at him. Eyeing him down. Getting all revved up over my big hunk of man."

"Marge? Please."

"Don't deny it. I know there's something going on between you two. All the girls want him."

"Hon, that ain't true. You know you're the only one for me."

"Oh baby, you mean it?"

"Yup."

The two stood quietly exchanging goofy looks of affection. Jonathan, never one for the mushy stuff, began searching for a barf bag. He climbed to the shotgun position and turned on the radio. Anything was better than a bad holographic soap opera.

By the time Jonathan found an acceptable station the two had reconciled and said their good-byes. Marvin touched a big red button and Marge's image vanished in a burst of light. Marvin lowered the antenna and began packing up the contraption.

"See guys, it's all about how ya treats your woman. Sure I might seem like a kiss-ass from time to time, but trust me, boys, she knows who really wears the pants."

The machine beeped itself to consciousness and returned Marge's image to the sky.

"Oh really? You wear the pants, huh? You know how to treat me, huh?"

"Honey, I . . . ah."

Excuseless, hopeless, Marvin stuffed his hands in his pockets and began shuffling them about in an attempt to dry his sweating palms.

"What's that?" she asked.

"What's what?"

"That. That thing on your leg."

"Where?"

"There. Lift up your pants."

"Oh no," said Grimis quietly, sinking into his chair. "I kinda forgot about that."

Marvin uncovered the tattoo as instructed and shot an evil glance towards Grimis. The hell he would catch for this would be beyond human comprehension. Earth wives were easy. Marge had centuries of nagging practice. It was an art for her. Marvin was just the unlucky, unthinking canvas.

"What the?" she asked. "Grimis!"

She hurled a ten-minute barrage of threats and dispersions at the two delinquents. Jonathan even caught a few for being a bystander. When the tongue-lashing ended, she pulled a rolling pin from kitchen drawer and began tapping it on her palm.

"Just wait'll you come on home, honey-boy. We'll see whose wearing what."

Marvin tried to weasel his way out of the situation, but in a moment he was talking to air. Grimis and Jonathan snickered. They knew what it was like to grovel. Say what you will about traditional gender roles, but women ruled the relationships they entered one way or another. They'd been there, of course, but they'd never admit it. For men, there's nothing as fun as tormenting a buddy caught in the act of sucking up.

CHAPTER 20

Separating the Bronx and New Rochelle is a tiny political disaster known as Co-op City. The densely populated area is comprised of several dilapidated high-rise units, none of which are owned by the inhabitants. Originally envisioned as a stepping stone for those on their way up in the world, it soon became a den for uptown crack dealers, pregnant teenagers, and delinquent fathers. Clearly more people were on their way down.

A virtual bubble, the Earthly answer to purgatory is connected to the civilizations on either side by a pair of single-lane, two-mile-long roads. Both run through undeveloped marshland and neither is terribly busy. New highways take the business folk where they need to go. The locals keep their distance.

Sam maneuvered his Honda through the stretch on the Westchester side. His car twisted and turned in compliance with the will of the wetland. Narrow bridges, hills, and turns too sharp to be navigated at speed had killed many an inebriated teenager over the years. Sam eyed the shoulder as he drove. It was littered with broken beer bottles and burnt-out bombs. He smiled to himself and patted the Honda. One more breakdown and he'd add it to the list of insurance jobs.

About halfway between Westchester and Co-op City the shoulder expanded into a small parking lot. He pulled in, clicked off the lights, and stepped from the car. He remembered the place well. They'd called it "the Point" when he was young. Probably still did. The name fit, like the bonfires, the dope, and the lies its male inhabitants told about girls they never knew. A large part of his growing up had happened in this realm the congressmen forgot. But he remembered. He saw a Corona in a steel trashcan. They drank Bud in his day. Clearly the place lived on.

Sam thanked kids older than he for hacking away at the shrubs, expanding the lot's dimensions. Those ghosts discovered the rocky pier not more than a hundred yards from the road. He consumed many a beverage on its ledge. He lost a few things there, his wallet, a fight or two, his virginity.

Sam straightened when the car pulled in. A new Lexus. It figured Donato would be stupid enough to trade in the Beemer for a Jap knockoff. He shoulda bought a Toyota and taped thirty grand to the hood.

"You got good news, I hope," said Donato.

He shut the door and set the alarm. Anal fool. Who would

rip him off? He stepped closer and Sam remembered his size and the beating he had taken last year for paying off two months too late. He was a big man, all business. He wasn't tall, just big in an ominous, crush-your-skull-in-one-quick-maneuver kind of way. It took a lot of balls for Sam to ask him for a favor, especially when he owed on an account. The request had intrigued Donato. His curiosity and their history were the only things separating Sam from a trip to the hospital.

"Well? I'm here. So what's this plan you're so hot about?"

Sam pushed up his sleeves and sighed. For a grunt bookie, Donato was an intelligent businessman who could smell a lie like a fart in a Ford. He'd get one shot at a pitch.

"How would you like to make a half million?"

Donato laughed and walked back to his car. He deactivated the alarm and opened the door. Sam called out before he could sit.

"What?"

"Don't you wanna hear it?"

"The only thing I wanna hear from you is that you got my five grand. I don't know what's up with you and Franky, and I really don't care. Just remember that I get mine first. Understand me? You got six days left on the loan. No extensions."

"What if I could get it to you sooner?"

"Great. I don't buy it, but great, Sam. Do that and I'll buy you an ice cream. For now, stop wasting my time. I got some things of my own to talk to Franky about."

"He ain't there."

Donato slammed the door and walked back to Sam. He

began twisting the diamond in his left ear, an unconscious habit that told the careful observer that his fists would soon fly. Sam felt them before and wanted to avoid a repeat performance.

"Franky's been kidnapped. I ain't playing with ya. He called me this morning."

"Bullshit. Why would he call you?"

"'Cause I'm the reason they got him."

"Who?"

"The Campellenas."

"Well, it was nice knowing him. Six days, Sammy."

"I need to borrow five hundred grand," said Sam desperately.

Donato's face dropped. He shoved Sam to the Honda and belted him in the mouth. He watched Sam slide down the car and plop to the dirt. There was blood on his lip and a tooth on his tongue. Donato sighed.

"It didn't have to be like this. I thought you were through. Shit, Sam, I'm a bookie and I'm telling you to lay off the betting. What's the matter with you? Two years clean, then right back in the saddle. If you weren't who you are, you'd be in the ground by now."

Sam used the car as a crutch and pushed himself to his feet. It's a tough thing standing up. Difficult for any man, day-to-day, year-to-year, but with the load he carried, the task was almost impossible. Donato sensed the weight, but had long ago run dry of feelings.

"Thanks," said Sam. "I know the difference between the things you did and the things you shoulda done. I appreciate the slack."

"So no more bullshit, Sam?"

"It's not bullshit. See for yourself."

Sam pulled an envelope from his coat and passed it to Donato, who removed its contents and glanced it over.

"An insurance policy?"

"Yup."

"For who?"

"My father. And you'll see there that I'm soon to be the sole beneficiary of $1.6 million."

"How so? Says here your one of four . . . ah, three without Jonathan."

"Grayson's been dead for years, and as far as Windy . . ."

"Yeah."

"He's real sick, Don. Even if he lives, he won't be walking around on his own for much longer. The drinking finally got him. Liver. Kidneys. They're pretty bad."

Donato ran a flat hand across his flat head and joined Sam on the hood of his car. They sat together for a moment in silence, thoughts drifting to the kids they once were. Times were good back then. Granted, maybe a little better now with the euphemistic filters of time and distance, but they were good nonetheless. So much had happened since stickball in the street. The players were the same, but the game had changed drastically. There weren't any teams anymore.

"He's a good guy, that Windy. Always liked him."

"Yeah."

"Look Sam, I'm gonna let this one go."

"What?"

"Forget the five. I've been doing good lately, raking in the bucks. It ain't gonna break me. Consider it a gift for the old days. Okay? But you're cut off, Sam. No more loans. No more beats. And I'm gonna spread the word, too. You're done. That's it for you. Time to get well. Sound good?"

"No."

"What?" cried Donato, jumping from the car. "I do you a solid and you throw it back in my face? Are you nuts?"

"I pay my debts, Don. Maybe late, but I always pay."

"How?"

"Loan me the five hundred. I can use that to pay off what Franky owes. It's partly my fault they got him and if I don't straighten things out, he's dead."

"They'll kill him anyway."

"Maybe, but I gotta try. You're right about me Don. It's time to get well, but I can't begin with this thing hanging over me. If Franky dies like this I'll just use it as an excuse to keep gambling. You know I will."

"That's your deal, something you need to get a handle on. I like Franky. We go way back. But I don't know if I like him that much. Know what I mean?"

"Come on. Loan me the money. It's good business. Franky owes you, I know it. If you don't help me help him now he ain't gonna be around to settle up later. So what do you say? Do the right thing here. You know I ain't going nowhere. It's a sure deal."

"Ain't nothing sure. Sounds like good money after bad."

"No. No. You have the policy backing you up. The profit is built in."

Donato stepped from the car and walked towards the metal can. He began tapping it with his fist. He was tempted by the offer. It was real and as clean as anything a man like him could hope to be involved with. Five hundred would put him a lot closer to the island retirement he had planned. He looked over the marshlands. It wasn't his place anymore. The folks in his business were younger and faster and killed quicker for less. He was losing ground, influence, and the taste for the whole damn thing. It was time to move on.

"Five hundred is a lot a cash to have out indefinitely. That old man of yours has been hanging around for a while now. What makes you think he's gonna kick it soon? The doctors say anything?"

"Let's just say I got a feeling he's on the way out."

"How much this feeling cost you?"

"Enough."

"And you'll walk okay? The pot is that big?"

"Let's see, after my bills and debts, your cut, plus the little something Uncle Sam snatches, I should walk with about $250,000 or so plus whatever I can get for the garage."

"That's enough for you?"

"More than I've ever known. Get me a car and a condo in Florida. Who knows? Maybe I'll get a job selling Buicks or some shit. Hell, I might even set up an IRA, plan for my future. I think being respectable is the way to go. I'm getting tired of all this dirtbag crap and I'm sure as hell getting tired of this place. I wanna go somewhere where nobody knows the asshole I've been. Someplace warm."

"You and me both."

"So you'll do it?"

"Yeah. I guess I will."

"Great."

"When you need the cash?"

"Tomorrow night too soon?"

Donato grabbed at his ear again, but this time the itch was real. He put his hand to his mouth and looked up and to the right. He eyes widened as he performed the required accounting. The tally completed, he turned back to Sam.

"It'd be a stretch, but I can swing it. What say we meet here tomorrow night around eight? I'd come to your place, but the town's got eyes, you know?"

"All too well," said Sam. "But don't worry, this thing will be over by the weekend. And barring any hassles with the insurance company, we should get the check in a month or so. Can you hang out that long?"

"Normally no, but for a pay-off like this, it's worth using your own cash."

"So we're cool, then?"

"Just two things."

"What?"

"First, you fuck me and I'll kill you. Friend or not, you die. Number two, you get pinched on this thing and it's your ass. I don't do murder, not like this, anyhow. Understand me? As far as the world is concerned, my loaning you cash to free Franky has nothing to do with you bumping off your old man. Oh yeah, and number three: remember, prison or not, I hold you accountable for my money."

"I got ya."

"Fine. I'll set things up."

They shook hands and parted. Sam watched his taillights disappear around a curve. Another friend bought and paid for. No wonder the devil never carried a sword—temptation was the greatest weapon of all. In the end, men defeated themselves. With the lights gone and thick clouds shrouding the moon, darkness engulfed the lot. Sam relaxed, loving the simplicity of the sightless world. He thought of men's undoing and he wondered for the briefest of moments what would cause his own.

CHAPTER 21

It wasn't long before the travelers found themselves on the edge of a great metropolis. For the first time they believed they would complete the quest successfully. They just knew it would happen, as they were certain this would be a wonderful place.

Amber pointed to the river and all marveled at the lights dancing across the surface. Golden yellow moving in time with the sparkling blue of the tides. It was glorious, whimsical. They felt like children.

A drawbridge stretched out towards the river and disappeared in a circle of mist. There was no reason for the coverage. The sky was clear, the air calm. Yet it stood, separating the life they knew from the place humanity has searched for throughout the ages. Ironic. It was so easy to find. Just another bridge to cross, a lazy walk through the mist that was their existence.

Like all the questions, the truth revealed itself once the chattering racket of endless asking subsided. Faith, trust, hope, and belief brought them to the bridge. Those and the "kick-ass" determination that told its owner they knew they had the right to visit. Like most completed things, it seemed simple in retrospect. And as always, the view from the finish line was amazing.

Holy wars. Canon law. Religion and preachers and that ridiculous patch of sand in the Middle East. What did they have to do with this place?

The muscle car made its way to the edge of the bridge, stopping briefly at the request of a tall, uniformed man. The lanky fellow climbed from his tower and approached the party.

"I say, who goes there?"

"Ah, we're here to see the Big Guy," said Grimis.

"Indeed."

"Yes."

"Well, I'm sure he'll be delighted. I'll notify him at once of your arrival. Judging by your appearance, you undoubtedly have some fascinating bowling stories to pass on. It should be quite a hoot."

"Was that a dig?" asked Jonathan, more for confirmation than actual inquiry.

"Whatever is a dig?"

"You know—a cheap shot, an insult."

"Oh right, right. I see what you mean. Then yes. Yes, I'd

say it was a bit of a dig, my good fellow. Though a well-deserved one, I might imagine. Now, how long will you be staying on the North End?"

"Not more than a day," said Amber.

"Good. Good. I hope your trip is a pleasant one."

The guard took her hand and kissed it gently. Grimis grew tomato red and seized the fool by his collar.

"Listen, Romeo, knock it off and open the gate."

"Fine," said the guard, smoothing his shirt. "That will be four quid, please."

"What the hell is a quid?" asked Jonathan.

"Madam, please explain to the gentlemen. Really, I can't bear it myself."

"A quid is the local expression for British pound," said Amber. "It's also used occasionally by kids in Australia, though not a very proper word in either place. I expected more from a learned man such as yourself, Mr. . . . ah . . ."

"Wilson," said the guard, fighting off a blush.

"Wait a minute," said Jonathan. "We gotta pay to get in here?"

"No. Admission is free. You're paying for bridge maintenance, minus a small fee for myself, of course."

"How small?"

"Umm . . . I'm not quite at liberty to disclose that information."

"How much?" asked Jonathan, displaying a clenched fist.

"Three . . . ah, three of the four actually."

"Figures."

"Well I have children, you see, and . . ."

"Save it. Government workers. You're all the same."

Both Sides of Broken

"So what's the total?" asked Grimis. "In American dinero."

"Hum, that would be about eight of your dollars."

"And that's the current exchange rate? asked Amber.

"No, no. What I mean is that it *was* eight, but is now most definitely seven, yes, seven is the price for a one-way pass."

"Christ, and I thought the Throgs Neck was bad," said Jonathan, mostly to himself.

Grimis pulled out a wad of bills, paid the man, and asked for a return trip. Though enticed by the possibility of scoring another few bucks, the man declined the request, noting that most who entered never wanted to leave. According to him, application for citizenship after entry was ninety-seven percent. He assured the travelers they'd be no different.

"Just give me the token."

Grimis tossed the coin into the ashtray and slammed on the gas. The tires spun, leaving the guard encased in a cloud of purple haze. He choked and waved and cursed the stupid Yanks and their wretched automobile. They never heard him. They were gone, barreling towards infinity. He smiled slightly as the dust cleared. There was a reason he set up camp on the border, and it sure as hell wasn't the pay.

* * *

Somewhere in the mist the bridge transformed itself into a tunnel of white stone. They were bumper to bumper with cars going to and fro, but there were no slow-downs, no traffic, and the air about them was as fresh as a flower shop in April.

Grimis spotted an exit, clicked on his signal, and began to turn the wheel.

"What the hell?"

"What?" asked Jonathan.

"The car, it's not moving. It's like we're on rails."

"We are," said Marvin, stirring from a nap. "It's just like a choo-choo, only smaller and Grimis isn't wearing a hat. Where's your hat, Grimis? Conductors gotta have hats, you know. It's the rule."

"Sometimes I like him better when he's sleeping," said Jonathan.

"Relax," said Amber. "There must be a reason for this."

Grimis looked around at the other drivers. They were reading and typing and watching television. It was like the Long Island Expressway, only without the accidents. He gave the horn a try and rolled down the window.

"Hey pal. What the hell is going on?"

A thin man of about forty folded over his paper and looked at Grimis.

"Excuse me?"

"What's with the rails?"

"Oh," he said, smiling. "A new guy. It's the auto train. Just think where you wanna go and you'll get there. No worry, no tickets, no stress at all."

"Thanks, Mac. Say, what you got there?"

"*Daily Examiner*. I'm about through. Here, take a look."

The man tossed the paper to the convertible. A moment later his car merged right and exited the tunnel. Jonathan grabbed the paper from the floor and looked it over.

"I don't get it."

"What?"

"There's nothing here. Look."

Both Sides of Broken

The paper was blank on all sides. Useless, but not pointless. A blank paper had to mean something. Things always did. Marvin snatched the paper from Amber, quickly folded a section into a party hat, and used the rest to cover his eyes. A rumbling in his nose told all he was unconscious again.

The car moved crisply along the tunnel route for about thirty minutes. Without warning, it broke right and entered a small lift barely large enough for the vehicle. The doors shut with authority and the compartment began to rise. The travelers felt a slight pressure about their faces as G-forces played havoc with their internal organs. They were going fast and far, then not at all. The sudden stop woke Marvin and turned him green.

"I'm gonna be sick."

"Here?" asked Jonathan. "It's probably not the best—"

Marvin lurched forward and started puking over the side of the GTO. The way he ate, it would be quite a load.

"Watch the paint!" said Grimis, pushing the poor fool farther from the car.

"Don't throw him out," said Amber.

"Better that than ruin the shine. You realize what barf does to chrome? Worse than pigeon poop, let me tell ya. He'll understand. Jon, grab his other leg."

The two men held Marvin upside-down about six inches from the car and began jerking his ankles. With each gyration, Marvin heaved up some more candy.

"It's best he gets it all out."

"Best for who?" asked Amber.

"You don't understand men at all, do you? Come on Jonathan, give him a good yank."

175

Just as Marvin disposed of his last load the elevator door opened. A distinguished man in tie and tails entered without thought and stepped in the center of the debris. The sight turned his own stomach and sent the poor fellow scurrying down the hall.

"We're gonna do real well here," said Jonathan. "I can feel it."

The travelers climbed from the car and entered a massive marble hall. The floor was fifty yards wide and stretched farther than the party could see. They tried to follow the sequential squares of black and gray as they made their way to the horizon, but their eyes lost themselves in the dizzying array of whites speckles spread about the floor.

"What's wrong with you?" Jonathan asked Marvin.

He was standing slouched with his hands in his pockets, head drooping. He kicked at the ground and muttered to himself.

"What?" asked Jonathan again.

"I wish I'd brought my roller shakes."

"Roller skates?"

"Yup. This place is perfect for 'em. Skateboards too, but I don't much like skateboards any more on account of I fell one time and lost my left pinkie toe. Remember that, Grimis? That was my favorite toe too. Guess now it would be my right pinkie toe, only they're probably bad luck. What do you think?"

Jonathan tried to picture a nine-toed fat man on a skateboard. Knees bent, belly shaking, arms outstretched hoping to avoid another collision.The art-covered walls ran thirty feet high before sloping to an arched ceiling. The only illumination came from an assortment of skylights spread haphazardly about its length. It was magnificent at first, interesting a mile later, so-so soon after, and before long just plain dull. The human ability to adapt can be an amazing handicap. How sad that eventually we reduce any event, no matter how glorious or evil, to normalcy. But so it goes.

A whistle sounded as the group passed the three-mile mark.

"What's that about?" asked Amber, turning towards the sound.

"I'm not sure," said Grimis "but I have the feeling we should get out of the way."

"What are you talking—"

"Look out!" said Grimis as he pushed his friends from the center of the hall.

They toppled to the ground and rolled uncontrollably as a gale-force wind sucked them into its clutches. Jonathan tried to speak, to see, to stand upright, but there was nothing to stand on and no one to speak with. His friends were unconscious, and in a moment so was he.

* * *

Jonathan awoke to find himself seated in an immaculate subway car. Surprisingly enough, Marvin was awake and chatting it up with a suited man over a game of checkers. He crowned a king and laughed and clapped like a child.

Grimis and Amber were sleeping. He had his arm around her, and Jonathan thought that the greatest thing. Perhaps he'd come around after all. Perhaps he'd realize who he wanted was who he'd always had.

A woman to Jonathan's left noticed him stirring and offered a smile.

"Want a blow?" she asked.

"A what?"

"You know, a blow pop," she said, producing an old-fashioned Tootsie candy.

"Man, I haven't seen one of those since I was a kid. What flavor?"

"Cherry and chocolate."

"I'll take cherry, if you don't mind. You know, for a minute there I thought you were a . . . ah . . . forget it."

She blushed slightly as she handed him the candy.

"So where you headed?"

"I was hoping *you* could answer that. We were just walking down some hall when this wind started up. The next thing I know I'm here sucking on a blow pop with a beautiful woman."

"Thanks. I'm married, but thanks."

Strike one. Years ago he'd have tried for two, but not now.

"Sorry," he said, hoping to gain a friend.

"No problem. You must have caught the express. They can be jarring if you're not expecting them. Wasn't there a guide waiting to meet you when you came in?"

"Yeah, but we kinda . . . well, it's a long story."

"I bet. Well, this is my stop. Take care."

The doors opened and people began to calmly exit the car. No pushing, no mugging, no fat winos bumming change and stinking up the station. Just nice people, neatly dressed, going about their lives as though nothing was wrong. For the first time Jonathan wondered if anything was.

"Wait a minute," he called. "Where do I go?"

"You'll know when you get there."

Jonathan was getting tired of riding shotgun to fate. He had plans and agendas and people to meet. Infinity or not, he had something terribly important to do, and so far the whole process was moving like a horse-drawn aircraft carrier. He stared out the window as the car began to move. He watched the woman laugh as a sharp-looking man ran to her and held her close. They kissed. Two children appeared at their feet. They were happy and foolish and wrinkle free. Jonathan hated them for some reason. He hated Ken dolls the same way, but never knew why. Maybe he was jealous, or maybe they were too perfect to be believed. Another lie orchestrated, perpetrated, propagated to make him feel like total shit.

Jonathan woke Grimis and Amber at the next station and told them to get going.

"Is this our stop?" asked Amber.

"Yup."

"How do you know?"

"I just do. Let's go."

The stone subway chamber emptied into a wooden hall. It was bare except for the sound of their heels on its floor. Soon even that was gone, and the wood gave way to plush carpeting. A bust of Fred Astaire forced them to turn left. Jonathan wondered if it had something to do with the tapping. Maybe it was symbolic of his passing. Something to say that the dance was done and they'd arrived. He was tired of dancing for an invisible audience. He wanted to gather the roses and go home.

They walked on, passing an endless row of statues carved

from either onyx or white marble. They were famous folks facing each other. Black to the left, white to the right. Jonathan frowned. Even in this realm, it seemed, little was left to the gray.

An arched doorway appeared, stunning the travelers. It was mighty, made of English oak, and studded around the edges with bits of stained glass. Jonathan wondered why it came to be, if he had somehow summoned it, and how they would ever get it opened. They didn't have to strain, for with his thought came the answer. The double doors parted slowly as the group backed away.

The doorway led them to a reception area. It was stylish contemporary, overflowing with space-age coffee tables and smoked glass figures. The receptionist put down her magazine, greeted them warmly, and offered refreshments. They declined and sank into the leather chairs.

"The Holiday party is here to see you, sir," said the receptionist to the intercom.

"Fine, Gladys. Just give me a second to wrap things up in here on the McKensie project."

"The what, sir?"

"Just have them wait."

Twenty minutes passed before the intercom crackled to life. A sleepy-sounding voice instructed Gladys to send them in.

"And hold my calls," he said.

"Oh, yes sir," said Gladys with a hint of sarcasm. "I'll keep the natives at bay."

She waved the travelers in and went back to her fashion magazine.

CHAPTER 22

Sam sat eating breadsticks and sipping beer. He had never waited more than five minutes for a first date and now here he was twenty gone and not an angry thought in his mind. For the first time, he let things be and enjoyed the moment for what it was. Him, a bottle, and the often-tricky chore of removing the label without a single tear. It ripped.

He called the waiter over and asked if anyone had called for him. No luck. The kid was young, but had been around a while. He knew the habit, the look, and filled in the rest for himself. He kept quiet and brought another cold one without asking. Sam nodded his thanks and the kid disappeared.

Sam checked his watch. He intended to wait a half hour, maybe even eat alone, but he wasn't hungry anymore. His thoughts chased the yearning away. He threw some money on the table and retrieved his coat from the chair. She wasn't coming. The job kept her busy. He figured that and understood. Clearly something had come up.

His waiter was busy taking an order from an elderly couple two tables away. Sam walked over and thanked the kid. If there was one thing he appreciated in this world it was a good waiter. Most were a pain in the ass. The change was refreshing.

"Thanks, mister, but I wouldn't be taking off so soon."

"Why's that?"

"Look."

Samantha was talking to the hostess.

Sam smiled. "How'd you know that was her?"

"She's the only one in here worth the wait."

"You got style, kid."

"Thanks. Should I bring a bottle?"

"That you should. Make it red."

"Will do."

The waiter returned to the kitchen and Sam met his girl halfway to the table. He took her coat and pulled out the chair for her. She was worth the little things and if she'd let him, he'd do them until they were gray.

"Sorry," she said. "Something happened with the case."

"The rape thing?"

"Yeah."

"He didn't attack another girl, did he?"

"This time in broad daylight. He's getting sloppy, Sam. It's like he's rushing things, getting impatient."

"You know him that well?"

"He was my case before your brother got hold of him. Well not officially mine, but I told you the story. All cops hate rapists, but it's different for women. We lie about it, but truth be told, we take it very personally."

"I bet."

The waiter returned and filled their glasses. He suggested the pasta primavera. Sam was hungry again and in the mood for veal, but with the kid's track record he decided to go with his suggestion. Samantha concurred.

"So did you get him?" he asked.

"No. I tell you Sam this thing has been eating me alive. I grew up around here. This is my home. I can't see having people like him in my backyard."

"You look tired."

"Can't sleep. The boss ordered me home. Says I'm overdoing it."

"Well look, if you need to sack out for a while I'll understand. I wanna spend the time, no doubt, but I'm worried about you."

She reached across the table and took his hand. It had been a while since someone said that and meant it. Her friends were busy and the guys she dated rarely saw past her breasts. She wasn't blind to Sam's desire, but she knew there was more to it than a roll in the hay.

"I'll be fine," she said. "I don't have to be in until four tomorrow."

"What's with that, anyway?"

"What?"

"Your schedule. When I met you were working four-to-twelves, right?"

"It's not like that exactly. I'm a detective. We have the same shifts as the blues, but nobody sticks to them. When you're on a case, especially one like this, you gotta keep to the bad guy's schedule. Night usually works best, but there's a lot of overtime."

"Must be fun."

"A thrill a minute. Does wonders for your social life. Hope you're not the jealous type."

"Not my style. I'll worry, though."

"Fair enough."

They clicked glasses and sampled the wine. The kid brought their pasta and waited for them to taste. Sam gave him the thumbs up. He'd come back again. So far the place was an oasis of good fortune.

Sam wanted to know more about what was going on. He sensed that she was an overachiever, kinda like a bulldog with great legs. For a city boy he didn't know much about the way cops worked. Images of stakeouts and covert operations danced through his mind. He saw the movies and heard the stories about young cops going too far, too fast. He wanted to protect her from the evils that lay waiting. He laughed at himself. She was in great shape and packed a Glock. Chances were she could kick his ass in a second or so.

"So, you hear anything from your brother?" she asked.

"No, and I tell ya, I'm starting to worry. I wanna file that report if it's not too much trouble."

"Why don't you give me the details and I'll write it up tomorrow? Unless, of course, you wanna do it now."

"No. No. I don't know. Maybe I'm overreacting. It's just not like him is all. What do you think?"

"Hard to say. I don't know him. You told me he has no enemies, no debts, really no place to be or go. Given your description, it's doubtful the guy was kidnapped. Is it possible that he got himself a girlfriend, or maybe just took off for a while?"

"He hasn't had a date in years and his car is in the lot at the station."

"You try the clinics? Maybe he checked himself into a center."

"Doubt it. Windy's a career drinker. He functions well enough and has no desire to quit. Doesn't even mention the idea. I doubt he'd get religion now."

"I'm running out of ideas here, Sam. How's his health?"

"Well that's the big question. I'm guessing it can't be too good, but he never talks about it. I asked him a few times, but he shrugs me off. I'm his twin, but Jonathan was his confidant. It's hard, you know?"

"Yeah."

"Maybe I could give his doctor a call. He hasn't been there in a while, but it might be worth a shot."

"You know him?"

"Not really."

"Then you'd be wasting your time. He couldn't say anything if he wanted to."

"Right. Right. Well I'm not ready to start checking hospitals and morgues. I think the old boy has more time in him than that. Let's file the report and give it a day or two. Maybe he did meet someone. Stranger things, right?"

She returned his smile and took his hand again. The coffee and cheesecake came. It was as superb as the rest.

"This is some restaurant," said Samantha. "Come here often?"

"No, but I plan to."

"Good. Then it can be our place."

Sam liked the sound of that. He liked everything he knew about this woman and he was eager to learn more. He was falling for her. Two meetings, one kiss, and a thousand thoughts were all it took to convince him that this was the woman he'd been waiting for, the one he was supposed to meet. His break-up, the months of heartache, the lonely nights spent wallowing in booze were forgotten in a blink of her eye.

It happens that way. Just when you think you'll never know the comfort of another's touch, the warm security of a hug, or the gentle treasure of bodies meeting in the moonlight, it happens. It happens all over again, and it's wonderful.

Samantha leaned across the table and whispered her thanks in his ear. Her breath was warm and sweet and inviting. She was a schoolboy's dream, but so very real.

"Let's get out of here," she said.

Sam flagged down the kid. He sensed the urgency and came with check in hand.

"What's your name, buddy?"

"Billy Joel."

"Get out."

"What can I say? Pop was a fan."

"Well, Bill, you're a hell of a waiter. Keep the change."

Sam patted the kid on the shoulder and ushered his girl out the door. They went to her place, only because it was closer. They fit like people are supposed to fit. No pretense, no games, no playing and saying the stupid little things people do in an attempt to mask what they really want. They wanted each other. Passion ran wild that chilly afternoon. Their first time was in the hallway. Crazy kids never even made it to the bedroom. New lovers are insatiable. A marathon in the hall, a quickie on the couch, and a fairly decent crack at a third go in the kitchen. They were comfortable enough to realize their limits without the awkward embarrassment that sometimes comes with a failed attempt. They just laughed it off and settled for ice cream.

She prepared the desserts and they ate them naked. She attacked him with the whipped cream. He countered with chocolate sauce. He pushed her to the table and spread it over her body. She squirmed endlessly as he licked the warm liquid from her breasts and thighs. He kissed her softly and danced a hand across her cheek. She grabbed him forcefully, bit his lip, and sucked the sweetness from his tongue. She was burning with want and her moans made it clear how wet she'd become. He smiled and then, without warning, slid down her body and put his tongue inside her. She screamed and came and begged for more.

* * *

Sam wanted to spend the night, but he knew that they'd never let each other be. She was tired and he exhausted. He kissed her goodnight, tucked her in bed, and let himself out.

Before leaving, he found some paper by the phone and wrote her a short note. It wasn't poetry, but he thanked her and kissed her as best his words could. He left his number and told her to call day or night. Their pillow talk revealed she didn't have much in the way of family. Sam could relate and he wanted to be there for her. His thoughts held her as he shut the door.

* * *

Sam came home to a blinking machine. Most days he'd let it lie, but now he'd have to get used to checking his messages again. He clicked the play button and waited as the tape rewound.

"Hey, it's me," said Norah. "How's things? Windy okay? Look Sam, I was thinking about the other day and, ah . . . I don't know, I guess maybe I was a little hard on you. Hard on us, you know? Anyway, I wanted to say I'm sorry and maybe we could go out sometime. Nothing serious or anything, just talk. That's normal, right? Not like there's a newly divorced protocol guide. Well, whatever. Talk to you soon."

Sam shook his head in disbelief. If there was one thing he'd never understand it was that woman. Hot and cold. Off and on. Yes Sam and no Sam and go to hell Sam. He was through with her and the whole deal. Thank God they didn't have any kids.

He walked to the kitchen and grabbed a beer. On the way back to the living room he clicked on his country station and plopped himself on the couch. He was asleep before the second sip.

CHAPTER 23

An enormous stone desk hid the Big Guy from the travelers. He was pecking away at a keyboard when they entered.

"Sit," he ordered without offering them a look. "I'll be with you in just a second."

His tapping continued for a long moment and ended with an authoritative slamming of the enter key. He turned from the monitor, raised his chair to an appropriate level, and peered at them over his black-rimmed spectacles.

"So, which one of you is the Holiday boy?"

"I am, sir."

"Come a long way, huh?"

"You could say that."

Jonathan began to analyze the giant of giants in an attempt to gauge his chances of success. So far they looked pretty good. He seemed approachable, talkative, and friendly enough. And, though he seemed overworked, his willingness to meet with them said something positive about his character. Sure, he was a little full of himself, but who wouldn't be. Maybe this smartly dressed tech-nerd wasn't the apathetic demon he'd learned to fear as a child.

"So what's the deal? Why the big meeting? I hope you didn't come seeking forgiveness, advice, or answers to the *what* and *why* of the world. Don't get me wrong, folks. I love to help out, but I've got angels and such for that, you understand. These ain't the old days when I could chat on a mountaintop with every other bearded nomad."

"I understand," said Jonathan.

"Do ya really? You see this thing?" he asked pointing to a computer. "I got tons of 'em, with more gigabytes of memory than mosquito bites in Brazil. And that's just my database for the living. You should see the system I have running to keep track of all the dearly departed."

"Must be some job," said Grimis.

"You ain't kidding. Talk about a workload. Who knew designing a universe would be such a full-time gig? I used to jog, play a little racquetball. Now look at me. I got love handles, a receding hairline, and I'm working on my third eyeglass prescription. I tell you, nothing's easy."

Jonathan looked at Amber in disbelief. Was the Supreme Being actually bitching about his career choice? She shrugged and turned to Grimis, but he didn't know what to make of it either. Marvin just sat cross-legged and bounced in his chair.

"You got any video games on this thing?" asked Marvin.

"Who is this guy?"

"Just a friend," said Jonathan. "Anyway, about my problem."

"Yes. Yes. What is it?"

"I need an Earth pass."

"Oh, is that all? Why didn't you say so? Need any company? Wanna raise a few relatives from the dead so you don't get lonely during the trip? Or how about I bring back Sinatra so you can have a little music in the car?"

"I'm serious."

"So am I. You think returning from the dead is like catching a cab? A lot goes into a return trip and there has to be a good reason. It's my game, remember, and I set it up so you only get one turn around the board."

"I don't want a new life. I just want a day or two to fix something."

"Well, I hope it's not your faucet."

"It's life and death."

The Big Guy leaned back in his chair and pondered the request. He reached for a drawer and retrieved a cigar. A gold lighter and several strong puffs brought it to life. The scent told them it was Cuban, probably worth more than everything Jonathan had on, including his watch. For all the bitching, the job obviously had its perks.

"I need to know more about the situation," said the Big Guy, blowing a ring to the sky.

"It's kinda personal."

"What? You wanna lose your friends? I can understand that, one of those no-laundry-in-public things, right?"

Jonathan turned to his companions and asked for the room. His plight piqued their curiosity, but they were better friends than snoops and agreed to let him be. They gathered their coats and stood.

"Nonsense," said the Big Guy. "No need for you to be ambling about the complex. You'll probably get lost and lost means paperwork. I don't need any more of that in my life."

He snapped his fingers and Jonathan's friends were frozen.

"Are they okay?"

"Of course. I just took them out of time's grasp for a while. They're still moving and living and doing the things they like to do. They're just not doing them in the linear realm."

"The what?"

"That one's probably a little above your head for now. No offense."

"Whatever. As long as they're okay."

Briefly, Jonathan relayed his tale to the Big Guy. He told him of his career gone bad and his plot to have his father killed. For some reason, he thought it wise to leave out the part about MacLoughlin. He still wasn't sure if the man was real and he didn't want to blow his chances by convincing the Big Guy he was crazy.

The Big Guy asked if he had come up with the idea alone. Jonathan had foreseen the question and had planned to give up his brothers. He figured their ill will would add to the urgency factor. Yet, for some reason, he lied and assumed full responsibility. Being a martyr wasn't his style. He wasn't keeping quiet to be a hero. There was something else that made him listen to the lump in his throat and swallow it down without revealing a thing.

Both Sides of Broken

When the tale was told, the Big Guy reached for his organizer. He flipped quickly through the pages, paused at the nearest opening, and reached for a pen.

"I can put you on the trial calendar for a week from Friday."

"The what?"

"The trial calendar. You know, like as in court."

"What do I have to go to court for? I thought you were the man in charge."

"I am. It's just procedure. Didn't you go to Sunday school? I like the whole legal avenue. Final judgment, the argument of good and evil, the trials of Job. It's my thing."

Jonathan dropped his head to his hands and began tugging at his hair. All his life he believed that bureaucracy was evil, that the ultimate fate of any organization is the corruption and dissolution of that organization. People band together under the shroud of rules and procedures in the hope that these regulations will bring about order. In fairness and truth, order arrives. But the further truth, the one his father could never believe, is that it leaves just as quickly.

Group-think kills creativity. Things are manufactured to the point that the process becomes more important than the product it produces. Faster, better, cheaper, newer. Carbon copies cut quickly. Pragmatic engineers who never begin with a blank page assemble all that is valued.

For the first time, Jonathan understood the men of the Middle-America militias. Politics and insanity aside, he knew what they were after. A rebirth. A fresh look at the government. A chance to edit a document that was never intended to be finished, never intended to be laminated and

193

stuck inside a museum. He wanted to break the glass.

"I can't wait that long," he said. "Time dances or not, I need to complete this thing."

"I see. Do you expect it to be a long trial?"

"No. I'm an attorney. I can handle my own case. No witnesses. No examination of the evidence. Just the opening I gave and a closing argument. Hear me out and make your decision."

"We have to assemble a jury."

"It's not a criminal case. I'm not seeking punitive damages. Let's call it arbitration. Me against the code book."

"I can live with that, but they'll have to witness it. Otherwise it means hiring a court reporter and they're backed up worse than the court."

"Fine. Wake 'em up."

To Jonathan's surprise, the ordeal went quickly. The Big Guy read back the initial statement, listened to his tale without interruption, and retired to his chambers for final consideration. Marvin didn't understand much of what transpired, but the others did and that worried Jonathan. He'd learned to love them and wanted desperately to convince them that he was worthy of the same.

"It was complicated," said Jonathan, mostly to break the silence. "A lot of things were happening to a lot of people. It was more for them than the money. It was—"

"It's okay, Jonathan," said Amber, rubbing the tension from his shoulder. "Mistakes are what people make. Even the big ones can be forgiven."

"That's right, buddy," said Grimis. "Everything's a situation. We can't judge you unless we know what the situation was, and I get the feeling that story of yours didn't cover the whole deal. Am I right or what?"

"As always."

Amber grabbed Jonathan by the shoulders and spun him around.

"You lied to him?"

"More like omitted."

"Why?"

"It's complicated."

"Fine. Just answer me this, regardless of actions past. In the *now* of this moment, as you sit here with us as timeless friends, is your heart in the right place?"

"I hope so."

"Do your actions follow your heart?"

"Yes."

"Then we'll follow you. Right, Grimis?"

"Right."

"Right for me too," said Marvin, looking up from his coloring book.

"Where'd he get that?" asked Jonathan.

"Where do we get anything in the worlds beyond Earth? You see, understanding is a wonderful place. The only restrictions are the ones you put on yourself. Even those who live challenged by defect can learn to fly in the After-Earth. All it takes is the guts to wish yourself wings."

Jonathan watched Marvin play. For the first time, he noticed the severity of his retardation. So many limits and so few recognized. Marvin willed himself happy and married and the greatest golfer known. Jonathan offered this teacher a silent thank you, for from him much was learned.

* * *

The door to the judges' chambers stirred. The Big Guy returned, notebook in hand, and plopped himself into his chair.

"Mr. Holiday."

Jonathan stood and approached the bench.

"The court has sought fit to deny your request for an Earth pass. The regulations regarding temporary reincarnation of negligent spirits require the unquestionable necessity of said spirit to the former world. Though there appears to be some danger with regards to your father, he is in the presence of several friends and family members who love him. Since your demise you have been relieved of such responsibility. It is advised that you return with your comrades to your prior location. This order is hereby dismissed."

"Sir, you don't understand."

"Really? I think I understand pretty well, Mr. Holiday. I don't know what your friends here have been telling you, but I'm very much on top of things. Your remorse is commendable, but guilt doesn't fix things. The sin you committed lives on. You can't be held responsible for the actions of others. It's beyond you. What is happening down there now, however, is indirectly related to your behavior. That cannot be rewarded or recognized by the court. Just go back to your life in the South and try not to make the same mistakes there."

"But if you would just—"

"Silence!" roared the Big Guy. "Son, this is not the South Side or that insignificant excuse for a weigh station in between. This is the North End and I'm the boss here. My rulings are final. The laws are clear. You wanna argue with someone, try that fellow's uncle, the one who used you for a weed-whacker."

Jonathan looked a question at Grimis, but he didn't respond. No wonder he had so much responsibility. Sometimes nepotism can be a burden.

The Big Guy snapped his fingers and the travelers were back in the waiting room. Gladys made them sign a guest list and showed them to the door. The Big Guy barked at her over the intercom as they turned to leave. He wanted her to cancel his next appointment. She laughed and informed him there was no one in the waiting room.

* * *

The travelers made their way back to the tunnel. Grimis' GTO zipped along on the rails, sending a crisp breeze through the opened top.

"Where to?" asked Grimis.

"Home?" offered Amber.

"No," said Jonathan. "I can't quite face that yet. Anyone up for a beer?"

"Sure."

They thought themselves to an Irish pub approximately ten minutes away. The clock told them it was happy hour, but the place was all but empty. The foursome took a table near the bar and ordered a pitcher of Coors. A lonely fat man rested himself on a stool. He was listening to a Billy Joel song, and making love to a gin and tonic that was mostly gin.

"Hey pal," said Grimis. "Where is everybody?"

"Who, exactly?" he asked, turning on his stool.

"People. This is prime time, right?"

"As prime as it gets, I guess. Fridays have been dead lately. Most folks stay home. Been there, done that. You know the deal."

The party looked at each other, wondering what exactly these folks did that couldn't be done again.

"No," said Grimis. "I'm afraid I don't get ya. Can you be a little more specific?"

"Sure, see for yourself."

The fat man pulled a yellowed paper from his coat and tossed it to Grimis. Like the newspaper he had received earlier, it was blank.

"This the *Examiner*?"

"Yup. The fountain of all knowledge."

"But it's blank," said Amber. "What good does it do you?"

"Used to do a lot."

"How?" asked Jonathan.

"Don't ask me. Ask it. Ask it anything about anything. Ask it how to ride a bike or be rich or levitate objects. Ask it anything you wanna know and it'll give you step-by-step instructions for doing the task perfectly the first time around. No failure. No embarrassment. No limitations of any kind. Try it."

Marvin snatched the paper and asked it which club to use to sink a putt on the ninth hole of the Devil's Den golf course from twenty yards out in high wind. The group was impressed with the complexity of the question but even more so with the answer the paper provided. Not only did it reveal the correct club; it discussed the proper footing and power-to-torque ratio of the swing.

"That's incredible," said Jonathan.

"I guess," said the fat man. "It even has audio and video modes if you get tired of reading. Just tell it what to do."

"Is that what the people were watching and listening to in the tunnel?"

"Yup. It's the only book around."

"If it's so important, why are you willing to give it away?" asked Amber.

"Like I said, sister, been there, done that."

"Are you nuts? Think of what you could do," said Jonathan. "Anything in an instant, talk about your cool places."

"If you say so," said the fat man. "Personally, I like a challenge every now and then. You know, taking a test without the answers. Keep it, you'll see what I mean."

The fat man paid his bill and left the foursome with his device. They switched it to video mode so Marvin could play and took turns blasting it with questions. A pitcher turned to four and the questions turned philosophical. Jonathan smiled at their inebriation and the sorts of things that intrigued them.

CHAPTER 24

The Honda's headlights bounced along the Point's unpaved entrance. Potholes deep as manholes made successful navigation a bleak prospect, but the car handled the gyrations without complaint. Sam collided with a newly formed rut here and there as he made his way to the edge of the strip, but he remembered the layout well enough to avoid the major depressions.

He parked on a grassy strip at the far right of the lot, idled the engine, and listened to the remainder of a Garth Brooks tune. He never cut off a song. The way he figured it, each melody was somebody's dream turned truth. He respected the achievement and refused to trample on its greatness.

The place was deserted, as expected. Kids rarely came

before eleven and soon they wouldn't come at all. The fog on his windshield told him the cold was approaching and, bonfire or not, the water's edge is not the place to be during a New York winter.

He was early, rested, and still beaming from his afternoon frolic. He thought of Samantha and wondered if she was still sleeping. He pictured her snuggled under her covers, blonde locks dancing about the ruffles on her pillow.

The Lexus pulled in a moment before nine. Donato was on time, which meant he had good news. If he had changed his mind he wouldn't have come at all. No call, no explanation, just his absence to tell you that he had revoked the favor. For a leg-busting bookie, Donato hated confrontation. He wasn't afraid; he just didn't have the stomach for arguing. His two modes of expression were silence and rage. Either he liked you or he punched you in the mouth. No small talk. No idle threats. Nothing was gray in his life and all things were taken to extreme. Sam eyed his powerful torso as he approached the Honda. He was glad to be off his shit list for a while. It wasn't fear so much as he was running out of teeth.

"Everything still cool?" asked Donato.

"Yeah. My father's deal is bought and paid for."

"When's it going down?"

"Saturday night. We'd do it tomorrow, but there's less hospital staff around on the weekends. Security is about the same, but all the doctors go golfing. My guy says it'll be easier then."

"Anyone I know?"

"Can't say."

"Right. Anyway, I got your package."

Donato tossed a brown file folder on the hood of Sam's car. He snatched it up, undid its leather ties, and peered inside.

"Holy shit!"

"Damn right," said Donato. "It was trouble and a half getting that much clean cash."

"What do you mean clean? You wouldn't let me give them anything traceable, would ya?"

"See for yourself. Non-sequential, decent denominations. The Campanellas should be happy enough. No sense blowing the thing before it begins, right?"

"Right. Shit, I didn't even think about that."

"Figures."

"Sorry."

"Don't be. A mistake like that tells me you're cool. If you were trying to dick me with this thing you'd be a little more concerned with the money. Forget about it. Hell, I'm just surprised they didn't say anything."

"Well, thanks anyway. Saved me from looking like a jerk or worse. I bet you're gonna ask for a bigger cut now."

Sam was joking, but Donato didn't smile. He folded his arms, fidgeted slightly, and began playing with his earring. He liked to consider himself an honorable crook, one with a good reputation. Sam's comment pissed him off. If he wasn't looking at making a big score on the deal he would have walked. But nothing washes down pride like a pot full of money. Donato swallowed his and let the joke slide.

"When are you gonna make the drop?"

"Tomorrow night. Wanna come? Lord knows I could use the backup. They ain't exactly girl scouts, you know."

"I wanna keep a low profile on this one. Franky can't know

anything. That's clear, right?"

"Crystal."

"Good. Let me know how it goes. Remember, that bag is your life. If it don't make it home, neither do you."

"I got ya."

Donato disarmed his car and opened the door. Sam watched him slide into the leather seat and fidget with the radio. It must be nice to have the wherewithal to come up with so much cash on a day's notice. Presidents of major corporations couldn't flip the bill without mortgaging their homes and yet some knuckle buster from Arthur's Avenue could swing it without thought and still manage to make the drop-off in a dream car.

Donato backed out of his space and pulled perpendicular to the Honda. He cracked the tinted window, wished Sam luck with the meeting, then drove off. The gesture was nice, but something in his voice told Sam he would enjoy things whatever the outcome. Big money or some old friends dead. Business must be really good to make them equal out.

* * *

Parking in Sam's neighborhood was brutal—even more so with the latest crackdown by the meter maids. Normally he'd squeeze his wreck in by the hydrant in front of his building, but his ticket collection was climbing into the felony zone. A few more and they'd boot the car. The last thing he needed was a day in court.

He circled the block again and noticed a gray Mirage. There weren't many around, especially with a dent in the left front quarter panel. It had to be hers. He knew the car and the girl all too well. He remembered the night he drove it home and tried to explain the accident. It was new then and she had beaten him up over it. He wasn't hurt, but she never asked and that bothered him. It's strange what you remember when the haze of love is lifted.

Sam made the trip a third time and caught an old man walking towards his truck. He waited with blinker flashing as the tired old gent lifted his legs into the cab. The engine took three turns, but idled fair enough upon ignition. Sam continued to wait as the man warmed his vehicle. He pulled in front-first as soon as the space became vacant. The awkward maneuver forced him to jockey for proper position, but rather that than back in and risk losing the spot. He wasn't the only vulture searching for scraps and in his neighborhood better folk than he came to blows over such things.

He walked a block and stopped at the Mirage. "What the hell does she want?" asked Sam aloud.

Norah was waiting for him by the entrance. Her nose was red with cold, but he didn't feel sorry for her. She had kicked him out. She had the house and the furniture, and would probably get to keep it all when the judge was through. He was stuck with a bare apartment in a dumpy building. So what if she was cold? It was about time she suffered a little.

"Nice night," she said.

"Yeah. Look, the star is out."

She laughed. She always laughed at his stupid jokes. He never told her they were borrowed from has-been comedians on cable.

"A little chilly though," she said.

"What's going on, Norah?"

Both Sides of Broken

She dragged her toe across the step. She wanted to say something important, something that should have been said before their feelings dwindled. She thought she'd found the right words, but even now, having gone so far out of her way to make herself look vulnerable, they wouldn't come. Thirty years old and still playing grade-school games, still afraid to speak her heart. It was almost annoying.

"Maybe we rushed into this thing . . . you know, the divorce."

"Norah."

"I'm serious. I know I've been running you around, but it's only because I've been so confused. We were a couple for so long, Sam. Dating in high school, married before I got out of college. We spent a lot of years together and I guess I just needed to see what was out there."

"What are you saying?"

"I've seen it, Sam. You're not perfect. God, I know that much, but you're mine and I see that now. You chased me even after I let you go, even after I told you to forget it and get on with your life. I want you back. I want us back."

Break-ups suck like Mondays, only the kind where you get hit by a truck on the way to work and then fired for showing up late. People of the world may not be able to agree on a single religion or currency or form of government, but they'd agree on that much. Someone always gets hurt because someone is always hanging on to the things that were when things were fine. Things hadn't been fine with them in a long while. He knew that only because she told him. Now the fear of being alone made her forget her own truth. That same fear made her burst into tears when his look told her he couldn't take her back.

Sam loved her. He wasn't about to lie to himself and say otherwise. He just wasn't in love with her anymore. He tried to explain the feeling, but he knew she wouldn't understand. She couldn't now, with good memories so fresh. Time and distance are the only things that let friendship blossom between lovers lost. You can't rush it or force it or will it into your life. It just comes when you're ready, when the two involved are ready to forgive, forget, and move on. You can only hurt so bad for so long.

She asked him if there was someone else, if she'd been too mean or pushy, or just hadn't cared enough. A part of him had dreamed of having this conversation and he'd endlessly rehearsed all the nasty, hurtful "I told you so's." But those were just defenses talking. He never imagined she'd actually want him again. Now, faced with the reality of her tears, he couldn't say a damn thing. He just held her and let her cry it out.

He wiped the wetness from her cheek and kissed her softly as old friends do. He said he'd call and then told her again so she'd know he meant it. She thanked him, declined his offer of a walk to her car, and turned away. She started crying again as she left. It made him want to die. He watched her until she disappeared around the corner. He swallowed a lump the size of an orange, dug his keys from his coat, and entered the building.

* * *

Bottle in hand, Sam went to his bedroom. He sat on the

edge of his mattress and stared at Norah's photo. She smiled back at him, all dolled up for one of those mini-mall glamour-shot deals. It was a birthday gift a couple years back, something she always wanted.

Sam laughed at himself. After all she'd done to him, the first thing he did for his new place was set up a shrine. He paid it homage on a daily basis. Nothing changed. Even after the split, she was the last person he saw when he went to bed and the first when he woke. For the longest time he couldn't figure out why he'd kept the picture, but the conversation reminded him of something he always knew. The girl was worth the trouble. She just wasn't his girl anymore.

He folded the cardboard stand and tucked the picture in his bottom drawer. A stronger man would have trashed it, but sometimes it's better to be weak. Out of sight was good enough. There'd be no out of mind.

He grabbed a note from the nightstand and dialed the number it offered. A man answered on the third ring. He sounded sleepy, but quickly changed his tempo when he realized who was calling.

"I got the money," said Sam.

"All of it?"

"Yeah. Let me talk to Franky."

"Where we gonna meet?"

"Later. Now put him on or lose the cash. I ain't talking about a drop-off until I know he's still alive."

"What? You don't trust us?"

"Now."

The grunt dropped the phone to the floor and yelled for Franky. There was a slight ruckus as the brothers cursed at each other over the television. A moment later Franky was on the line.

"You got it?" he asked. "How? Forget it, I don't even wanna know. Thanks."

"It ain't over yet."

"So how we gonna work it?"

"Hey, hey, hey, knucklehead. That's enough," said one of the goons as he snatched the phone from Franky. "No need for yous two to be making plans. Sammy boy, I told you he was fine. Now you gonna play nice, or what?"

"I want meet in a public place."

"No can do, friend. The cops are still busting our balls on this other thing. Too risky. It's gonna have to be a drop-off."

"You get half."

"What?"

"I'll leave half in one place. Then I get Franky. Then I give you the rest."

"Bullshit. You give it all first and maybe we don't kill him and you and whoever else we feel deserves a bullet. Got me?"

Sam turned red with anger. He was sick of playing games, sick of debating with untrustworthy assholes. He banged the phone on the table repeatedly, screaming with each blow.

"You listen, greaseball son-of-a-bitch. Tomorrow. Three a.m. In back of the old Co-op city theater. One guy. You hear me? One guy. I see more than one of you assholes and I'm walking. That's it. No debate."

"Why so late?"

"Last picture's at twelve. It's over at two. By three the place is dead. Get it? Got it? Good-bye."

Sam hung up the phone and took a slug of Jack. He knew

nothing could last forever, but the bad times were certainly giving it their best shot.

CHAPTER 25

Without sleep, the morning seemed a mere continuation of the reckless debacle of the night before. Jonathan felt lucky. Unlike the others, he impersonated a conservative drinker. The act earned him a clear head, some moments alone, and the wherewithal to make meaningful decisions for the group.

Grimis and Marvin pounded them back better than he had ever seen, and to his surprise, Amber did her damnedest to keep up with them. By the second pitcher, they had reduced the *Daily Examiner* from the all-important book of books to a not-so-amusing drinking game. By the fourth, the trinket's novelty had worn off completely. They switched to shots of Absolut and began playing quarters. Grimis tossed the mystical device on the bar and it was quickly forgotten.

Both Sides of Broken

Jonathan, however, remembered its presence all too well.

He excused himself from the game and started playing sad songs on the jukebox. He thought of Norah. He should have married that one, should have beaten his brother to the punch. Looking back, their relationship seemed so Shakespearean. Sam was always jealous of his brother because, in his eyes, Jonathan won everything. If only he knew how little those triumphs meant to the victor. An "A" in History, a decent part in the school play—how do those things compare to losing a soul-mate forever?

Jonathan conceded to being a more consistent winner, but it was clear to him who took the bonus round. Sam collected the grand prize with a smile, only to trade her in during the next show for a shot at whatever was behind curtain number two. Jonathan hated him for letting her leave.

They closed the bar and grabbed some coffee at a nearby diner. Amber wanted to spend the night. She rarely drank and was queasy, with a headache the size of an old Buick. She argued for rest, but as always Jonathan was in a hurry. He packed the car, clicked on some jazz to help his friends drift off, and began the drive home. Home. He smiled. It was the first time he had considered the South Side to be home. Maybe it was. Maybe it always had been.

The *Daily Examiner*'s audio mode helped him pass the time. He inquired about music and women and even asked a couple of questions that had stumped him on the bar exam. When he was certain that all were asleep, he asked about his case. He wasn't hoping for a reversal, a bit of missed evidence, or anything to make him look less dumb than he had proven himself to be. He had accepted his foolishness long ago, but the trial had cost him his career, his life, his everything. He was more than a little curious as to the *why* of what went wrong. He wanted to know how he had missed the truth, why he lost so big so soon, and, most of all, how his father would have performed under the same conditions. The answers surprised him and he slammed the device to the seat.

"What do you know?" asked Jonathan.

The machine took him literally. "Everything," it said.

Jonathan stifled a scream and punched the paper silent.

The GTO crossed the border at seven a.m. He should have been tired, but his thoughts were racing. His conversation with the machine began to drive him insane. What he was hearing was truth as pure as truth could be, and yet he doubted its merit. The more it spoke, the more he thought it full of lies. He was angry, but the emotions the debate inspired taught him a little about both parties. Suddenly, things started to make sense.

He knew what was wrong with things. Why the After-Earth avenues were all tragically flawed. And all at once he understood what the man in the bar was trying to tell him. He smiled at the realization. It was so simple, so easy, and it all started with the North End.

The device functioned as designed. It performed within specified parameters. And it seemed to serve the purpose its inventors intended. Yet, despite the apparent perfection, the thing just didn't work. It did what it was told and not what it was supposed to do. No conscience. No discrimination. No censorship of any kind. You asked and it answered. Complex programming and unimaginable storage capacity aside, its sole task was to be a giant encyclopedia. Free information, practical understanding, and instant applicability to any and all who inquired. What a nightmare. What a boring nightmare.

It figured Jonathan would stumble onto this truism with the help of a common man. Common people with uncommon sense always seemed to know the truth of things. The so-called important folk, however—the ones with the power, money, and influence to put things into practice—hadn't a clue. Strange: in a place where everyone could know everything, no one bothered to ask if the philosophy of knowing everything was the right one.

Jonathan saw it. He recognized the weakness for what it was and planed to capitalize on the shortcoming. No use in others having all the fun. He would have to pose the question of all questions. Is what we believe, what we were taught to believe by loved ones long gone, really believable? He couldn't wait for the answer.

* * *

Morning. Sunshine. Warm air dancing through shimmering blades of grass so green. Teacups. Feet up. Winter's cruelty fading to the sound of thankful bluebirds. The backyard feeders are a welcome sight to well-worn wings and, though they're a challenge to construct, the songs received are more than compensation.

A black pan. A soft sizzle. The spicy scent of sausages filling the air. One can never be certain of time in the life after Earth, but it was clear to the travelers that the workweek was over. Addresses aside, sausages mean Sunday, and there was a whole lot of frying going on.

The Boss flipped the patties again and slid them from the pan to a serving plate covered with paper towels. He dabbed away the grease, dished out the meal, and offered orange juice. Jonathan watched him fill their glasses. He thought about how many people he'd judged on rumor alone. Of all his sins, he thought that was his greatest. He knew now that each person deserved a fair shake, a handshake, a chance to keep the vows they took. They don't deserve to be reduced to one-dimensional caricatures. The Boss was dressed in sneakers, a Buffalo Bills sweatshirt, and faded blue jeans slightly ripped at the knee. Another man his age would have appeared to be foolishly clinging to days gone by, but he pulled it off. It was clear his morning runs served their purpose. He was trim, solid, and as together as his title suggested.

"Rough night?" he asked.

Grimis groaned and began searching his pockets for an aspirin. Amber pulled a bottle from her purse. They each swallowed a pair with some juice and chased them with black coffee.

"You too?" the Boss asked Amber.

She smiled at Grimis and shrugged. The Boss thought her cute and was glad to see she could have fun once in a while. For the longest time he'd worried about her and how she'd adapt to the place he created.

He didn't doubt that Amber was a capable woman. She'd had grown faster than he could have hoped. She had led a good Earth life as well. She could have gone anywhere, anyplace, any time she wanted, but she choose the South Side because she loved his nephew and wanted to be near him.

He looked at Grimis. He too could have gone anywhere.

Both Sides of Broken

His Earth life wasn't as triumphant as hers, but he'd handled himself well enough. Guilt brought him South, but he'd made peace with his decision and learned the rules of the game better than any other. He could have left the moment he arrived, but his loyalty was greater than his desire for exploration and vindication. He began to see the Boss's vision, and soon he too was fighting for the cause. But the war started so long ago.

The Boss loved them both. He felt responsible for them, like a father to his children. Indeed, he loved all his adopted children and wanted only the best for them.

"Where's Marvin?" he asked.

"With Marge," said Jonathan. "She wasn't too happy about his new tattoo."

"Tattoo? Grimis."

"What?" asked Grimis through a mouthful of eggs. "It looked good on him. Besides, the man's gotta start putting his foot down. That lady walks all over him."

"Well, she's gonna be walking some more if he was as drunk as you. No offense, buddy, but your breath is a dead giveaway."

Grimis exhaled deeply and began sniffing the air in front of him.

"What are you talking about? My breath is just fine."

Amber handed him a stick of gum. "Sure it is, honey."

When the meal was complete, the Boss began clearing the table. Jonathan laughed at his passion for performing the little things. When he was a lawyer on Earth all he could dream about was becoming so rich that he could hire a maid, butler, chauffeur, and someone to wipe his butt. Now he was faced with a man who could afford such luxuries ten times over and yet he was cleaning up after them.

The Boss finished the dishes, refilled the coffee cups, and joined the others at the table. The bags under his eyes were less obvious. Jonathan guessed he'd been sleeping again. Maybe whatever was troubling him had gone into remission. Then again, maybe the poor fellow had reached the state where hopeless depression feels little more than a minor variation of the normal day to day. Jonathan knew the feeling and hoped his host had a better time of it.

"So, did you manage to see the Big Guy?"

Jonathan nodded. He knew what was coming. He had failed. The Big Guy had ushered them out before he even got to mention the Boss. His visit had done little to win favor from either man. He could only hope that this giant would be a little more receptive to new ideas.

"He's still the same," said Grimis.

"A wannabe executive?"

"Yup."

"I can't believe so many people follow him," said Amber. "He wasn't at all how I pictured. He was arrogant and short tempered and . . ."

"He wasn't always like that, you know," said the Boss.

"No?" asked Jonathan.

"He used to be like the books said, helping little people, appearing out of nowhere just to toss about some fish and wine. But he got too big and important for the manual stuff. He's a desk jockey now; and, between you, me, and the Staten Island Ferry, he's not too happy about his new position."

"No kidding," said Grimis.

"You've meet him before?" Jonathan asked Grimis.

"I've been around a while."

Jonathan gulped down a mouthful of coffee. "So where did it go wrong?" he asked the Boss.

"When he went from a mom-and-pop shop to a conglomerate."

"Huh?"

"It's simple. What started as a friendly little venture snowballed into what can only be viewed as a huge corporation. When he hired his thirteenth partner I knew he'd get into trouble."

"Is that when you made the split?" asked Jonathan.

"No. I had a little more staying power than that. I hung around for a few centuries, hoping things would turn themselves around. No luck. He had the market cornered. It was the North End, witchcraft, or reincarnation. Not much of a choice when you consider the imagination of the average Joe. Half the dearly departed unconsciously willed themselves back as horseflies."

"No way," said Amber.

"I'm serious. Can you imagine buzzing around piles of crap all day? Folks soon realized the risk and started accepting the Big Guy's alternative. Besides, they were getting bored with virgin sacrifices to the volcano gods. I mean, let's face it. It was just a matter of time before that one blew over. Men weren't gonna continue to waste perfectly good virgins."

"Excuse me," said Amber.

"Ah . . . sorry," said the Boss. "Anyway, his business boomed. He kept expanding and building and dreaming up new features, a new development here, an updated transit system there. Hell, he had a city within the first decade and a planet soon after."

"It's that big?" asked Jonathan.

"Bigger. Didn't you look around?"

"Well we were kinda . . ."

"Drinking?"

"Yeah."

"And I thought it was a good idea to send Grimis along. I give you a trip to the North End and you spend the whole time in one bar. I'm surprised you didn't get thrown out."

"That can happen?"

"Ask him."

Grimis offered a devious smile and hunched his shoulders. He raised his mug to hide his mouth and whispered something to Amber. She laughed and smacked him playfully. Jonathan didn't know when they had become so friendly, but they wore it well. He smiled for them and politely changed the subject.

"Well, I guess you know I didn't get my Earth pass."

"I kinda figured you'd have a tough time of it. He's not too free with them."

"Why?"

"That's obvious," said Grimis. "He's scared."

"Of what?" asked Amber.

"Losing out."

"You're nuts."

"I don't think he is," said Jonathan. "In fact, that's what we need to talk about."

"I'm listening," said the Boss.

"I still need the pass, and you guys should know by now that I'm not the type to give up. Now, I know about your little plan to turn me into some After-Earth travel reporter. It kinda pissed me off at first, but I don't mind anymore. It was a decent idea."

"How did you ever . . . ?" asked Grimis.

"Come on, how does anyone know anything in the life after Earth? I caught the thoughts you sent. You told me, buddy; you just didn't know you told me."

The Boss leaped to his feet and began pacing the room. "That's amazing! You're not supposed to be able to do that for centuries. How'd you figure it out?"

"Yeah, Jon, what's with you? Grimis and I knew you were kinda special ever since that day on the pier, but this is something different. You read the thoughts of the Boss himself. That's impossible. Isn't it?"

Jonathan clasped his hands behind his head and leaned back in his chair. He could feel the understanding rushing towards him. It had started as a sprinkle his first day out of the DMV, but so much had happened since then. The knowledge was flowing now because he willed it so. An idea from Grimis, some encouragement from Amber, a little challenge from The Boss, that was his catalyst for learning and the answer to their ultimate problem.

"Boss, I know things haven't been too good here lately, but I've got news for you. They ain't too good anywhere else either. You may not be powerful enough to give me my Earth pass, but I've got a feeling that the Wizard of the North End isn't either."

"So what are you gonna do?"

"I think it's time we pull the curtain."

"Compete with the Big Guy?" asked the Boss. "How could

I—we—ever do something like that?"

"You tell me," said Jonathan. "You're the one who did it before."

"He's right," said Amber. "You have done it. Heck, you almost won."

The Boss smiled at the memories of battles long since waged. He enjoyed the challenge, the self-righteous idealism, the cause, and the angry young man he had been. What he didn't like was fighting an old friend. Pride would never let him admit it, but he missed that friend more as the years wore on.

"Maybe so, but it was different then," he said. "The world is too big now. We could never pull off a power shift using conventional tactics."

"Who's talking conventional?" asked Jonathan.

"You're devious," said Amber.

"No. Just desperate. I've gotta make this thing with my father right or I'll never be able to move on. If I have to step on some toes to get it done, so be it."

"Those are some pretty big toes," said Grimis.

"Well, like the man says, it's better to be dead and cool than alive and uncool."

"But I'd bet that man wasn't dead at the time he coined the saying," said the Boss. "I'm gonna need a little more of a plan, Jonathan. Can you give me something concrete?"

"Got a pen?"

* * *

Jonathan spent the rest of the morning explaining the plan

to his partners. He envisioned a historic battle between the North and the South, only this time around it would be about marketing, sales, and the construction of the kind of After-Earth that real folks with real problems actually expected upon death. If they could accomplish the task, Jonathan wouldn't need the Big Guy's permission to go to Earth. The Boss could just sign the permission slip and let him fly.

After much debate, it was decided that Jonathan's plan was the only way to go. The Boss disclosed that the South Side had been in the red for years. It needed the kind of facelift only a massive influx of clients could provide. In the end, it was decided to turn the whole thing into one big resort and casino.

Grimis just about shit himself when heard the idea. All he could talk about was being the greatest pit boss who ever lived and seeing Mr. Frank Sinatra perform again. Thoughts of blackjack, wild shows, alcohol, and dancing girls ran through his mind.

The Boss was also intrigued by the concept. It was Amber who needed some convincing. She didn't like the Vegas motif. Spending eternity in a big diner filled with slot machines wasn't her idea of paradise and she was certain that many others would feel the same.

Jonathan understood her concern. The last thing they needed was to create a haven for the negative people who populated the Earthly version. He assured her that the casino would be only the first in a long line of After-Earth fantasies. He called it the Eternal Wonderland: *Where dream vacations are but a thought away.*

There was some debate as to how the common person could be taught to will himself into a perfect scenario.

Jonathan offered himself as an example: "Ever since I got here you've been saying I'm special."

"You are," said Amber, glancing over Grimis' makeshift architectural sketches.

"Well, so is everyone else."

"That's nice, Jon," said the Boss, "but come on. I think we've all seen a few around here whose elevator doesn't go to the top."

"Brains have nothing to do with it. It's all about imagination. Think about it. As kids we went on cool vacations all the time. We played cowboys and Indians, cops and robbers, and Dungeons and Dragons. Every game seemed incredibly real because we wished it so."

"So?"

"So what I'm saying is that the reason the three After-Earths are doing so poorly is because they're filled with people who've forgotten how to use their imaginations. Think about it—even I, the supposedly amazing human, spent thirty-five years at the DMV. What the hell is *that* about?"

Grimis got up from the table, walked to the fridge, and removed a Coke. He waved it gently in front of the others and tossed one to Jonathan at the sight of his nod. He yanked the tab and took a long drink, then passed his sleeve over his mouth and looked at Jonathan.

"I see your point, but there's no denying your rapid understanding of the rules. How are we supposed to teach everyone to dream? And who would listen? You saw how useless the *Daily Examiner* became."

"You're right, Grimis, but people didn't believe it because it was too easy. Nothing they had ever known could be easy and real at the same time."

The Boss crossed his arms and regarded Jonathan curiously. "So by your theory, we should be doing a whole lot better than we are?"

"No."

"Why?"

"Because it's too damn hard here."

"What are you talking about?" asked Amber.

"Think. Enrollment is down in the North because there are no challenges. People can do whatever they want, whenever they want it, with no effort at all. Enrollment is down here because the challenges are overwhelming. We give them no guidance at all. Boss, I know why you split. Maybe not the whole reason, but I'm sure of at least part. You wanted to learn something new. You wanted to fail and try again. But in your quest to challenge people, you made life just as futile."

"How?"

"When I came here, Grimis told me I could do whatever I wanted, but that's all the information I received. If I didn't have a purpose to push me forward, I would have ended up like the rest, in a state of learned helplessness. That's why the Sticks is so popular. It may not be heaven, but at least they know the rules."

"So what do we do after we get people to our little palace?"

"We teach 'em like real teachers teach. We guide, we instruct, we set goals, and we cheerlead. But we don't do their homework for them."

"It kinda makes sense," said Grimis.

The Boss turned on the kettle and, at Amber's request, retrieved a pair of mugs from the cupboard. This little lawyer with a mission intrigued him. Perhaps he was too narrow in his views. Maybe it was time to widen his circle of friends. And perhaps the days of sole proprietorships were over. It would be nice to be successful again. And it would be nice to spread the wealth.

"When could we get started?"

"How long will it take you to finish your tea?"

CHAPTER 26

Sam went sleepless. Liquor, guilt, and endless sexual fantasies spoiled his slumber. He rose early, drove to the garage, and listened to his messages. The shop had been closed for almost a week without warning and several customers had called with complaints, demands, and legal threats. People were nuts when it came to their cars. Screw up the job and they'd sue. Disappear on them for a while and they'd come back with bats in hand. He decided to avoid further conflict and begin returning the calls after breakfast.

He started a pot of coffee, snagged what was left of an Egg McMuffin from the fridge, and began sifting through the mail. He took a bite of the sandwich and spit it in the trash.

"Jesus."

He pulled the bucket from under the desk and began tossing in the junk mail. Car washes, cellular phone services, dopey accountants with nothing to count. Talk about your environmental calamities. Direct mail was pure evil. He matched the new bills with the pile on his desk. There were a few doubles, and trashing them gave him a sense of accomplishment. He didn't need the company checkbook to tell him it would be a stretch to get the rest paid. Con-Ed, phone, some miscellaneous invoices from oil venders and the like. That was enough to kill the budget. Two weeks until rent day and he didn't have a penny in the till. He wrapped a rubber band around the remaining nuisances and decided to let them lie for a while. No sense plugging holes.

A customer or two happened by between phone calls. A tune-up, a couple of oil changes, nothing scam-worthy, but a buck is a buck. Some zit-faced kid with a 1987 Firebird came in at four-thirty hoping to get some emergency bodywork. Apparently, he'd "borrowed" his father's cherry while the old man was away on business and banged it up in a movie theater parking lot.

"Got insurance?" asked Sam.

The kid struggled a bit, as if speaking was a new skill. Sam knew the answer. He and the father had plenty of coverage, but using it would blow his cover and skyrocket his premiums. On a normal day, Sam would have demanded the insurance information. If the kid was a punk driving a Mercedes, he'd send him home until Monday and then rape his company blind. But for some reason, he wasn't in the mood to be a bastard. He liked the kid, the car, and the idea of him getting lucky after the show. It brought back memories.

"Is it bad?" asked the kid.

Sam ran his hand along the rear bumper. "The tailpipe needs some straightening."

"What about the bumper?"

"It's cracked clear through. If this were a '78 we could pound it out, but nowadays someone comes in with a shot like this and we just replace the thing. When's your old man coming home?"

"Tuesday night."

"Part won't get here in time."

"Shit. I'm dead. I'm so dead."

"Relax. That's why God made Bondo."

"So can you fix it?"

"Depends. Got any cash?"

"Are you kidding? I just started working at the Burger King down the street. I borrowed fifty bucks from my buddy, but I don't suppose that'll do too much. Guess I was hoping for a miracle. Sorry to bother you, mister."

"What sorry? I've been dying for a Whopper all day. Tell you what, you run down to that place of yours and fix me up a double with cheese and I'll see what I can do about this bird here."

"You're kidding?"

"No. I'm Sam, and you?"

"Tommy."

"Nice to meet ya, Tommy. You drive stick?"

"Yeah."

Sam tossed him the keys to his Honda.

"She's a bitch to get outta second, but she's got more pep then you'd expect. Made the modifications myself. Try and bring her back in one piece, okay?"

"Thanks man. Thanks a million."

"Forget about it."

Sam watched the kid run off, thrilled at the thought of getting away with his crime. He knew the feeling on a much larger scale and hoped that somehow his act of kindness would make him worthy of success. He wasn't a hero but, like most, he enjoyed playing the part now and again. Besides, it seemed to mean more when the bad did good. Lately he had been feeling so very bad.

He finished the tailpipe before Tommy returned. They broke for dinner and then Sam gave him a lesson on the wonders of Bondo. The kid was into cars and learning, and bombarded Sam with questions. The hour job stretched to three, but neither noticed, neither cared.

For the first time in his life Sam felt like a father. He wasn't naive enough to believe that a single conversation proves a man qualified for parenthood, but he certainly impressed himself. Those moments with the kid were better than any his old man had ever shown him.

Sam locked the door, turned on his redneck station, and began to clean up the office. He swept the floor, organized the shelves, and even sifted through some old files. He noticed the pile of bills on the desk, bit his lip, and attacked them. He couldn't be a kid forever.

* * *

The phone startled Sam. He'd fallen asleep on his office couch and his neck bore the burden of a disgruntled spring. He rose, cracked the kinks from his body, and reached for the phone.

"Yeah?"

"Mr. Holiday."

The tone in the man's voice scared the cobwebs from his head. He rubbed the sleep from his eyes and cleared his throat.

"Yes. What's wrong?"

"This is Officer Brod, Mr. Holiday. I'm afraid I've got some bad news about Samantha."

His words struck Sam like a blunt sword to the skull.

"What happened? Is she . . . is she—"

"She alive, but hurt real bad. We're at the hospital now."

"Is she awake?"

"No."

Sam felt his cheeks burning. Terror, rage, fear, and frustration wrestled for the catbird seat in his mind. He'd kill whoever did this to her. He'd fucking kill him.

"I'll be right there."

Sam hung up the phone, threw on his coat, and headed for the Honda. The streets were bare, but the drive seemed longer than a Monday morning commute to Queens. He was crying by the time he reached the parking lot and sat for a minute, blinking the redness from his eyes. He wasn't embarrassed by tears. He just wanted to contain the emotion, solidify it into hate, and bash the son-of-a bitch over the head with it like a rock.

He didn't need to ask for directions to her room. The trail of officers in the hallway pointed the way. It was clear they loved her, and Sam knew from the frowns they wore that he wasn't the only person seeking vengeance. A tall, thin uniform grabbed him by the arm as he approached the door to her room.

"You Holiday?"

"Yeah."

"I'm Brod, the guy who called you."

"Yeah. Thanks."

"Well, we figured she'd want you here. She doesn't have much in the way of family, you know, and you were all she's been talking about lately."

"That's nice to hear."

"She's some lady."

"Yeah."

Sam shook the officer's hand and entered the room. Samantha's face and neck were swollen, her lips cut, and dark bruises mottled her cheeks. He took her hand. Her knuckles were red and scraped, as though she'd fought back. Sam figured she had. She wasn't a token skirt by any means. A Nidan in GOJU, a brown sash in Wing Chun, she could take care of herself all right. Whoever did this to her had been big or trained or both.

The thought of some oafish brute tossing her about forced its way into his mind. He shook off the image, kissed her softly, and left the room. Officer Brod met him at the door.

"Was she . . . you know?"

"No. No. Thank God. The doctors suspect rape was intended. There were marks on her legs and such, but no penetration, no vaginal bruising. She fought him off. She fought him off alone."

Brod blinked rapidly and turned his head a moment. He looked back at Sam, cheeks flushed, eyes red.

"Who did it?" asked Sam.

"We don't know yet."

Sam ran an angry hand through his hair.

"Come on, man," he said, as quietly as he could. "You must know something."

Folks forget sometimes that cops are people like any other. They get jealous and hurt and pissed-off that things are never the way they're supposed to be. Brod studied Sam's expression and decided he was worthy of some disclosure. "We know who did it. Not officially with leads and such, but we know."

"That crazy kid, the one who got off?"

"Yup."

Sam felt a twinge of hatred for his dead brother. He blamed him for the attack and silently swore to get even.

"You gonna bring him in?"

Brod looked at a senior officer standing a few feet away. The man nodded and Brod answered.

"Of course, Mr. Holiday. All criminals are brought to justice. Even the crazy ones we can never convict. It's their right, you know. We just hope the poor sick man makes it to the station house okay. It's a very dangerous city, you know."

Sam returned his smile. Those words made him forget every tongue-lashing and ticket he'd ever received. They'd get him. They'd hurt him. And he deserved every blow.

"I'm gonna get some clothes and a few things for her," said Sam. "I wanna thank you guys again for the call and the . . . you know. I just wish I could be there."

"No. You need to be here, with her, for her. Understand? We'll take care of him. You just take care of her."

Sam exchanged concerned glances with the group of officers who had assembled to witness the latter portion of the conversation. An alliance of trust was formed in that moment. The men in the hall leaped from strangers to friends in an instant. They would keep the secret of secrets for as long as they lived because they believed that the crime they would commit was justified. Sam respected them for the risks they took and the loyalty they showed. He loved them for loving her.

* * *

Sam's apartment seemed barren. Samantha had never spent the night, had never even been there, and yet it ached for her presence. He didn't have a key to her place so he couldn't gather any of her personal items, but he managed to pack a case of what he imagined were essentials. He stuffed in a fresh shirt for himself and turned towards the door. A vision of Franky tied to a chair popped into his mind. He picked up his phone and dialed. One of the brutes answered on the second ring.

"It's Sam."

"What?"

"Something's come up. I'm not dicking you. I got the cash. I just can't make it to the theater."

"Buddy, it's 1:30. That gives you an hour and a half to get where you're supposed to be. If I don't see you there, he's dead."

Sam was tired of thinking about death and threats and money and games. His mind, heart, and soul were lying in a bed with a wounded woman. He longed for closure, a chance to end it all and begin anew. He'd be damned if some muscle-bound bruiser was going to steal that chance away.

"Fine. Kill him now. You might as well, 'cause I can't show."

A rumbling on the line let Sam know the goon had dropped the phone. Franky screamed as though someone had stuck a poker in his eye. A moment later he was on the line.

"What the fuck is going on, Sam? We've sung this song already."

"I've gotta go to the hospital."

"What happened?"

"You don't wanna know."

"Oh yes I do, Sam. This isn't exactly fun I'm having here."

"Just tell them that I'll call tomorrow night with a new location and a new time for the meeting. We'll do it tomorrow, for sure."

"They won't buy it. You're playing too many games."

"Not anymore. I'll meet them face to face and I'll bring all the cash at one time. If they wanna kill me, fine. I just don't give a shit anymore."

"You sure about that?" asked one of the goons from an extension phone.

"Yeah," said Sam. "All I want is my friend alive. The money's yours. Give me the night and our lives when we meet. That's all I'm asking for."

Sam sensed the man believed him, but he also sensed the fear in Franky's voice. He'd be there. He'd end things. He'd do whatever was required.

"Fine. Tomorrow. But no more bullshit."

Tim Toterhi

The thug slammed the phone, missed, and slammed it again. Sam laughed. He replaced the receiver and grabbed his coat.

* * *

Sam stopped at a minimart on the way to the hospital and bought an ugly stuffed bear and couple of magazines. A few cops were still roaming the halls when he arrived at a quarter to three. An orderly harassed him about the visiting policy, but a look from a well-built officer changed his mind quickly enough. He thanked them again, chatted for a while, then ordered them home. He figured they needed the rest and were just waiting for someone to tell them what to do.

Samantha was still unconscious. He watched her for as long as he could keep his eyes open. Then he fell asleep in the chair and dreamed he watched her still.

* * *

Morning's glare met Sam's sleeping eyes and stirred him slightly. He turned in his seat hoping to avoid the growing brightness. He was tired and battle-worn, and for a moment mistook the hospital room for his own. That changed when he felt a hand softly squeezing his. He looked up to find Samantha staring at him with the same loving look he had given during her slumber.

Her awakening had been the greatest gift he'd ever received and he wanted to convey the feeling. He wanted to say so many things in that moment, but for once he relaxed and spoke the right words: "I love you," he said. "I'll love you forever."

She smiled as best her wounds would allow and mouthed the refrain. It was the sweetest sound he never heard.

CHAPTER 27

It opened on a Friday. After twenty-seven years of planning and building and arguing with large-bellied contractors, Jonathan's dream became reality. It was colossal, combining futuristic slopes and curves with the ornate gothic style of palaces past. It was Athens and Rome and Versailles rolled into one. The travelers doubted they would ever witness construction's end for the city was crafted from the fibers of imagination, a material as flexible as it is sturdy, as timeless as it is fleeting. It would forever be and yet constantly change.

The massive set of silver structures stood atop a mountain whose peak was out of sight in the sky. During the day, the sun bounced from the casino's stained glass. At night, the moon's reflection provided a backdrop of pale light on which the stars danced and played.

Grimis was often found in the center of the main hall, shaking hands, making rounds, saying the stupid little things people loved to hear. He was born for the job. People loved him and he loved to see that they had a good time.

He looked good. Gone were his dirty coveralls and worn work boots. He shaved and washed and willed his once disheveled and thinning hair to health. The neatly crafted mane was trimmed short on top, but allowed to flow freely down the back of his neck. It came to rest on shoulders reintroduced to free weights and bounced proudly as he ambled about. He was handsome—handsome enough to attract many of the tight young bodies strutting among the slot machines. He eyed them, of course, but was beyond the point of wanting more. He knew his metamorphosis had occurred out of a desire to please the one who pleased him. She never requested the change, wouldn't have minded much if he stayed sloppy forever, but in an honest moment, Amber confessed to Jonathan that she found Grimis' new look more than appealing. Jonathan laughed when he noticed her mischievous schoolgirl smile had returned. He was proud to know a couple so in love.

Due to his experience and position of authority, the Boss took on a senior management role. He oversaw the running of the operation, forecasted future trends, and strategized as to how those trends could be turned into productive attractions. With the casino complete and a theme park under construction, plans were already in the works to develop a tropical-island resort and country club. The possibilities were endless and the position kept him happily overworked. Yet, despite his schedule, he was determined to find balance. The last thing he needed was to make the Big Guy's mistake and become a pompous bureaucrat. To that end, he forced himself to spend at least thirty percent of his time on the floor with Grimis. He complained every now and then about the hassle of walking the rooms, but Grimis knew he was just blowing smoke. The old man loved the hours he spent making small talk and kissing babies.

Amber and Jonathan had less prominent, but equally important assignments. A whiz with numbers, Amber orchestrated the day-to-day bookkeeping operation as well as the asset management and financial planning for the entire project. Naturally, Jonathan began by handling all legal affairs, but his chores lessened considerably once the palace opened. The Boss saw that he was growing weary of playing counselor and gave him a staff to perform the more mundane tasks. Jonathan could then serve as floater, helping his staff with complex legal matters, Grimis with personnel, and Amber with the financials as required. He performed exceptionally well and, before long, became the Boss's unofficial advisor.

Shortly after the change occurred, the foursome decided to take a night off and discuss their amazing string of accomplishments. Grimis, aware of Jonathan's tendency towards promptness, arrived at the selected bar and grill a few minutes early. He saw Jonathan at the bar, gave his hat to the coat-check girl, and called across the room to his friend.

"Hey, Jonathan."

Grimis walked to the bar, ordered a scotch for himself and a Coors for his partner. He hoisted himself onto a wooden stool and put his arm around Jonathan.

"Whaddaya say?"

"What *can* I say? Things are great. We already doubled occupancy, the expansion is going better than I hoped, and so far there haven't been many hassles with the construction boys. Knocking wood, man, you know?"

"We certainly have been kicking some ass."

"A couple more years like this and we'll be beyond the black. I'm talking big time rich. It's great."

Grimis took a slug of scotch, fidgeted with his bar napkin, and grew silent. Jonathan knew he was building to something.

Finally, Grimis said, "You know I don't like getting all wimpy like in front of Amber, right?"

"Yeah."

"Well that's why I'm here a little early. Jon, I just wanted to tell you that I think you're doing a hell of a job with this thing."

"Thanks."

"No. It's more than that. I'm proud of you and the man you've become."

Jonathan almost blushed. He wasn't accustomed to receiving praise, especially from those he respected and admired. The comment meant a lot to him and he'd hold it in his mind for years to come.

"I don't know if I ever told you, Jon, but my boys aren't packing live ammunition."

"Huh?"

"Blanks, Jon. I shoot blanks."

"Sorry to hear that, buddy."

"I've been over it for centuries. Never really too big on

having rug rats anyway."

"And Amber?"

"She's about the same: take 'em or leave 'em."

"That's great. Coulda been a big problem."

"Yeah, maybe, but I think we're both past the procreation stage. It's just that seeing you, you know, watching you grow up like you have in the years you've been around—it kinda makes me think about what coulda been. I mean, I know I'm not your old man or anything, but ah . . . I guess what I'm saying is I wouldn't mind it so much if I was."

Jonathan was stunned. He wanted to say something, anything to show how much those words touched him, but Grimis couldn't bear another emotional moment. He clicked Jonathan's glass and slugged back the rest of his drink.

"One more over here," he barked at the bartender.

Amber and the Boss entered as his second scotch arrived. The foursome chatted about the simple things as they waited for their table. It was funny. With all their power, prestige, and material wealth, they could have eaten anywhere, anytime. Instead, they agreed on a tiny, out-of-the-way place where no one would recognize them. It seemed they were finally beginning to understand the Boss' passion for reexperiencing the little things. Indeed, burgers had never tasted so good.

The conversation turned to business before the waitress returned with the dessert menu and the party had to awkwardly stifle themselves to avoid detection.

"Everything okay?" the waitress asked.

"Fine, fine," said Grimis. "What you got in the way of goodies?"

"Ice cream, ice cream, and a la mode pie."

"Big on dairy, huh?" asked Jonathan.

"Yup. So which one of you folks wants the chocolate, the vanilla, or the coffee that comes with the apple pie?"

"I'll take the pie with vanilla," said Amber.

"No can do."

"Why not?"

"I know it sounds nutty, but our chef is a retentive fellow of the anal variety. He thinks coffee and pie go together like . . . well, pie and coffee. He wouldn't go for any of that mixing and matching. Understand?"

Amber shook her head in disbelief, ordered a dish of chocolate, and waved the waitress away. The rest of the party placed their orders and the conversation returned to the matter of personnel.

"I think it's a great idea to get Marvin involved with the new country club," said Jonathan. "We know he's the best golfer in the universe. He's got real hero potential."

"But do you really think he's ready for that much responsibility?" asked Grimis.

"No. I don't. But if we always waited until we were ready for something, nothing would ever get done. No marriages, no babies, and no handicapped people learning to break free of their chains. Nothing."

"You think he'll come through?" asked Amber, more of the Boss than Jonathan.

"Don't know. But I'd sure like to see him try. Besides, we're getting Marge out of the DMV. People don't need it anymore. She'll run the pro shop and be there to handle anything that really stumps him."

"She doesn't mind playing second fiddle?" asked Jonathan.

Grimis laughed and looked at the Boss.

"He still thinks learning is about upward mobility and pay checks. New Yorkers, what can you do with them?"

"So what's it about then?"

"Uncharted territory. Finding the beauty in something you used to loathe. Marge has been working on her patience. That explains her time at the DMV. Now she's looking to take a support role. After all those years running a Fortune 100 on Earth, she was ready for a new challenge, something she never even considered during her Earth life."

"Marge was a CEO?"

"One of the best," said the Boss. "You never know what you'll find in people when you dig beneath appearances."

"Ain't that the truth."

"So, what do you say, guys?" asked the Boss. "One more before we get back to empire building?"

"Sounds good to me," said Amber. "But make mine a coffee. Tomorrow starts end-of-the-month closeout. It's gonna be a busy day."

CHAPTER 28

Despite the overabundance of tolls and potholes and men at work who really aren't, New York is blessed with an amazing transportation infrastructure. A string of complex tunnels, bridges, and roadways offers alternate routes to every destination. Throgs Neck closed? Take the Whitestone. Traffic on the GWB? Head north and cross the Tap. Most take it for granted, bitching endlessly about the lack of choices and the slow-go to work. If only they knew the problems faced by rural commuters. A fallen log blocking I-84? You best turn that Ford around and call in sick. River overflow covered Yeehaw Junction with mud and cow turds? Hope you're driving a truck, buddy.

All New Yorkers know their power and place in the

pecking order. Albany may wave the flag, but the boroughs wield the swords. Not everyone votes because not everyone needs to. Big business and big money reside in the city. Nature pisses misfortune on them and it gets cleaned up the next day. No questions. No debate. No lies about a budget that never balances anyway. The check writers spend the necessary bucks or Brad in Scarsdale won't just write his congressmen, he'll cut off his yacht privileges. Can't have his shiny off-road vehicle actually going off-road.

It's funny when one thinks about how little of the state is city. Pick a point, any point; drive north for an hour or so, and you're surrounded by country so sweet the south gets jealous. Trees and rivers and horses clopping along mountain tails. It's a beautiful place, the New York that tourists ignore.

Sam's Honda bounced and twisted its way up the Taconic Parkway. Most of the leaves were scattered on the ground, but enough colored samples remained on the branches to make the trip memorable. A collage of rustic reds, yellows, and oranges speckled the barren branches. The days were growing colder. Winter didn't sneak up on you—it marched on over and punched you in the face. He could identify with the season. Perhaps that's why he hated it so.

It was nearly noon when he exited the highway. The people of Fishkill were running Saturday morning errands. The bank, the post office, snagging their Sunday suits from the local laundry. Sam hadn't been to the town since he was a kid and he'd forgotten how white the people were. American-made pick-up trucks outnumbered cars of any kind. Several of the monsters boasted lifted suspension systems, oversized tires, and working gun racks. He even spotted a few rebel flags—

startling after years in the multicultural Bronx. Even the fast food places had white employees.

Sam suffered seven blocks of traffic, keeping to the center to avoid the turn-related slow-ups on either side. The place was busier than he remembered. Car dealerships expanded, a Walmart sprouted where a field once stood, and a Home Depot rousted the local hardware store. Sam watched the blinking arrows inform drivers as to when it was safe to enter the crowded lots. He missed the fields.

A sign for the airport told him it was time to leave the Route road. He frowned as he complied. There never used to be a sign for Dutchess Country Airport. Folks never needed one. Things were where they always were, but that was changing. Men came to no-man's-land, men with money, plans, and construction hats. They brought new things and new people. Now even the old timers had trouble finding their way to the local market.

He parked his car in the visitor's lot and walked to the flight school. A fat bearded man in an Action Aviation sweatshirt sat on the office couch eating donuts and thumbing through an old copy of *Flight Training*. He looked at Sam, noticed he wasn't his one o'clock lesson, and went back to the magazine.

Another man burst through the double glass doors leading from the commercial portion of the airport. He noticed his fly undone, clenched his Styrofoam coffee cup in his teeth, and began tugging at his zipper with both hands. He completed the task, patted his stomach, and sat in a chair next to the fat man. Sam stood at the counter for a few moments watching the two men ignore him.

"Excuse me, man," said Sam finally.

"The name's Duncan," said the fat man, glancing up and immediately returning to his article.

"I was looking for an old guy, used to be an instructor here."

"Tall guy? Fluffy gray hair?"

"Tall yes. Don't know about the hair. Haven't seen him since I was a kid."

"Got a name?"

"Grayson, I think. At least that's what my father used to call him. He gave me some half-assed directions. I figured you guys might know something. He's supposed to live around here."

Duncun grabbed another donut and bit it in half. He walked to the coffeepot, refilled his cup, and chugged it down without pausing.

"Who's your pop?"

"Tom. Tom Holiday."

"Oh, the shark. You one of his boys, huh? Been a while since I seen him up this far, though. Heard he started renting from the guys down at Westchester. Keep closer to work and all. Nice guy, that one."

"Who's the shark?" asked the skinny man.

"Before your time, Pete. Some crazy lawyer me and the old man used to fly with back in the day."

"Any good?"

"Had commercial, instrument, and multi-engine ratings. Kept them up, too. Never went for the instructor's ticket, though. I guess it wouldn't be much good to a guy in his line."

"You fly?" asked Pete.

"No," said Sam.

"Shame, sounds like your pop woulda been a good teacher."

Sam shrugged off the image of being trapped in a tiny C-152 with the demanding old bastard. The fear was vivid, but unlikely. Thomas Holiday was too busy to teach his sons to shave or throw a ball or ride a bike. Flight lessons would never have happened.

"So how is the old son of a bitch?" asked Duncan.

"Dying," said Sam. "He's been in a coma for two years. Heart failing. Lungs not as strong as they should be. Doctors think he'll be lucky to stretch it another month."

Pete laid his magazine on the table. "How'd he end up like that?"

"Surprised you didn't hear. It happened out west, but the way you pilots talk, I figured . . ."

"What?" asked Duncan impatiently.

"He went down in a Piper Cub. Killed my mother, laid him up pretty good too, obviously. They ruled it mechanical error, a snapped aileron cable. Supposedly there was some rough weather too, but you know the FAA. I never really got the details."

Duncan walked to the desk and clicked off the ATIS report. The two men faced the runway in silence for a long moment and then lifted invisible beer glasses as a sign of respect. Pilots don't like to hear about other pilots dying, especially careful ones who follow the rules and keep up their training. They'd drink tonight. His father's old friend, the young wingman, and a bunch of flyboys he never knew would stand around the pilot's lounge and toast his memory.

Duncan's student walked in and apologized for being late. He said he had called for a weather briefing an hour before and things didn't look too promising for their cross-country. Duncan told him to recheck and request an outlook forecast. If things were still looking bleak they'd have a ground school on cross wind landings. The kid nodded and headed for the classroom. Duncan returned his attention to Sam.

"Grayson got a huge place a few miles from here, but he's been living in a bungalow out behind the hanger. Just follow the service road past the tower, hop the fence by the white building, and it'll be the second shack on your right. If any of the fuel guys give you shit about being inside the gate, tell 'em Duncan said it was all right."

"Thanks. He's there now?"

"Now. Later. He'll be there whenever you go. He doesn't do too much anymore. Lung cancer got him pretty bad a while back."

"He's dying?"

"Supposed to be dead already. I don't know how he made it this long. Crazy old man, pushing eighty and still takes in more smoke than air. Too bad you're bringing bad news."

"Well, I figured he should know. They may have had a falling out, but I know my old man loved the guy. Who takes care of him, anyway? Anything I can do?"

"No. Doesn't need much. He's got people taking care of his estate. As for him and the trailer, he has a girl who comes two, three times a month to clean, do laundry, and such. The boys and me take turns checking on him about once a week. You know, talking planes, buying him booze, smokes, and dirty magazines. Nothing big."

Both Sides of Broken

"You're kidding."

"What? He's bouncing on the springboard of the abyss. Might as well enjoy what time he's got left. Hell, I half expect to find a corpse every time I go in there. Which reminds me—Pete, the moron here, skipped his turn. The old boy is due for a check. Would you mind bringing him some stuff?"

Duncan reached under the counter and pulled out a couple packs of unfiltered Luckys. He removed a lighter from his pocket and slid the items over to Sam.

"Make sure he doesn't have any matches. He'll hide 'em, so you gotta check good. He hates Bic lighters on account of they're tough on his arthritis, but better that than burning to death."

"I'll let you know if he's stopped kicking."

"Better you see it than me, man. I hate that sorta shit. Take care, Holiday boy."

His thoughts wandered as he walked. Duncan wasn't the first person to express concern over his father's situation. But how could they care for him? Didn't they see the man he'd been? For a moment Sam doubted his feelings. Perhaps his father wasn't evil. Maybe things seemed worse than they were. No. The terrible times he had weren't fictional. They happened because the man made them happen. The only thing the conversation with Duncan proved was that his father had the wherewithal to be a decent person. He just chose not to be one around his family. It was the choosing that hurt Sam the most.

A light rain was falling by the time Sam reached the bungalow. He knocked, waited, then entered without receiving an answer. Drawn shades darkened the tiny room. It was quiet and cluttered, with the musty air of the aging. He called out again. Nothing. Sam felt for a light switch, but found the window first. He drew back the shades, but the light was less than he expected. Rain started pounding the tin walls. He closed his eyes and thought of the lone airman turning touch-and-goes. He'd never spent a moment in a plane, but there was a time when he'd wanted to. He'd stolen and studied every manual his father brought home. He knew the procedures, the regs, everything but what it was like to be airborne. That was the one thing he couldn't swipe from a briefcase. Sam hated his father for never taking him up. All the brothers did. Maybe that explained why Jonathan had put flight school before law school. Maybe that was why Sam never flew at all, even commercially. Different people, different ways to cope. His eyes opened under the weight of a memory.

He watched the craft from the window. Wings steady. Two thousand two hundred feet, the proper pattern altitude. His rectangle was straight enough as he turned downwind. Sam pegged him for a pro. The plane dipped slightly, losing a good twenty-five feet. Wind shear doesn't care about your ratings or how many hours you have. She's a bitch to all. He'd have to stretch out final, land slightly faster than the handbook recommended, and hope that ground effect didn't kick his ass.

Sam closed his eyes and performed the landing in his mind. First thing, call the tower.

"Dutchess County Airport, this is Cessna 4668-Lima on left down wind. Inbound for full stop on runway 24."

"Cessna 4668-Lima clear for full stop runway 24. Information Mic just updated. Current wind is 016 at 120. Be advised pilot report indicates low level wind shear at 0500."

"Thank you tower. Cessna 4668-Lima clear for full stop runway 24."

Got clearance. Now let's land this puppy.

Carb out. Power down to fifteen hundred RPM. Dip slightly, bring nose up, and maintain a five hundred feet per minute decent rate. Stretch out downwind a little. Okay. Good. Now check for traffic and turn crosswind.

"Okay Sam, high, low, fast or slow?"

"Speed good. A little high, right? Yes, but I'll need the altitude to compensate for the shear."

Select ten degrees of flaps. Descend to nine hundred feet. Check for traffic and turn final.

"Cessna 4668-Lima turning final."

"Roger."

Power back a hair. Align with glide slope.

"Let's see if I remember. White over white and your high as a kite. White over red and your dead. Red over white and you're all right. Guess I'm doing fine."

"More Flaps? No. Too bumpy."

Pass through three hundred feet. Double check alignment. Two hundred feet. One Hundred. Slowly close the throttle. Fifty feet. Thirty. Flare nicely. Main wheels touchdown. Nose wheel a second or so later. Very nice.

"What wind shear?"

"Dutchess ground, this is Cessna 4668-Lima on Taxi way F. Request permission to taxi back to the hanger."

"Cessna 4668-Lima, permission..."

"Nice landing, huh?" asked an old voice. "Sure sounded like a nice landing. A Piper, right?"

Sam turned to find Old Man Grayson in his wheelchair. He

was smoking and coughing and trying to convince his heart to continue pumping blood to a body that seemed more like a skeleton.

"Well, is he on the ground?"

The old man tapped an antiquated transmitter with as much strength as he could muster.

"Damn thing doesn't work in the rain. So?"

"So what?"

"The plane, boy. Look for the plane."

Sam turned to the window. The weather worsened still, but the landing had gone well enough. The pilot and his baby sat on Taxiway E awaiting further instructions.

"Everything's fine."

"Good. Good. Hate to lose another pilot."

"Where's Windy?"

"Here, but not quite here. Depends on what you believe, I guess."

Sam grew red in the face. The old goat was toying with him. More games. Bullshit had become the national pastime. It made him sick. He wanted to reach down and yank up the geezer by his throat. Rage filled him. "Listen old man, take me to my brother or—"

"Or what?" asked Grayson. "Or you'll kill me? But that's why you're here, isn't it? To kill us, to kill us both?"

He laughed at Sam's unconscious shrug. He may have been old and nearly blind, but he'd seen enough of life to know what this young man had planned. He didn't fear him. Standing there helpless, defenseless, feeble, and slow. He feared no man. His age and disease took him past such trivial concerns.

"You have no power over me, Samuel. You may have thought it so, coming here with that ridiculous gun of yours, but it's all an illusion. My time is done, I fear only my maker now."

"Pretty, but I don't buy it and I don't give a shit."

Sam awkwardly pulled the piece from his pocket and brandished it in front of Grayson.

"One more time. Where's my brother?"

"Silly boy, so much like your father. All business. Point to point. Never stopping to question what you do."

"Where?"

"Right where you told him to be. He's in the other room, dying."

Sam bumped past Grayson's chair and walked to the next room. Windy was sprawled on the bed, clothes disheveled, smelling and looking worse than the old man. For a moment Sam wondered if his brother was already dead.

Grayson entered and slowly guided his chair alongside the bed.

"What happened to him?" Sam asked. "He was fine a few days ago."

"Hardly fine," said Grayson. "His insides are shot. Only a matter of time before he caught a lungful of the flu. His body's fighting too many wars to handle another. It got the best of him."

"Why didn't you call me?"

"So you could kill us quicker? I thought you'd be pleased. Natural causes, winning without risk. You get your money without murder. How nice for you."

"It's not about the money, asshole."

The old man shook an angry fist and struggled to his feet. He took a labored step toward Sam and scowled as best a tired old man can.

"The hell it ain't," said Grayson. "Everything's money to you people. But let me tell you son, I had it, lost it, and had it again. It don't mean a damn thing. Life . . ."

Grayson began coughing wildly. He hunched over and spit a wad of blood-soaked phlegm to the floor. Sam stepped back in disgust and watched as the old man gasped for air. He found his breath and slowly straightened.

"See this?" he asked. "My fortune makes your pop's look like candy money. But nobody's here. Nobody's at the house. Nobody's nowhere for me."

"That's your problem, old man. You fucked up your life, not me. I'm not responsible for you and you're not responsible for my father. A man's screw-ups are his own. I know the story. You gave advice. He didn't take it. So what? Still pissed that he went behind your back to the partners and got the job without your help?"

"I was trying to spare him from the life I had. No time. No family. Stress. Booze. Money, yes, but at what price? You know nothing about what I did, even less about the man your father was before he sold his soul."

"Oh, I know, mister. I know shit happens and money makes it happen. Talk about remorse and regret if you want, but I don't do either. He was a bastard and I'll never be like him. I found my life. Soon I'll be rich, married, and out of this fucking place for good."

Grayson extinguished a cigarette on the arm of his chair and struggled to light another. Windy let out a deep breath and moaned slightly. Grayson was right. Windy may have been strong, but he was fighting a battle no man could win. He'd die soon—any moment, or so it seemed. A part of Sam wanted to reach for the phone and dial for help, but the old man was right about his intentions. Neither of them could be breathing when he left the room.

Sam took Windy's hand and looked into his eyes. They were glazed, distant, as if he'd already started the journey to the next life. Sam missed him already. He was a worthless pain in the ass, but they were twins and that counted for something.

"He's in pain," said Sam. "Where's his pills?"

"Finished. I saw no reason to get more. Figured he'd be . . . you know."

"You figured, huh? You fucking *figured*?"

Sam exploded with the weight of endless frustration. He spun Grayson around with a shove and watched him topple to the floor. He groaned on impact, then was silent and still. Sam knew he'd killed him, but guilt was nowhere to be found. Grayson was arrogant, self-centered, and completely oblivious to the pain of others.

"Fuck 'em," said Sam, looking at the corpse. "You're better off."

Windy's labored groan turned Sam's attention from the corpse on the floor. Sam walked back to the bed and patted his shoulder.

"You'll be all right, buddy. I'll take you home. I'll take you home. I promise."

Windy shook his head and made it clear to Sam that he wasn't about to go anywhere. He needed to die. His life was through and he needed to move on there and then. If only his body wasn't so stubborn.

Sam felt pressure on his hand. He knew what Windy wanted. He knew the way twins sometimes know things. How convenient for him that Windy's wishes fell in line with his plan. Sam swallowed a lump, covered his brother's nose and mouth with pillow, and watched his eyes as he suffocated. They seemed thankful, restful, more at peace than he'd ever seen. It took only the better part of a minute, but Sam cried the entire time.

* * *

The storm intensified, providing coverage for Sam and the corpse he carried. He put Windy in the trunk and drove back to the flight school.

Duncan didn't seem at all disturbed when Sam explained how he'd found Grayson's body sprawled out on the floor. He shrugged, scratched his scalp, and picked up the phone.

"Shit," said Duncan. "I don't even know who to call."

"The morgue?" asked Pete.

Duncan put down the phone and began tapping the table. The rhythm helped stir his thoughts. He turned to Sam.

"The cops, right?"

"Probably the best idea."

"Yeah. They probably have reports and shit to file. You know, it's funny."

"His dying?" asked Sam.

"Hell no. We've been waiting for that. I mean, I've been on this planet for forty-seven years and I never seen somebody die. I sure as hell ain't never been responsible for a body before. It's funny the things you don't know about until they happen."

"I guess so. Well, I better get going. Long drive ahead."

"Sure," said Duncuan. "Thanks again."

Sam shook his hand, tipped an imaginary hat to Pete, and walked towards the door.

"Hey," called Duncan. "Snag yourself one of my cards from the desk, will ya? You may wanna try your hand at flying some day. It really is a way of life."

"Maybe I will."

Sam patted his pockets, noticed a bulge that wasn't his keys, and removed the smokes.

"Catch," said Sam, tossing the cigarettes to Duncan.

"Don't want 'em?"

"I quit."

"Looks like he did too."

Sam nodded and lifted a card from its holder. He stuffed the card in his jeans and stepped into the storm.

* * *

He pulled into a deserted rest stop on the Taconic Parkway, wrestled Windy's body into the front seat, and called the police. He gave them his location, then explained how his brother had fallen asleep in the car and hadn't woken up. He acted upset, confused, everything he thought a person would feel in the situation. The lying was laughably easy for him. They offered soothing words, had him perform some basic tests on the body to confirm death, and instructed him to bring

Windy directly to the hospital.

He knew the cops would investigate, but wasn't too concerned. Questions would arise concerning the father, the money, possible links to Jonathan's death. They'd question Sam big time, but Windy was a sick drunk and an endless string of doctor reports would detail his failing health. In the end, things would be fine. Sam wasn't sure of much anymore, but he was certain of that.

CHAPTER 29

Grimis stood in the center of the hotel's main kitchen, directing deliverymen like traffic in downtown LA. He sported classic restaurant garb: black slacks, white shirt buttoned to the neck, and a pair of comfortable sneakers.

"Say, Mac," said a tall Irishman. "Where you want your shrimp?"

"How much you got?"

"Six cases here. Seventeen more in the truck."

Grimis pulled a stack of invoices from his pocket. He shuffled them awkwardly, stopped at one marked "Battered Around Seafood, Inc.," and scanned it quickly.

"Says here there's supposed to be twenty-five cases in all. Where's the other two?"

"Oh, those two. There ah . . . well. Let me see that invoice."

Grimis handed it to the man, wondering how many times he had pulled this scam. A box here, a box there. Skim ten from the orders in a day and you could make yourself a killing on the docks.

"Yeah, I guess I made a mistake. I'll check the truck. We should have another two on board."

"No problem," said Grimis.

A man in a flower cap tapped impatiently on the counter. He'd planned to make a bundle himself ripping off the big boys, but after witnessing Grimis in action, decided against it. Fortune Flowers won the account on a fluke. If he blew it, he'd lose his job. Better to smile and give honest play if it lets you live to scam another day. He unconsciously smiled at the saying.

"What's with you?" asked the shrimp man.

The smaller flower man shrugged, lost the smile, and went back to his tapping.

"Let me get with this guy," said Grimis. "Give me the papers for the shrimp. I'll sign for 'em now. Just put the rest in same spot. Any questions, ask Carlos in the back."

He pulled a pen from his shirt pocket and signed the invoice.

"Don't you wanna count 'em?"

"You said you have what I ordered. I trust you. Mess around, and you're a thief and I'm a dope. Until then, I'll assume we're grownups."

He dispatched the flower man, argued with the liquor people, and renegotiated the server's contracts. Throughout the chores, he took calls from the band, the band's manager, and the band's girlfriends. He hated musicians. There were a lot of asses that came with the job, but musicians were the hemorrhoids.

A few moments huddled together in silence and offered him a break. Jonathan entered to find him sitting on a crate sipping a glass of Chablis.

"So this is what you do all day?"

Grimis grumbled, smiled, and stuck out his hand. "How's things?"

"Same as here, I guess. Busy as hell. But who knows, maybe it'll die down after the anniversary festivities."

"You believe that?"

"No."

"Good," said Grimis. "Hate to see you disappointed."

"Ever think it would be this big?"

"No. You?"

"No. It's nice though. The Boss sure is happy."

"Still wanna leave, don't you, Jon?"

"That obvious?"

"You've changed everything but your tendency towards stubbornness. But what the hell, nobody's perfect. So you gonna ask him for some time off?"

"That's the plan."

"Well, now's your chance. He's in the back office. Should be getting off the phone in a few minutes. All the luck, buddy."

"Thanks. Hey, what's the latest with you and Amber?"

"You know. We been seeing each other a lot and well . . . I, ah . . ."

"Jesus, and you call me stubborn."

The two laughed like the children they were. Jonathan knew what Grimis was feeling and Grimis knew Jonathan knew. They exchanged smiles and then Jonathan left Grimis with the ringing phone and set out to see the Boss.

* * *

Success hadn't changed him much. Same clothes, same car, same God-awful office. You'd think with all the money, he'd hire himself a cleaning lady.

"Jonny boy!" said the Boss, leaping from the desk.

He'd been training again. Weights, martial arts, morning runs. He looked fantastic. Jonathan examined his own figure. Over a hundred years in the After-Earth and he still hadn't stuck to his diet. He'd learned to levitate objects, read minds, and was but a decade or two from teleportation. All this and he'd yet to lose the ten pounds he'd put on during law school. Amazing.

"Don't you sleep?" asked Jonathan.

"Too much to do. We're kicking some serious butt. Have you seen the latest rating reports? The last six months have been a bitch for the Big Guy. For the first time in recorded history, population growth in the Sticks has leveled."

"Great."

"Better than great. We're doing it, man. The four of us are actually doing it."

"That's what I need to talk to you about. I gotta go for a while."

"You what?"

"My father. It's time to set things right."

262

Both Sides of Broken

The Boss dropped his head to his hands and ran his fingers through his hair. He knew Jonathan would never forget his quest, but deep down he kind of hoped he would. The whole thing had been bothering him a lot more lately, and all could see the worry within. In a place where everyone actively lived their dreams, Jonathan was miserable. He didn't deserve the anguish. The Boss wasn't the Big Guy, but in his eyes the young man had paid for his sins long ago.

"It's not up to me, Jonathan. It never was."

"Come on. Look around. This place is amazing. Maybe you're still not as powerful as the Big Guy, but it must have gotten better."

"I don't know. Maybe it has."

"You're scared of him, aren't you? After all this work, you're still scared of him."

The Boss frowned slightly, amazed at Jonathan's perceptiveness. He had never told anyone of the fear. Grimis had guessed long ago, but he had denied it successfully. In truth, the emotion had lessened, but even after centuries had passed, it stirred still. He may have been the Boss, but he wasn't perfect. He was learning and living and making mistakes just like the rest. On some level he suspected the Big Guy was going through the same things, but the thought offered little comfort.

"Well?" asked Jonathan.

"Once, maybe. But now it's more like guilt."

"Over what? An idea. A difference of opinion. You're not evil or vicious. There's no flaming balls of lava swallowing people. No bloodthirsty hounds of hell. Come on. If anyone should feel guilty it's the Big Guy. Hell, if I thought I could get away with it, I'd sue him for defamation of character. Forget all this capitalistic nonsense. We could just win the North End in a settlement."

"You're nutty, you know that, Jonathan?"

He smiled at the thought of putting the Big Guy on the witness stand. It might be fun, but he'd hate to see what happened to him if he lost.

"Maybe a little."

"So what do you want from me?"

"The pass. I need the pass."

"Okay. No promises. You hang out until the festivities are over and I'll see what I can do."

"That's a little vague, don't you think?"

"You're a pisser. Okay. Okay. You set up a meeting between me and the Big Guy and we'll try to work things out. Deal?"

"Yeah, like I can just call him at his ranch house."

"Why not? You're an important guy. You've got a twenty percent stake in the South Side."

"I got what?"

The Boss smiled and pulled a couple cigars from his breast pocket. He lit one for himself and passed the other across the desk.

"That's right. I forgot to mention. I'm giving the three of you twenty percent each."

"Why? I mean . . . yeah, why?"

"Don't ask. Just act stupid until dinner tonight. I haven't told the others yet. Don't wanna spoil the surprise. It should be quite a show."

"I'll say."

Both Sides of Broken

The partners turned off the phone's ringer and allowed themselves a few minutes to sip brandy and smoke their Cubans. The Boss would thank each of them that night for making his dream a reality, but he wanted a special moment with the man who breathed life into the concept.

It is said that visionaries and geniuses rarely get along. Their egos, often larger than their intellect, tend to foul up even the closest of friendships. The Boss suspected that's what happened between himself and the Big Guy. He had regretted the split since the moment it occurred and vowed never to be on the opposite end of things. He liked Jonathan and he'd be damned if he'd make the same mistake twice.

CHAPTER 30

Twenty-five minutes into the hour-long trip catastrophe swatted another human off the planet. A mile or so ahead of the Honda some foolish, middle-aged man Sam had never seen was riding a motorcycle. He was speeding. No helmet. No boots. No leather gloves or jacket. Only experience stood between him and the asphalt. Riders will tell you that there are only two kinds of bikers. Those who've fallen and those who will fall. The only thing one can do to delay the inevitable is exercise caution and be prepared. He did neither.

The turns of the Taconic were clearly more challenging than he'd anticipated. He lost control. No pothole. No oil leak. No definable error, mechanical or otherwise. Just him upright, then not. Poor judgment in the highest form. He slammed to the pavement at eighty-five mph and bounced helplessly for thirty yards. His folly ended at the metal guardrail. It held him . . . well, part of him. His head bore the weight of impact, ripped from his torso, and bounced backward along the road. The rest of his smoking carcass slid under the rail and dropped thirty feet to the river below.

Doctors would comfort the family with lies about how he died on impact, but truth be told, he lived longer than reports conveyed. He felt his shoulder shatter on initial contact. He watched in horror as his fingers melted against the rubbing of the road. Instinctively, he folded his arms and tucked his chin, but the sudden movement sent him spinning from chest to back. He burned until he blacked out, but the rail woke him almost out of spite. In the instant before decapitation he saw many things. The trees, the sky, a picnic he had with his little girl when she was five, then blackness. Game over. Earth life done.

Drivers close to the scene watched in horror as emergency teams made their way to the accident. Traffic backed up for miles, but no one beeped or cursed or left their cars. It seemed many had heard reports of the wreck via the parkway's emergency AM frequency. Sam heard it and tried to understand what power would let such a thing happen to a family man, to any man. He couldn't justify the actions of a god so cruel. The man was being stupid, for sure, but was the punishment worthy of the sin? He doubted it. He doubted so many things as he sat in his car with Windy's body.

Fifteen minutes into the wait, people began to stir. It was horrid, but it was history. The New York minute ticked away and folks returned to thinking of themselves. Horns sounded.

Babies cried. Sam began to imagine the stench of the body he carried. He wrestled the vehicle to the shoulder, exited, and walked twenty yards to a roadside phone.

Samantha sounded better. She still wasn't the vibrant girl who bounced about the precinct, but her voice was a lot stronger and she even managed to joke about her situation. He hadn't planned on telling her about Windy. He wanted to wait until she was released, but his guilt was getting the better of him and he needed some advice.

"He just died?" she asked.

"Yeah."

"God, I'm sorry. Are you okay?"

"I don't know? I feel numb. Two brothers in six days. I just don't know."

"Where was he?"

"Dutchess Country Airport. He was visiting a friend of my father's. I didn't even know he knew the guy."

"What made you think to go there?"

Sam felt as if she was unconsciously prepping him for the questions the investigating officer would ask. He'd prepared for them thoroughly days before he ordered Windy to the airport. Repeating his lies like a mantra, he memorized every aspect of what he'd say. He chorused the proper tone, tempo, pitch, and pace endlessly. He knew it all, but the words seemed harder to speak when someone was listening. He fumbled and slurred as if his tongue knew the truth and rebelled against the vocal cords. He settled soon enough, however, thankful for the practice session.

"He called me, right before he died. Said he needed to talk. He sounded spooky, like he knew or something. I just wish I could have found the place in time. I wish I coulda been there for him."

The silence she offered disturbed him greatly. Perhaps it was paranoia, but for a moment he wondered if she doubted him. She was smarter than he and more experienced in this arena. His fear of what she might know turned his tension to sweat.

"Take him to the hospital," she said.

"Yours?"

"No. You don't have to come all the way here for me. Besides, it might raise questions, seeing as how you don't live in the area. Where would you normally go?"

"New Rochelle when we lived at Pop's place. County if something happened at work. Haven't been in years."

"Go to County. It's bigger, more chance of getting lost in the shuffle."

"Why would I wanna get lost? You don't think . . ."

"Of course not. But young detectives like to make cases out of air. The last thing you need is to go a few rounds with a Colombo wannabe. Just go to County. I know people there. I'll find out who's working and give you a name. Call me before you talk to anyone."

"Are you sure you're okay, babe?"

"Yeah, just a little spooked. I'm sorry. I just freaked when you said the Taconic. I couldn't stand to lose you. That accident is all over the news, you know?"

"Why? Just another road kill, right?"

"Isn't your radio on?"

"No. I turned it off after I heard what happened to the guy. They found his head twenty feet from the rail. Jesus, can you imagine?"

"It was Paul Wilson."

"Christ. The actor?"

"Yeah, people are coming in from all over. Looks like you'll be there for a while."

Sam managed a nervous laugh. His thoughts returned to Windy. He had to get back to the car. People were only going to believe he was sleeping for so long.

"The fun never ends, does it?" he asked.

She promised him things would get better, and though his every instinct screamed otherwise, he believed her. He thanked her for the help and the smile he couldn't see. He told her he'd come by after the cops finished with him. Then he kissed her good-bye.

* * *

Sam met the officer in the hospital cafeteria and answered questions over coffee. The conversation was short. No smoke-filled room. No wild accusations. No light bulb in the face. It was nothing like he imagined. Perhaps movies weren't real after all.

The stocky Italian officer asked a question or two about the estate and one confirming his relationship to Jonathan. The majority, however, focused on Windy's medical history and the events leading to his demise.

"Hear anything about Wilson?" asked Sam, as the officer completed his notes.

"The headless horsemen?"

"Yeah."

"Not much. They say he was drinking."

"You're kidding?"

"Nope. Figures. Guy like that, has everything and he throws it away for a bottle and a joy ride. Makes me sick."

"Yeah. Anyway, officer, what happens now? I'm not exactly experienced in these things. Got a few speeding tickets, but that's about the extent of my familiarity with the law."

"Really? I hear you're getting pretty familiar with Ms. Simms. Must be nice."

Sam caught the officer's smile and tossed it back at him.

"Please," said Sam. "I don't wanna jinx myself. She's a great girl."

"Sure is. Can't wait to get my hands on the SOB who laid her up."

The officer folded his pad and rose from the table.

"People die, Mr. Holiday, and almost always from natural causes. Bury your brother. The insurance company may break your balls over this thing, but I wouldn't expect any hassles from us. Just make sure you take care of our girl."

"Will do."

The officer wished him well, offered appropriate condolences, and shook his hand before leaving. It was the handshake that convinced Sam he had gotten away with the crime. People don't shake hands with someone they believe to be a murderer. Sam was in the clear, and he felt like celebrating.

* * *

Traffic from the hospital was light, allowing the Honda to move crisply about the city streets. On some level, Sam knew his actions were going from bad to worse to outright sick, but that didn't bother him much. He was performing with precision, a feat that had escaped him his entire life.

The garage seemed like a high school reunion upon entry: strange and familiar in the same moment. He found the phone without the usual search, lifted the receiver, and spun the numbers to Samantha's room. He eyed the device as it rang, wondering if he was the only person under seventy with a rotary phone. He thought it strange that people still said the word dial. There were high school kids who had never dialed a phone in their lives, never had to wait for the spinning wheel to come full circle. Misdials were a pain, but he could appreciate the wait. The procedure required effort and somehow made the call mean something.

Samantha sounded better. A nap and some pills had done her good. She brushed off his thank-yous and told him she was being released in the morning. She missed him and conveyed the feeling via a sensual whisper.

He wanted to be with her, love her, hold her until the end of time. But how do you say something like that without sounding like a greeting card or a complete jag-off? You don't of course. You take the risk, wait, and hope she loves you enough to say the same silly things without noticing their silliness.

He asked her if she wanted company; if she needed food, magazines, anything. She did. She needed him, but declined, knowing that he had to make arrangements for his brother's funeral. They kissed their good-byes and she left him alone.

Only after he'd replaced the receiver did he realize how little he knew about the procedures following a death. Jonathan had handled their mother's funeral arrangements. Windy had handled Jonathan's. Hell, he had managed to juggle most of the day-to-day things at the garage as well.

Sam was lost. He hated being lost, but unlike most, he readily admitted the failure. A moment later he bit his lip and called Norah.

"Tonight?"

"Yeah."

"Oh Sam. I'm so . . ."

"Yeah."

She cried, and the sound of her tears returned a memory that had never truly left. He missed her. He loved her. He knew that no matter what went on in the lives they'd built apart, he'd miss and love her endlessly, as she would him. So for once he didn't try and talk her out of sadness. He let it be. He let her grieve, for Windy, for Jonathan, for the man and family she lost to another. It wasn't much of a good-bye gift, but it was something. She quieted herself, wiped the ruined mascara from her eyes, and sniffled herself to composure.

"I'll be right there."

"No," said Sam. "I've got something to take care of. It won't take long, but I was hoping I could make the arrangements from your place."

"What's going on?"

"Nothing. I've just got some running around to do. This way, if you stay there, we can get twice as much done."

"Sam, if you don't wanna see me . . ."

"That's not it. Come on, Norah, I think we're past the point of bullshitting each other. Besides, I could really use a friend tonight. Just later, okay?"

"Okay," she said, still hoping for something that wasn't. "My place?"

"No. I was thinking . . . No. Forget it. You'll think I'm nuts."

"What?"

"The movies."

"What?"

"Yeah. I don't wanna sit in a diner drinking bad coffee and wallowing in self-pity. I loved my brothers, but frankly, I'm spent. Emotionally bankrupt. I wanna sit in a cushy chair with a bucket of popcorn and lose myself in an action adventure. I know it's denial, but only a couple of hours worth. It that so bad?"

"Ten-thirty show or the twelve?"

"I should be back in time for the first. Tell you what. You set up things for Windy. Sunday wake, Monday funeral? Whatever you can get, just fast, okay? I'll do my thing, visit Pop, and find out about the movie. I'll pick you up soon as I'm through."

"Sure."

"Hey Norah, I want you to know this means a lot to me. I don't have that many people I can count on and it's just—"

"Sam. I know. It's all right. Really. See you later."

She hung up the phone and Sam instantly remembered why he had married her. On a practical level, he knew why they fought, divorced, and were miserable for more years than not. But he knew the good stuff too, and was thankful for the memories.

Both Sides of Broken

He clicked the button, began dialing Franky, thought an outside line would be wiser, and put down the phone. He grabbed his pistol from the top of a metal filing cabinet and headed for the car. Twenty minutes south of Scarsdale, he found a McDonald's and made the call.

"Where the fuck you been, asshole?" asked one of the goons. "I want my friggin' money or fat boy here is dead."

"Don't you get tired of saying the same things? You sound like a cartoon."

"Fuck you."

"Ah yes, it's the amazing Vocabulary Boy! Let me remind you that *I'm* running the show. You do what I say and maybe you get your cash. All right, now that we have the preliminaries out of the way—God, I love using multi-syllable words in front of you Neanderthals—we can get down to business. Where are you?"

"Yeah, right, like we'll just tell you and have you bring the cops."

"Clearly you're not getting me. In about twenty-five minutes you will receive a call from me telling you to meet me somewhere exactly five minutes later. The location will be close enough to your present one so as to allow you access without getting pulled over for speeding. In order for me to pick the spot I need to know where you are."

"Bullshit. We meet at the theater, like you said."

"Sorry, we meet where and when and how I say or we don't meet at all. One guy and Franky. No guns. You get the location five minutes beforehand. I'm not into you guys being prepared and I'm certainly not into being hit by a sniper."

"Neither am I. No deal."

"Okay. Bye-bye, Mr. Money. Bye-bye."

Sam tapped the phone against the receiver. The goon on the other end called out frantically, ordering him not to hang up.

"Okay, okay. Just don't screw me."

Sam refused to dignify the comment. Don't screw me? They were in the business of screwing people.

He called them five minutes ahead of schedule and ordered them to the playground behind PS 141. They argued about traffic, parking, and the time it would take to reach the area. Sam cursed mildly and gave them the dial tone.

* * *

His white hands shook as he purchased two tickets to the latest Harrison Ford flick. He tried to seem as calm and normal as the others in line, but couldn't. He was sweating, despite the evening chill. Sam thanked whatever God had allowed him to roam the Earth for the teenage employment rate. He was certain the spaced-out ticket taker seemed more of a freak than he.

Sam stuffed the tickets in his pockets and called Norah from a pay phone outside the theater. It rang twice and he used the moments to slow his breathing.

"Hey Norah. Things go okay with Windy?"

"Yeah. Wasn't much I could do being that it was after hours. Left a message with the church, got some flowers, and notified some friends."

"What friends? Windy had friends?"

"Sam."

"Kidding. What about the funeral place?"

"They were actually there. Felt terrible about Windy having just buried Jonathan."

"Sure. Mr. Feathermore gonna give me a rate?"

"No. But they'll squeeze it in tomorrow if that's okay."

"Great."

"Deposit twenty-five cents," said the phone's automatic voice. "Please deposit twenty-five cents for the next three minutes."

"Where are you?"

"The movies. I figured there'd be a line for that new Ford film. I got the tickets, though. Show starts in ten. We can make it if we skip the previews. I'm sorry. Stupid idea, huh?"

"No. I can get there in time. Just hang outside."

They made the opening credits. It was a great movie, but Sam didn't get word one. It's kinda of hard to lose yourself in a cinematic Neverland after having killed four people.

The scariest thing is that the first three weren't even hard. They were big-time criminals who sold drugs and threatened his life. The rationalization made them paper targets at the circus. Franky was the tough one. Looking a father figure in the eyes, watching him realize the rescue attempt was nothing of the sort, pulling the trigger. Yeah, it had been tough, but not tough enough.

Sam thought of his real father as Harrison disarmed a nuclear warhead. All those years he had smacked him and his brothers around. Calling him stupid, crushing his dreams, ruining the family he'd brought into existence. No more.

Four men in five bullets. Sam was almost proud of the balls it took to pull it off. The old man would die. Maybe not for a while. Maybe not by his hand. But he'd die certain as sunshine. Happy birthday to me.

CHAPTER 31

Jonathan wasn't much for people, let alone placing them on pedestals. If one was worthy of accolades, word would spread without him yakking it up. No sense in belaboring the point. This is not to say, however, that he was without heroes. He had several, including Sam Walton, the former head honcho at Walmart.

He remembered reading an article about how the guy started the company. No money. Small office. Day-to-day and hand to mouth for longer than he'd like to admit. There wasn't even enough cash to buy a decent desk for the president. Old Sam made do with two sawhorses and a sheet of plywood. Rumor had it that he'd grown accustomed to the makeshift workspace and continued to use it throughout his career.

Jonathan thought that was the coolest thing and adopted the practice.

His office was barren. Plantless. White walls. No hairy pencils or silly figurines floating about the terminal. Just the plank of wood, his computer, and two stacks of paper: a huge pile marked "To Do" and a small one labeled "Done." He pressed the "Enter" button and pushed another paper over to the "Done" side.

"You really should call yourself a decorator."

"Windy?" said Jonathan, looking up from his work. "How did you—"

Windy stepped from the doorway and took a seat on the couch. He was dressed plainly in jeans and a polo, but the garments were clean and he looked good in them. So much had changed since Jonathan had last seen his younger brother. He was healthy, with color about the face and the extra pounds a proper diet brings. He was clean, shaved, sharper than ever with his hair combed back and held in place with a touch of spray. But there was an aura about him sparked by more than the physical alterations. He seemed confident, happy, pleased to be the person he was. He stuck out his hand, but Jonathan pushed it away and pulled him in for a hug.

"I can't believe it. My God, I thought I'd never . . . How?"

"Relax, Jon. It's just me."

"Just you my ass. Wait, but if you're here then you're—"

"Dead. Yes, I know. For quite some time now, actually. It was rough at first, but I seem to have grown accustomed to the After-Earth."

"Well, shit. This calls for a celebration. I know I must have a bottle around here somewhere."

"Save it."

"What?"

"I don't drink anymore."

"No kidding. That's great. What, you get hooked up with some kinda After-Earth AA group? Don't tell me you found Jesus or some crap?"

"No, nothing like that. Just found my way."

Jonathan smiled at him, cocked his head, and nodded the way fathers do when their sons bring home the first-place baseball trophy. He was proud of the man his brother had become, the man he'd always been. Windy caught the look.

"How long have you been here?" asked Jonathan.

"Who knows? Years. Decades. Long enough to learn some things, to keep what I need, and toss what I don't. How about you?"

"Seems like forever, but my buddy Grimis tells me that it's only been a couple hundred years. Listen to me. Only. I sound like a regular resident."

"From what I hear, you're a lot more than that."

Jonathan brushed off the compliment and hugged his brother again. "Okay," he said. "A million questions."

"Shoot."

"First, what time is it on Earth?"

"You mean like Eastern Standard?"

"No, wise ass. The date."

"Well, for us it could be any time."

"Yeah. Yeah, I know that whole deal, but when did you die?"

"Less than a week after you."

"A week? Oh my God, only a week. How?"

"Natural causes, supposedly. You know, the problems with my liver and kidneys."

"Sounds like you don't buy it."

Windy took a labored breath. He had traveled far to find his brother. So much to say, ask, feel, and remember, but he couldn't afford to dance around the topic. "Sam killed me, Jon, not like with a chainsaw or anything, but he sent me packing, for sure."

"Come on. *Sam?*"

"I'm serious, Jon. He did. I was fading to final slumber, but he shut off the lights and put me to bed. He killed Old Man Grayson too. Not really on purpose, but, well, he did it for sure. I think he's gone wacko, Jon. He's in deep with the gambling thing and I think it's made him flip out."

Jonathan rose from the desk and began pacing the floor. Windy watched him for a moment, then stood and took him by the arm.

"Believe it, Jon. He's gone."

"How? Why? Franky wouldn't hurt him. Sure it was a lot of money, but come on. What could be so bad that he'd plot to kill you?"

"It wasn't about Franky. It's higher up the food chain. All sorts of people are involved and none of them any good. Pop's next, and you know it. Why else would you be trying so hard to get an Earth-Pass?"

"How did you know about that? How do you know about any of this stuff? No one said anything."

"I don't live here Jon. I'm a Northender. I heard because your life and this casino wonderland are all the rage up there. You're big-time, man, a regular celebrity. Folks love the concept and the people who dreamed it up. The scalpers are selling T-shirts, for Christ's sake. You got a fan club, a breakfast cereal, everything. Hell, I'd bet they know things about you that you can't remember yourself."

"No shit. Why didn't anyone tell me?"

"What, and have to cut you in on the profits? Get with the program, Jon. No one likes paying royalties. This is black market capitalism. I tell ya, you guys are really missing the boat. It's all about merchandising."

"Huh. Well whaddaya know? I guess it is a cool idea. Could you run something like that for us up there, you know, if we came up with an official logo and product line?"

"Don't see why not."

"Great. I'll have to check with the others and draw up some papers, but I'd say it's a go. How's forty percent sound?"

"Like too much. You're a good with ideas and law, Jon, but you're a terrible negotiator. I'll do it for twenty-five, and I'm still robbin' ya."

"Done deal. I'll get you the papers in the morning. There must be some kinda inter-dimensional fax machine, right? The Boss will know what to do."

"Great. Thanks for the opportunity, Jon."

"Like hell. You're doing me a favor. Good looking-out, kiddo."

Windy wished he could leave on a happy note, but he had to press the issue. "So do you believe me now? You know, about Sam?"

"No way, Mr. Imagination. I just can't picture Sam doing the deed. Okay, I'll admit I was concerned for Dad and wanted to get back to Earth, but that was more over guilt and fear of what MacLoughlin might do. I guess he was full of shit after all, huh?"

"Maybe not."

"What do you mean?"

"I died on a Saturday. He said he'd kill Pop in a week or so. He's got another day or two to complete the task."

"Then he's the one to watch, not Sam. Look, Windy, I know you mean well. We're all trying to find answers, but I can't see Sam doing what you say."

"Well, you better work on your imagination skills, buddy, because he killed you too."

Jonathan didn't think. The words stung and he stung back. Hard. He punched Windy straight in the jaw, snapping his head across the room like a rubber band. Windy stumbled to the wall and slid halfway down before realizing what had happened.

"Get out," said Jonathan. "I love you, man, but you must be nuts or something to say such things."

Windy cursed a chipped tooth and wiped some blood from his lip. He got up, shook the stars from his eyes, and regarded Jonathan curiously.

"Nice shot, Jon. Working out?" Windy offered a synthetic chuckle and walked over to Jonathan. Do you remember your accident?"

"Of course."

"Well, I checked the car after the police were through. He screwed with the brakes. Not so much as to have them fail straight away, but enough to weaken their effectiveness. He couldn't have been certain as to when they would give, but he knew that they would eventually. Guess it was lucky for him you decided to play chicken with a semi."

"No way."

"Come on. Think about it. Those brakes of yours didn't work as well as they should've, did they?"

Jonathan closed his eyes and tried to remember the accident. "I can't accept that, Windy. Believe it if it makes things easier for you, but don't mention it again. I'm not calling you a liar. I can see you're above it. But if he did it, he'll confess someday. For now, I'll remember him as I see fit."

"That's one of the cool things about memories," said Windy sarcastically. "They're yours to screw with."

"You got that right."

"Fine, you stubborn SOB. I'm not here to sell Jonny dolls or argue about brake lines anyway. I came because of Pop. MacLoughlin's little game is still playing out and you're right to believe he's a hell of a lot more dangerous than Sam. I don't know what you're doing with all your backpacking around, but I do know that you're running out of time."

"Can you help?"

Windy looked at his watch and cross-checked it with the darkened sky beyond the window. Only grains remained in the hourglass that was his vacation.

"Afraid not. I've got to go. Bye, Jon. I'll be expecting that fax."

"Wait, wait. Don't go yet. Where's Mom? Have you seen her? Is she up there with you? No, Windy. Don't leave me. Please."

Windy's body faded to shadow and the shadow to nothingness. Jonathan stared endlessly at the spot where he'd been standing, wondering if it was all an illusion. No. His luck was such that it could only be real.

He wanted another word, another hug, another answer, but there was nothing in the room but unfinished paperwork. He paced the floor trying to make sense of the conversation. His faculties failed and tossed him to his chair. He imagined the stack of papers laughing at him, mocking him with their size. It seemed as though the pile would never decrease and things would never finish. He tried to contemplate the weight of an unending quest, but it was too much to handle.

A moment later his head plopped to the desk. Instant slumber. Well deserved.

CHAPTER 32

Sam's radio alarm clock belted out a classic Vince Gill tune. Six-thirty: amazingly early for a workday, let alone a Sunday. Sam rarely woke before eight, but there was much to do in the hours ahead and he'd be useless without his cherished quiet time. He rose reluctantly. The second verse began before he could rub the sleep from his lids. He showered, pulled on some loose-fitting blue jeans, and ran a comb through his hair. He thought about starting the coffee, but the kind he made tasted like wastewater from an industrial plant. With the day he was going to have, he'd need something a little more palatable.

By nine, he'd gathered the nerve to call Donato. He'd been up for hours, fielding calls and mapping out the spread charts for the day's games. People bet on everything: pros, college games, even a few on the local high school rivalry. The action on the Giants game was a little slow, but even so, the money he took in was staggering.

Gamblers are funny in that everything means something. The Yanks lost the series, so even die-hard New Yorkers eased up on the Giants. Donato figured they thought the bad luck would spread. The quacks. No matter, with the unexpectedly long baseball season out of the way, he could direct his attention to his pet sport. Business would pick up.

"Hey, Sammy. Things go okay?"

Sam swallowed hard and tried not to think about the man's hands around his neck.

"No, they didn't. Not at all."

Donato's face tensed in a way that Sam could feel through the phone.

"What happened?"

"Everything. Franky's dead. They killed him before I got there. Probably the night they took him. Who knows?"

"So how come you're still walking."

"'Cause I had the money. Christ, I'm sorry, Don, but I gave them the case for my life."

"That was five hundred grand of my money. You know what that means, right?"

"Yeah, but no. This shouldn't change anything between us. I'll still face up to what I owe you. You'll get the million when the old man goes. You don't have to kill me."

"Yeah. I'm afraid I do, Sam. You ain't got the balls to off your pops. I shoulda seen it coming. Sorry, Sam, but that's the way it's gotta be."

Both Sides of Broken

Sam swallowed hard, unable to believe Donato could be so nonchalant about murder and losing so much. He would do it, too. Donato was never one for humor.

"Twenty-four hours," said Sam. "Give me that much to set things in motion. If the old man isn't gone, then do what you gotta do, but at least give me the time."

"Fine, but don't go nowhere."

Sam listened to the dial tone for a moment, wondering if it was similar to the last sound you heard before you left the Earth life. It seemed fitting. Life as a conversation. Sometimes it's abrupt and to the point. Sometimes it's painful. Sometimes it's long and warm and so sweet you never want it to end. But it does. They all do. And when it's over there's nothing left but a sense of emptiness and that awful noise.

He pulled Donato's suitcase from under the bed and clicked it open. So much love given to so much money. Hand-counted, neatly stacked and wrapped. The thought made his stomach turn. He had once thought that money was the greatest thing. No more. For all his plans, his devious thoughts and actions, nothing could stop the transformation he was only beginning to see. No explanations, but in a weird way he was becoming a decent man. The only thing that puzzled him more than its occurrence was why he fought it so. Both truths wrestled inside him, trying to shape the man he'd be. The struggle was greater than he'd anticipated and his potential champion was having a tough round. He knew that the moment he dialed Jeffrey's home.

"Hello?" said Jeffrey.

"It's Sam."

"Holiday? What the hell do you want? Know what time it

is, for Christ's sake?"

"Sorry, but I thought a family man like you would be up and about by now. Don't tell me you've got the world's first late-sleeping two-year-old?"

"Hardly," whispered Jeffrey. "Diana and the baby are at my mother's this weekend, not that it's any of your business. The wife and I wanted some quiet time. She's still sleeping. Wake her and we both die."

"Oh, stop with the theatrics. I didn't call for chatter about the family. I got a job for you."

"Hold on. Let me go to the other phone."

It took a few minutes for Jeffrey to pick up the kitchen line, sneak back, hang up the phone in the bedroom, and return to the kitchen. Sam laughed at the thought of the two-hundred-pound beast tiptoeing through his own house. He killed people for money and yet he was scared of waking up his wife. Funny how things work.

"You got a job? Please. You couldn't find your ass with both hands and a road map. How do you got a job for me?"

"Look, Jeffrey, I know we didn't get off to the best start, what with you beating the shit out of me and all, but that doesn't mean we can't be friends."

"I'm hanging up, asshole."

"I want you to off Donato."

"Franky's boy?"

"Yeah."

"That could bring problems for me."

"Not from Franky. He's dead."

"How?"

"Me."

Both Sides of Broken

"When?"

"Last night."

"Bullshit. I don't buy it."

"Fine. I'm not selling it. All I'm saying is you got nothing to worry about from him 'cause there ain't no him no more."

"Why you telling me this?"

"'Cause I know your rep and I know you won't say a word. You've got old-school morals about these things, like one of them gangsters in the movies. Probably comes from your being a Jew and everyone breaking your balls all the time. Who knows? Who cares? Prove what you gotta prove to whoever whenever. Life goes on. All I can say is that I'm trying to clean the slate and I need some outside help. Donato's next on the list and I can't do him myself. So, you want the job or what?"

"Why you going after him? You owed Franky the big cash, right? If he's dead then you're in the clear."

"I thought you never ask questions."

"Don't usually, but I know Don. I can't just whack someone I know without asking why. At least give me a reason."

"I've got four hundred thousand reasons."

"I thought Windy was the drunk. Good-bye, Sam."

"I'll pay in advance. Tonight. Say eight o'clock my place. No. Better yet, make it the garage. This is no bullshit. I'll pay tonight. You do it by tomorrow. What have you got to lose by showing up? Deal?"

A moment of silence. Jeffrey was performing some calculations, trying to weigh the price of a man's life. He'd killed for less, much less, but he was younger then and without a family. His children had taught him the value of life. He hadn't done much more than rough people up since they were born. Didn't need to. His reputation carried a lot of weight and most folks stayed out of his face. He made decent money, kept the business from his wife, and was able to spend time with his kids. He hated the lying, though, and, like everyone else, wanted to stop pretending. All he wanted was a way out of the life that had seemed so cool when he was a boy. The thought of becoming an average Joe made the decision for him.

"Deal. I'll see you at eight."

Sam hung up the phone and smiled to himself. For a loser, he was doing pretty well.

* * *

Sam arrived at the hospital just before ten. Samantha was talking with one of the nurses while collecting her paperwork from the desk clerk. She was popular everywhere. The nurse's smile made that perfectly clear. She giggled and pointed as the nurse shuffled through pictures of her grandchildren. Samantha made some comment when the show was through and the nurse walked away beaming, her day made.

She turned, tossed her hair, and gave Sam a smile that melted his heart. He watched her as she walked to him. Blue jeans hugged her curves and a loose button-down caressed her shoulders. In the face of her beauty he failed to notice the fading abrasions on her cheek. Love does that sometimes.

"Hey hon," she said, wrapping her arms around him. "I missed you."

"How do you feel?"

"Better. Great, actually. Just glad to be out of here."

"Then let's go."

Sam opened the door for her, started the car, and asked if she was hungry.

"No. I just really wanna get home."

"Gotta work?"

"You can call it that. I'll be off the street for a while. God, I hate riding the desk. I start back tomorrow."

"Don't waste any time, do you?"

"Never."

"All right, home it is."

She ran her hand through his hair as he pulled from the space.

"You sound disappointed."

"It's just that I was looking to spending some time with you."

"Well, who says you can't? I was hoping you'd come in and stay a while."

Sam blushed. He was never insecure around women. He told them up front what he was about and what he wanted from them. If they didn't like it they could hit the road. No deals, no debate. He wasn't a lady-killer by any means, but he didn't bullshit them either. Most girls found that a turn-on and it provided him with more than his share.

But there was something different about Samantha. She made him feel silly and self-conscious. He never walked into a room she was in without double-checking his fly and running a nervous hand through his hair.

"Wanna swing by and get some movies?" he asked. "I'll even go for the sappy ones if you want. We could cuddle up on the coach and, you know, maybe make out a little. That is, if you're up to it. I know you've been through a lot and I don't wanna push you."

Her eyes thanked him for the selfless thought. She'd never said it, but the ordeal had shaken her. Part of her wanted to crawl into a fetal position and hide under her bed. The other wanted to pull him close, close enough to prove she still had faith in the existence of good men.

"Make out? You're so cute. Sure, but eighty-six the sad stuff. Let's get an adventure flick."

They spent the day together, kissing, hugging, telling each other the little things that lovers do. Favorite colors and songs, family tales and first-time stories, schoolyard pranks they thought they'd forgotten. By mid-afternoon it seemed as though they knew everything about each other and yet they talked on. Promises broken and kept, dreams lost and found, and plans. They spoke of the plans they'd made and how their meeting had changed them all forever. Neither said, "I love you" because they didn't have to.

They made love at her prompting. He was worried that she wasn't ready for it, but changed his tune the moment she grabbed his hair and pushed him to the wall. They disrobed each other wildly. Cloth ripped. Skin scratched. Her desire spread quickly and she nearly screamed when he bit into her neck, sucking like a vampire at his first kill. He rolled her to the wall, ripped off her panties, and thrust himself inside her. She lifted her leg towards his shoulder and ordered him to lift it still higher. Grabbing his ass, she pushed him deeper inside, wanting more, needing more, begging and commanding in the same breath. He couldn't speak. It was the best sex he'd ever known and he came until he thought he'd die. They collapsed together, sweaty, exhausted, laughing the way you do when you're breathing too fast to speak.

"Oh my God!" he said. "Incredible!"

"Come on, cowboy, let's see if we can make it to the bedroom for once."

They rested a while, sipping soda and talking of the *what else* they wanted. He was hard sooner than either expected, and they made love again, but this time slowly, tenderly, passionately. He pleasured her with his mouth. Eyes closed, arms wrapped around her thighs. Candy had never tasted so sweet and her soft moans made it all the more delicious. He kissed her after she came and she smiled at the surprise of her own taste. Then he nibbled her ear. She guessed he was just as tasty and a moment later confirmed the hypothesis by putting her mouth to him.

* * *

Sam left her place at just after seven. He wanted to stay, but she had work in the morning and needed the rest. She offered to take the day off and accompany him to the wake, but he explained that Norah would be there and he'd rather not rub his new love in her face. She was impressed with his tact and rewarded him with a deep kiss at the door. Sam tasted the kiss again as he drove.

He stopped by the house, emptied one hundred grand from the case, and packed the remaining four in his trunk. He got to the station at quarter to and found Jeffrey waiting at the door.

"Well, at least you're punctual," said Jeffrey. "Got the

money?"

Sam retrieved the case, raised it above his head, and tapped it proudly.

"Right here."

"Open it."

He did as instructed and marveled at what appeared to be Jeffrey's very first smile.

"You got it. You really got it."

Jeffrey was already dreaming of the life the money would build. Fast cars, big houses, a fishing boat named *Killer* or *Jobber* or something else senselessly stupid and macho. Then he thought of his children and the images turned to college funds and cul-de-sacs. He liked those thoughts and continued to play them in his head as he took the case.

"He'll be gone by noon tomorrow. That fast enough?"

"That's why you get the big bucks."

Jeffrey nodded, got in his car, and drove off. He'd do the deed, Sam knew that much, but he also knew it would be the last time he'd see the Jewish hitman. He wondered what would become of him and his family. Then he didn't. Other problems pressed harder.

CHAPTER 33

Amber was never one to ask for things, but when she wanted something bad enough she could charm the rattle off a snake. Grimis knew this all too well, so he wasn't surprised when she announced that the Big Guy had agreed to meet the Boss in a neutral location.

"The Sticks?" asked Jonathan. "Why there? I hate that place."

"'Cause that's what the Big Guy told me," said Amber. "He wouldn't do it any other way."

"Great."

"Relax, Jonathan," said the Boss. "I know how you feel, but it could've been worse. At least he didn't ask us to go North."

"He did," said Amber. "Talked him out of it."

"Is she a peach or what?" said the Boss, beaming.

Amber dealt another hand of cards. She called the game No-Peek Baseball and smiled as Grimis groaned. He hated any kind of no-peek poker. Always lost, and judging by the pile of chips Amber accumulated, the other boys weren't too good at it either.

Jonathan flipped a ten to start. The Boss turned over a king and threw in a five spot. All saw the bet and later watched poor Grimis flip over seven cards without beating the king.

"I hate this game," he said.

Amber flipped an ace and called him a baby. He feigned annoyance then tried to hide a smile in a bag of chips.

"So where exactly are we meeting the man?"

"Some place called Greasy Nick's. He said you'd know it."

The Boss looked up and away, lost in images of days gone. He used to hang out in that famous burger-and-corn joint when he was younger. Having the meeting there was the Big Guy's way of saying "I knew you when." The Boss acknowledged the point scored and vowed to return the blow.

"Fine," said the Boss. "Grimis, you take Amber in the goat and I'll introduce Jonathan to my baby. Just follow along."

"You're taking out the 'Stang?"

"You bet. She's due for a cruise."

"What's so big about this car?" asked Jonathan.

"You'll see," said Amber. "You'll see."

The Boss flipped the rest of his cards, then pushed the pot to Amber.

"You're a shark, kid. I just hope I have better luck at the meeting."

Both Sides of Broken

He sent Grimis and Amber packing, then led Jonathan to the garage. Together they lifted the dusty cover from the lemon-yellow 1968 supercharged Ford Mustang. The Boss wasn't one for keeping things original. He valued performance and took it any way he could. In his opinion, Ford had a crappy motor year in '68 so he ripped out the stock 302 and threw in a 455 rocket, the biggest block alive. It had taken some creative maneuvering and a bucketful of engine braces to cram the monster inside such a small frame, but the job got done. So what if she stuck out a little? That's what hood-scoops were for.

She purred on ignition, dual exhausts rumbling like a hunter after the kill. Sexy. Poetic. Beauty as only a motor-head could understand. And she wasn't all engine either. The baby had some body. Red flames shooting down the side. Chrome everywhere chrome could be. Tint so dark you'd think day was night. Politically correct? Like hell. A note airbrushed to the back of the trunk proudly stated, "NO RESPECT FOR FUEL ECONOMY." The car was a woman all right, and the woman was a bitch.

They made it to the greasy spoon ten minutes ahead of the others and secured one of the plastic picnic benches that passed for a dining table. The Boss seemed to know everything about the place, but what amazed Jonathan even more was that people seemed to know him.

"Excuse me," said a dopey-looking kid of about twenty. "Are you the guy who came up with the Eternal Resort and Casino idea?"

Puzzled, Jonathan looked at the Boss.

"Yes he is. He's Jonathan Holiday."

"Wow, dude, could I like have your autograph?"

"My what?"

"Oh wow, man, right, like that was so totally uncool of me. Dude, I don't even have a pen. Bummer of major proportions."

The Boss snapped his fingers and a pen dropped to the table.

"Whoa! Nice trick, old-timer. You like play parties or something? My band could use an opener if you're into it. Ha ha . . . not!"

The kid walked back to his table and proudly displayed the signature to his friends. They stood in awe for a moment, chanted some slang that Jonathan didn't understand, then lost themselves in the corn.

"Doesn't that bother you?" asked Jonathan.

"What?"

"Being who you are and nobody knowing it."

"Used to a little, but not anymore. I'm happy when people fail to recognize me. When they do, they throw stones. I've learned to enjoy the anonymity. I'd enjoy it more if they saw me for who I was, but I guess you take what you can get."

"Take what you can get? That's a shitty way to look at things."

"Hey, that's life."

"But we aren't even in life anymore. I really expected something better, you know? A little more from people."

"Why? Is there some rule that says all must evolve? And as far as this not being life, let me tell you, mister, the After-Earth is just as important as your first life. Maybe more so."

"But this isn't where I'm used to being."

Both Sides of Broken

"So? Were you used to being in school when your mother sent you to your first day of kindergarten? Were you used to being at work when you landed your first nine-to-five? Jonathan, life has nothing to do with what we are used to doing. It's about the journey, the exploration from infant to child to adolescent and so on. It's about growth, man. You're just a baby in the next stage, that's all."

"What if I'm not ready for the step? What if I'm scared of what I might find on the other side?"

"Then don't go. You always have the right to be stupid, scared, and bullied into making the wrong decisions. There's a million examples. Be liked and say yes to drugs. Be cool and have sex at sixteen. Be daring and do the drive-by shooting because some other kid is wearing red instead of blue. It's your choice. You can be scared any time you want."

"But I never did any of those things. I never stepped that far out of line."

"No you didn't, and you should be proud of the choices you've made. But you're approaching another fork in the road. This time the decision will not be so black and white because there are no footprints to follow. It's all about you this time; you and faith and whether you believe in the person people see when they look in your direction."

"I don't get it."

"The Sticks, Jonathan. The Sticks. I know they've been calling to you. I know, for all your talk, that you feel the need to lose yourself in another normal life. To run, hide, forget everything you've learned, and go back to being a lawyer."

"Is that so bad?"

"No. But I ask you, is it any good?"

The Boss called over one of the younger kids, slipped him a twenty, and told him to run inside and grab them a couple of Cokes. The kid nodded, eager for a possible reward, and took off with the cash.

"No waiters?" asked Jonathan.

"Not here. The place is open from May to September and it does enough business to allow the owners to travel the globe the rest of the time."

"You're kidding. *This* dump?"

The kid returned with the drinks and the Boss told him to keep the change. He almost jumped with excitement, thrilled at not having laughed at the stranger's request. He'd keep the deal quiet though, afraid that his buddies might hit him up for a piece of the treasure.

"Look around, Jonathan. It's a simple but effective operation. No overhead. No inside dining. No help to steal you blind. Just a couple of cooks and a whole lot of cooking.

"People pay six bucks for an onion burger and a corn on the cob. Pricey, but worth every dime, let me tell you. Hand-grilled wonders you can smell for miles. And the corn! Jon, just wait until you wrap your mitts around one those puppies. That's the real attraction: good old American corn on the cob, soaking up a basket of real butter. Man, I miss this place."

Jonathan smiled at the Boss's memory. He was a cool guy, a toast-maker, the perpetual best man at a wedding. Too bad others never noticed. Too bad for them.

Grimis and Amber pulled up to the curb. He let her out and began the daunting task of securing a parking place. The warmer it became, the harder it was to find a spot in front of the popular eatery. Most folks biked it, walked it, or parked illegally and chanced a ticket. At home, Grimis would have opted for the latter, but the last thing he needed was to spark an Inter-After-Earth dispute over some local traffic violation. City courts might be small in some spots, but they spelled trouble in any dimension. He'd been around long enough to know that much.

He squeezed the monster behind a bread truck, willed an alarm to existence, and activated its sensors. The Boss wasn't the only one who remembered the neighborhood and Grimis wasn't about to let some punk walk off with his beauty. He hopped from the car and pulled up the top. He cursed his chivalry when he realized he'd have to walk the full four blocks alone. He hated being alone and liked to joke that he just couldn't get along with himself.

Grimis approached the table as the Buy Guy's limo pulled up. A bumbling chauffeur bounced about his seat unaware that he'd forgotten to undo his lap belt. He realized his mistake, popped from the vehicle, and scurried around to the opposite side, only to find the Big Guy had let himself out again.

"Sir, you really should let me get that for you."

"Nonsense, Morgan. Now run along."

Morgan echoed the Big Guy's words in a sarcastic mutter, returned to the car, and drove away. Just once he wanted to call him an asshole out loud, or maybe take him out back and sock him one good. If only he wasn't the being of beings. But he was, so the mutter would have to suffice.

"Nice car," said the Boss. "Getting old?"

"Just classy. You still driving that dog of a horse?"

"Blow your doors off."

"Hardly."

The Big Guy took the seat on the bench next to Jonathan and willed himself a Coke.

"So, young lady, why am I here?" he asked.

Amber looked at Jonathan and nodded.

"Well, you see sir, it's just that—"

"Oh come on, not another pitch for an Earth-pass. Son, I thought I told you to forget about that nonsense. I'm just not in a position to honor such a request."

Jonathan cleared his throat and took a sip of soda.

"That's just it, sir. I know that you're not in a position to give me one. You don't have the power anymore."

The Big Guy laughed, patted Jonathan on the back, and smiled at the Boss.

"Where'd you get the kid?"

The Boss' face turned cold and chased all the warm looks from the table. Sometimes the worst enemies are old friends.

"Doesn't matter where. But if I were you, I'd get used to hearing his voice."

"Coming into your own are you there, Boss Man? Don't let that rat trap of a resort go to your head. You got a lot more of my clients during the crusades and I still managed to whip your ass by the end of the century. People flow to me, Boss Man. Always will. I'm the beginning, the end, the only road to take. You're just a pothole on a dead-end street."

"That right? I'm a nothing and you're the all-be-it?"

"You got it, Boss Man."

"And what about this place?"

The Big Guy shrugged in amusement and waved his hand about.

"A rest stop at best. A closed weigh station at worst.

Nothing of consequence either way."

"Getting a little too into our analogy, aren't we?" asked Grimis.

They ignored him and stared at each other in silence.

"You always were full of yourself," said the Boss.

"As were you."

"Well, let me ask you something, since you seem to know everything about everything. If you're so damn wonderful, if the North End is so great, why are people recreating Exodus? Shooting a movie up there, bud? Or do you just like living in an empty palace?"

"You son of a—"

The Big Guy hopped to his feet, reached over the table, and seized the Boss by the collar. The Boss grabbed back and stepped over the bench to face his opponent square on. They struggled for a moment, neither able to topple the other to the ground. Grimis and Jonathan hooted like couple of teenagers, but Amber wasn't impressed. She pushed her way between the wrestlers, put each in a wrist-lock, and dropped them to their knees.

"Are we going to behave?"

Her tone was as firm as her grip. She hated the pretense of bravado and was no longer willing to play the good little girl. Their meager response was inaudible in the face of a woman's roar and she doubted their sincerity. She applied pressure to the hold and roused a yelp of pain from each. There was no need to ask a second time.

Jonathan and Grimis looked at each other in amazement as the two giants slowly rose to their feet. All four men turned curious eyes on the tiny lady before them.

"Moriesh Usheba, the master of Aikido, was five-two and trained for eighty of his eighty-seven Earth years. I'm five-four and, well, I've been around a hell of a lot longer than him. You figure it out."

The men nodded at the woman, filled with a newfound respect. Amber thought it an insult that such respect wasn't given freely to all from the start. Was violence really the only thing that could arrest their attention? Surely one should expect more from men so great.

"Let's walk," she said. "And talk this through."

The men followed without objection. The Boss stopped suddenly when he came upon a remarkable Mustang parked directly in front of his own. He turned to the Big Guy and raised his eyebrows.

The Big Guy nodded. "I picked her up last year. The limo was just for show, you know, to throw you off balance."

"So you still race?"

"Still win."

"What happened to your Cobra?"

"Too flashy. Needed more of a sleeper."

"You call this a sleeper?"

"Okay, I confess I liked your design."

"So you stole it?"

"Stole is a harsh word, Boss Man. Besides, it wasn't exactly up to my standards. It needed a few modifications to take it to the next level. But then again, you always did fall short of the mark."

"That so?"

"History doesn't lie, friend. Let's face it, taking the 455 out of a Pontiac Bonneville was a nice touch, but not the biggest thing you could've done."

"First of all, hot shot, it was from a Buick Electra. Second, the 455 is the biggest block on the planet. It's the be all, end all of gas guzzlers."

The Big Guy smiled and popped the chopped hood.

"You're forgetting the Cadillac 525. *That's* biggest of the big."

"You put a Caddy motor in a Ford? Are you sick? That thing was made for a seven-thousand-pound geezermobile. You truly have no respect for anything."

The Big Guy hopped in the car and revved the engine. She sounded like thunder with PMS. No laws too big to break.

"I'd race ya," said the Big Guy, "but you don't have the balls or the car."

He pulled out of the space and back up towards the South Side party.

"I know what you're planning, Boss Man. It's wartime. Anything goes. Anything's fair. And I'm here to tell ya that I'm gonna kick your ass."

He screeched away, leaving his enemies standing in smoke. When it cleared, the Boss wore a look of determination that Jonathan had never seen before. Grimis had seen it once a long time ago, and smiled at its return. The man he knew was back in action, and this time he was stronger for the company he kept.

"He's scared, isn't he?" asked Jonathan.

"Shitless," said Grimis. "The revolution is on its way."

"Well, hell," said Jonathan. "I'm up for a little anarchy, but not on an empty stomach. I think it's time to see if this corn is worth the road trip."

"Sounds like a plan," said the Boss.

CHAPTER 34

Mr. Feathermore tugged at his tight-fitting suit coat and tried to smooth the wrinkles from his shirt. He jostled his tie about his oversized collar and braced himself for another encounter with the most difficult of the Holiday boys. He knew Sam thought him cold. Most did, and they were right. Living with the dead day in and day out would steal the warmth from any man, or so he imagined. He'd given up on being liked long ago. Cash was so much easier to get along with.

"Mr. Holiday, I'm terribly sorry for your loss."

"Sure, sure. The next session starts at four, right?"

"Yes, four to seven. Well, then . . . I've got a bit of work to do."

Sam knew he was hoping for a nod or something to excuse him from the awkward situation, but wasn't inclined to grant the favor. He simply stared, jarring the man to small talk.

"Sure was a decent turnout this morning. Seems he had more friends than you expected."

"Yeah," said Sam with a smile. "Who knew he was so popular with the AA crowd? A guy like him. Never made a meeting. I thought they stick to their own."

The old man made a career out of watching people deal with grief. He'd seen every rationalization, from laughter to anger to tears to flat-out denial. He knew where Sam stood on the spectrum and chalked up the sarcastic comment to something other than his usual abrasiveness. Mr. Feathermore could also sense what his customers needed, and though he hadn't cared in years, something about this interesting little Italian man stirred his feelings.

"He was one of our own, Sam, and believe it or not, he made more than a few meetings. Just never caught the wagon. Never wanted to, I guess."

"So you're in the club too?"

Mr. Feathermore eyed Sam curiously. He didn't like him, but for some reason he felt he could trust him enough to lend the peace of mind he needed.

"Yes. I was a friend of Windy's sponsor. He was a good man, your brother. Not stupid, not worthless. He knew he was lost all the while, but he liked habit too much to be found. I've never seen someone with so much control."

"Control?"

"Yes. On his terms, in his way, most definitely yes."

Sam stuck out his hand and offered Mr. Feathermore a

solid shake. People tend to confuse the two but, respect often has little to do with fondness.

Norah entered the room shaking an umbrella. She looked harried, tired, and dark about the eyes. "You holding up okay?" she asked.

"You're the emotional one. I should be asking you."

"Not bad. He was a sweet man."

"I'm beginning to see that. Wish it hadn't taken so long. I'm just about out of family, you know?"

"Oh Sam." She took his hand and held him close, but he pulled away. She wilted. There was a time not long ago when she had to keep him from pushing too hard, too fast. Now the tables were turned and the view from the other side wasn't what she expected.

He didn't have to tell her. She didn't have to ask. She'd been replaced. It was clear enough, but she wanted to hear the words anyway. It wasn't out of a need to feel sad or self-pity, she just wanted to know for certain.

"Who is she?" she asked.

"Does it matter?"

"Yes. No. Is she pretty?"

"Norah."

"Is she?"

"Yes."

She ran a hand across her matted hair. Sam could feel her self-esteem dwindling. He wanted to reach out and grab her. He wanted to hold her and tell her that what had happened between them had little to do with beauty and everything to do with the something more. He wanted to caress her into happiness, but he feared he would cross the line with the first

311

touch.

"I should go, Sam," she said. "I have a client meeting and some calls to make, and—"

He took her hand and kissed her on the forehead.

"Don't go, not because of me."

She forced a smile, walked to the coffin, and cried. He watched her keeling there, whispering something to the friend long gone. Sam wondered why people talked to the dead. He chuckled at the thought. Maybe it was their only chance to get the last word in on an old argument. But Windy argued with no one and cared about little. Her whispering remained a mystery.

She rose and walked back to Sam.

"I can't make the funeral tomorrow. They got me flying to Washington for a proposal."

He looked. She nodded.

"Is that what you were telling him, that you couldn't make his send-off?"

"That, and how much I loved his brother."

She turned and walked away. Sam called to her when she reached the door. She stopped and looked around.

"I love you too," he said.

She smiled at the little lie and left. He knew it would be a while before they saw each other again.

* * *

The rain had stopped by the time Sam managed to escape from the funeral home. He had been spending too much time in the house of death and it was beginning to wear on him.

Both Sides of Broken

The outside seemed as fresh and bright as it would to a convict upon release. The sky was black by the time he reached the garage. It was cold too, even for a normal November. It seemed the weathermen were premature in their triumphant ejaculations concerning the effects of El Niño. Stupid little weather ball, as lazy as the country whence it came.

Sam kicked open the door, tossed his keys to the desk, and began rubbing his hands.

"Chilly, Samuel?"

He didn't have to turn around to know who had broken in. It was the man with the stick—the only man to call him Samuel and continue breathing.

"A little. Aren't you?"

"Never. Cold, hot, it's all a state of mind. I've gotten past it."

"Great. Here to talk a little philosophy?"

"No, I'm here to tell you that I can wait no longer. Jonathan was one thing, but Windy's death was a mistake, Samuel. Your mistake, and one for which I cannot be held responsible. I will not delay for you."

"So what, you turning me in?"

"Hardly. I'm simply here to tell you that I will kill your father tomorrow night as promised. Make sure you have yourself an alibi. Would hate to see the state wind up with all the money. Wouldn't you?"

"Forget it. The deal's off. I've got your hundred grand at the house."

"What?"

"I don't want you to kill him anymore. Hell, we can go get the cash now. I just want this to end. No more killing."

"But the game isn't finished."

"So?"

"So, it needs to be played out. Everything finishes Samuel, everything."

"Not this."

MacLoughlin drew his stick like a sword and held it towards Sam's chin. "*Especially* this, my friend."

* * *

The phone in Sam's apartment was ringing when he entered. He rushed across the room and grabbed it, surprised to hear Jeffrey's voice on the line.

"I'm around the corner, two blocks down. I'll be there in five. Pour some scotch, will ya? Two fingers. No ice."

Sam mumbled some questions, but the dial tone didn't respond. He tossed off his coat and started clearing some empty Chinese food containers from the coffee table, then caught himself. He laughed. Straightening up for a contract killer? He threw the containers back on the table. The doorbell rang.

Sam buzzed him in and poured the requested drink. Jeffrey had three flights to climb so Sam took the moment to make himself one, just as strong. He sipped it slowly. There was a knock at the door.

"What's up?" asked Sam, as Jeffrey walked to the couch. "It's done."

"Great, but what's with the visit?"

"You don't stay in this business this long by trusting AT&T. Everything that comes from me is in person."

"Hear ya."

Sam handed him the drink and they toasted Donato's death. Jeffrey called him a good man. Sam called him a prick. Jeffrey laughed and changed his vote.

"He was pretty bad, wasn't he?"

"Why, feeling guilty?"

Jeffrey fell silent. He pictured the murder in his mind. Slow motion. Frame by frame. One shot to the back of the head. A quick kill. Nothing fancy. Professional. By the book, just not the right book. Synagogue would be a tough go this weekend.

"I always feel guilty, Sam. The moment you go numb you have to leave the business."

"Why?"

"'Cause it's the fear that keeps you alive and the guilt that draws the line. All other emotions can be lost, but toss those and you get dead in a hurry. No job too hard. No cause to small. No discrimination or judgment or beliefs. No decision. When only the *how much* means anything you know you're lost. I've seen it happen to men in this line. It always gets them killed."

"But you have emotions, Jeffrey. Not like Bambi's got emotions, but I've seen them."

"That's why I'm getting out of the business, Sam. I have too many and they are getting harder to hide. I'm taking the wife and kids out of New York."

"Where? No, forget I asked."

"Anyway, I just wanted to thank you for the job. It means a lot to us that I can start living a normal life."

"You love them, don't you?"

"My family? More than life. You should try it, Sam. Might

be for you."

Sam swirled the remaining liquid around the bottom of his glass. He waited for it to settle and drank it down.

"Never was much good with family. Seem to do better on my own."

"You must suck at poker, friend, 'cause I can see you're lying like a dog."

"How do you mean?"

"Everyone's got at least one someone. Maybe they don't have the same last name, but true family rarely does. You gotta do what you think is right, man. Maybe get away like us. This place takes its toll."

"Ah . . . maybe Jeff. Maybe."

They shook hands and Jeffrey thanked him one last time before leaving. So many people were walking away that Sam was beginning to question his deodorant. He missed them. Franky, Jonathan, Windy, even Tony and Donato in a weird way. He missed them all.

He paced the room for a moment or so, gathered his courage, and picked up the phone. Samantha answered on the first ring, got rid of another caller, and returned to the line.

"Hey," she said.

"Look," said Sam. "I've never done this before and I know I'm gonna flub it all up, but it can't wait and I just need, I mean I—"

"What?"

"I love you. You know, like real forever love. I wanna marry you, Samantha Simms. Maybe not right now, but someday. Someday soon, if you'll have me."

The words shocked them both so that neither could breathe.

Both Sides of Broken

He was talking fairy tale come true and she felt the sincerity in his voice. Another time, another place, perhaps if he was there holding her hand. Then perhaps she would have said yes. Instead, she offered a maybe and his heart sank beyond Atlantis.

Despite her answer, they talked for hours. Kids, pets, schools, rent or buy, brand of toothpaste. They talked through the night, hoping to convince themselves that they were ready to accept what the other was willing to give. In a perfect world they would be. They'd fall into each other's arms and be one. But this was a world filled with lies, promises lost, and fears of what might go wrong. In this world she needed time to think. He knew it, and would wait until that time was over.

CHAPTER 35

With time meaning so little in the After-Earth, momentum ruled. Years passed as quickly as minutes because the Boss's team willed it so. The people of the South Side built wonders in moments and triumphs in the seconds they contained. They expanded and invented and created and discovered until no passion went unsung. Simply think your pleasure and it was possible.It was a simple scheme, this plot that foiled one so great. They cared for all who entered the South Side and asked honestly about their dreams. Once defined, the team gave them exactly what they had sought throughout their existence: enough direction so they could find the goal, an example to prove it possible, and a kick in the ass to get them started. Here, in this heaven labeled hell, achievements were actually earned.

Jonathan liked to joke that the new South was like the Earth that should have been. In truth, it wasn't much different than the one that was when he was there. It had challenges, fears, and obstacles to overcome. Pain, setbacks, and mountains to climb. There were no North End handouts, no flaky mysterious rules that didn't make sense, just one thing that no realm thought to teach: faith in oneself.

Simple as it sounds, conveying faith to the masses was all it took to transform a faltering, privately held enterprise into the largest tenant-owned organization in the history of life. Why? Because there were no rulers, no kings, no gods to make you think you could never achieve the things you desired. In the new South there were just subjects. Together as friends, they laughed and learned and leaped light years beyond the nonsense in that silly little book.

It was a glorious age for all but one.

* * *

He came to the Boss's office on a Thursday morning. He was old and tired, angry and sad at the defeat he had suffered. But he would not give the Boss the satisfaction of seeing him completely broken. He still had a suit, tattered as it was, and he wore it with as much pride as he could muster. Shoulders back, head held as high as a beaten brow could handle, he walked into the Boss's office and awaited instructions.

"Sit."

He did as commanded, though it was tough to swallow his pride. He was choking down his existence.

"Why the smear campaign?" the Boss asked. "You knew I was winning. Why sink to such a level? Why attack us in a manner whereby our only course of action would be to return in kind? You knew you wouldn't survive the press war. So why? Why toss in the towel that way?"

The Big Guy swallowed hard, feeling like a child at a parent's lecture. The words made sense. They were correct in form and logic. Yet he had an inexplicable desire to object, to ask why it was necessary to stop at the red and not the green. The parent would assure him that that is just the way things are, but the answer never satisfied any child. It could not hope to satisfy one so wise.

He wanted to scream, to rage against the being he had become. He stared at the Boss, wondering how long he'd wait for an answer. His eyes narrowed with impatience and for the first time the Big Guy felt the fear that he had put into people. He silently sent out a million "I'm sorrys."

"It was my last chance," he said. "I knew the campaign was wrong from the moment I began, but you can't imagine what it's like to lose all that you've built, all that you've loved. I was desperate. You were banishing me from my own plane of existence. You can't imagine how that . . . you just can't . . ."

The Boss's laugh chased away his words. "Can't I? Did you not banish me from your world for simply seeking to express my views of life and beyond? There is no one way, old friend. We know that now, and that is why there are no rulers here. Only brothers and sisters seeking the same goal. You failed, but that is not your sin. Failure is just a step to success in my eyes. Your sin is refusing to let others succeed. And any being, God or not, who would stand in the way of another's growth is the worst kind of soul. You, Big Guy—that soul is you."

The Big Guy bowed his head in defeat, acknowledging his error. He had been blind, not out of evil or wanton villainy, but from simple neglect. The ivory tower on which he stood was too tall to be functional. Age had bested him. His eyes grew weak. He could no longer see the subjects he used to visit on every occasion. He forgot them and slowly, all people, Earth and after, returned the favor.

"I am ready to accept whatever punishment you see fit."

The Big Guy dropped to his knees, lowered his head, and offered up his hands in despair.

"Stand up," said the Boss. "It won't be that easy for you. Your deeds over the last century have caused harm not only to my partners and myself but to the community we were elected to represent. It is they who will sit in judgment upon you, not I."

The Big Guy shivered at the thought of undergoing a trial. Given the precedent of detail he set, even Earth lives took years to examine. His would surely take a millennium. He'd prefer death to torture and banishment everlasting. But there was no death for the soul. No one knew that better than he.

"When will the trial begin?"

"It already has."

The Boss snapped his fingers and the darkened walls surrounding the barren stage erupted in a sea of light, exposing the countless lives housed by the enormous coliseum that served as his court.

"They can hear and have heard all that was ever said between us."

"How? So quickly? It could not be done."

"It was," the Boss assured him. "It was because we willed it so. They know you now, better than you know yourself, perhaps. They are capable of making a fair judgment, could even hand it down now, I suppose."

"No!" yelled the Big Guy. "I'm all alone here. I need help, counsel, someone to assist me in preparing a defense. Please do not let me go it alone."

The Boss' eyes tightened with contempt. "Why should I offer you company? You did not seem to need it when the walls about your castle came crashing down. You fought me until your last subject turned against you. You stood for weeks alone, fighting a personal war that had nothing to do with what we were seeking."

"Not true. I was stubborn, yes, but no more than you when you fought for what you believed in. You stood alone for longer than I did, if memory serves."

"Yes," said the Boss, "and you banished me for my ideals and tarnished my name for all eternity. Old people curse me in the street. Children cower in fear at the mention of my name. Father to son, spanning the generations and conceptual religions. You made all fear, and oppose me for what reason? So that you might be king in a land where all could be and think like you? Why should I grant you counsel in the face of your deeds? Old friend, I find I like you less with each word you utter."

The Big Guy sighed, wanting to shrink himself to nothingness, but like his sense of worth, his powers had faded. No more could he amble about as a carefree soul. The bell rang. Play time done.

"So be it," said the Big Guy. "I revoke my request for council and invite those in power to cast their sentence on me this instance. I have but one simple request before it is read."

"Yes?"

"That you, my old friend from ages past, review it and lend your input to its content."

"You ask *me*, the one you tortured all those years?"

"Yes. I once commanded you. Now I bow before you and beg for forgiveness."

The Big Guy tore his clothes from his body and knelt naked before his conqueror.

"I have no more pride. I put myself at your mercy and will abide by any ruling you choose to support. I have seen the error of my ways. My faith in you is strong."

The Boss willed a set of casual clothes and tossed them to the Big Guy.

"Get dressed. We do not teach each other to have faith in a single being. We believe in life and have faith in ourselves. Your words are still confused, but at least it seems your ego has diminished."

The Boss motioned for a guard.

"Take him away."

"Wait, wait!" screamed the Big Guy as the well-built bailiff dragged him from the room. "I thought you said you could rule now?"

"We could, but I want you to spend some time in the cell you gave me when I was in your court."

"No! Please at least tell me how long."

"You never told me, did you?"

The Big Guy was still screaming as the guard shut the door.

He begged to know when the trial would begin, but the Boss refused to answer. He remembered fearing the unknown. Neither man could stand the waiting. Those years before the trial were perhaps the worst the Boss had ever known. Torture, fire, loneliness for ages would be better than wondering about the decor of the hell you were to face. Knowing is everything. In the cell one knows nothing.

Only when the Big Guy's screams faded into the recesses of the institution did the Boss decide to answer.

"Tomorrow," he whispered. "The judgment will be handed down tomorrow."

He dismissed the crowd of observers and retired to his chambers. Grimis, Amber, and Jonathan hounded him with phone messages in an attempt to gain some insight beyond the words heard, but he shrugged them off.

For all his chatter about the will of the people and the new South Side, he knew his heart would never let the case get bigger than the two of them. It didn't need to be.

Folks would understand if he explained, but they never asked and he loved them for their silence. They simply nodded when he asked if he could be the sole member of the jury that would hand down the Big Guy's sentence. Perhaps it was their gift to him for fighting the early battles, or maybe it was because they knew how important the judging was to their hero. In either case, it was wonderful.

He drank alone that night and made a toast. It wasn't to victory or revenge, but to friends, old and new.

CHAPTER 36

Sam spent the rest of his Monday afternoon removing an alternator from a 1977 Chevy Nova. The work was soothing and he lost himself in the bitter smell of gasoline and the silky textures of oil and grease. He loved manual labor. He loved the attentiveness it required. His father had never understood the attraction and Sam had never tried to explain. He only knew that he did good work, sometimes even at a fair price. He found a sort of Zen in those moments—each nut twisted, each screw turned. In his eyes no office position could offer such reality of the now.

He finished the job and began a tune-up on a 1982 Ford. The garage had been all but closed since Jonathan died the week before. A sign taped to the door claimed that the establishment was under repair, but most folks figured the brothers had run into tax problems. The truth was never an issue of importance. Unannounced closings for unspecified lengths of time were common in the neighborhood and most accepted them as a part of the business cycle. A few jobs remained in the pipeline, however, and those with their cars in the lot were not as forgiving. With all that had happened recently he doubted he'd be able to keep the place, but better to finish the work accepted than to risk legal entanglements with nasty neighbors. Sam smiled. Given the area, he'd be lucky if they vented their anger via the courts.

The Ford was in better shape than he expected. New cap and rotors, some wires and plugs, and it was a done deal. He walked to the office, called the owners, and told them they could pick up their vehicles in the morning. The Chevy boy agreed, but the lady with the Ford was fuming after three days without a word. She demanded that Sam stay there so she could pick up her car immediately. He wasn't in a fighting mood, so he agreed. He called back the Chevy owner and offered him a ten percent discount if he'd swing by and pick up his car right away. He offered some stupid excuse for the urgency, but none was needed. The customer was there grinning at him before Sam heard the dial tone.

The lady entered shortly after the first customer departed. She announced that she wanted to give Sam a piece of her mind. He smiled and advised her she didn't seem to have much to spare. She huffed, threw her cash on the counter, and stormed out. Sam silently counted to five, then watched her reenter, embarrassed as could be.

"Forget something?" asked Sam, dangling her keys.

Both Sides of Broken

She hurried over, snatched them up, and stomped out again. She muttered something as the door swung shut, but it was lost in the wind.

With the last of the customers taken care of, Sam turned his attention to the financials. They were as bleak as before. Overdue rent, second notice on the gas and electric, and even the phone company was breaking his balls. The only account the twins managed to keep current was with the guy who stocked the water cooler. They were actually paid in advance on that one. Amazing where one places priorities.

By early evening, he'd had enough of paper shuffling. He was in the Honda again, cruising the streets in an attempt to sort through his life. Five dead, a girl in need of love, a father in need of something he doubted he could provide. So much so soon. Fred Flintstone was right. A rolling stone gathers no moss, but it sure can leave a hell of a bruise. Sam braced for impact, sensing some how that his worlds would soon collide.

He drove past the chained schoolyard, past the crackhead park, to a deserted alleyway where he had played stickball as a boy. He remembered pretending chewing gum was tobacco, the spray-painted box on the wall serving as home plate, the senseless arguments over whether a hit was a single or something more. Silly upon recollection, but so important back then. Sam watched the boys argue over a pitch that to him seemed high and away. Time changed nothing. Rules still were of the essence, at least to those who longed to follow them.

Sam frowned as he pulled away. Darkness would soon chase the boys from the lot. The thought sobered him like no coffee could. Somewhere, right now, a little boy was playing his last game of stickball. The saddest part, of course, was that he wouldn't even realize its passing.He lost himself in the driving daze, the kind that brings us to work without any memory of the journey. When he awoke he was a block from Samantha's apartment. Though he couldn't recall making the trip, he knew for certain the reason he had come. He found a spot a building down, parked, and walked the block to her place. He removed the ring from his pocket and kissed it softly.

"Don't fail me, baby."

She buzzed him in and met him in the hall.

"Hey sweetie," she said. "Didn't expect you tonight."

"Yeah, ah, I . . . just wanted to see you. You're not busy, are you?"

She wrapped her arms around him and smothered him with kisses.

"No. Never. What's up?"

"A lot of things. You know, I was very serious when I proposed this morning."

"I know."

Sam pulled the case from his coat and handed it to her. She opened it and almost cried.

"It was my grandmother's. I know she'd think it would look great on you."

"Oh. Sam, I—"

"I know," he said with a sigh. "You want more time. I understand that now. I just wanted to let you know that I need you more than I need to breathe. I guess I thought showing you the ring would help me convey the feeling."

"You don't need any help. It's in your eyes."

"Maybe, but there are things about me, things I've done that you need to know about before you make your decision."

She shook her head and held him close. Her lips nibbled his ear as she whispered, "I don't need the time and I don't need to know anything about anything. I was scared because we were on the rebound, because it was too soon, because it was so great. I was terribly scared, but I'm not anymore. I love you, Sam. I always have, ever since you were that goofy kid in grade school."

"Goofy? I thought I was cool."

She pulled away and grinned. "That's what made you so goofy. Now shut up and kiss me, Mr. Cool Guy."

They kissed so long, so deep, so wet, that somewhere in an After-Earth yet defined, Audrey Hepburn got jealous and began to pout. When they finally pulled apart, Sam had almost forgotten what he had come to tell her. Almost.

* * *

He sat her down and told her the whole tale. From his father to Donato to all the murders in between.

She stared at him in horror as he told the tale, and when he was done put her hands to her cheeks. She was pale. "What now?" she asked.

"I don't know. Last week things were so simple. But now so much has changed."

"That's not an answer, Sam."

"I know."

"Well."

"I want to make things right. That might be impossible

now, but I've got to try."

"How?"

"MacLoughlin. I feel as though he orchestrated every event. I'm not blaming him for my actions, but he certainly started all this and he's the only one still standing. That has to mean something."

"So what?" asked Samantha, eyes wider than he had ever seen them. "Are you going to kill him too? Do you really think that's the way out of all this?"

"No. His death is not the answer, but neither is my father's. I have to stop him. I have to at least try. I just need to know if you're with me."

Her silence tortured him like no weapon could. He expected her to slap him, to yell "No!" in his face, and run away. Yes, run away fast or arrest him there on the spot. But she did none of those things. No melodrama. No theatrics. She just calmly asked a simple question.

"Was it all for the money?"

"Yes. At least at the start. But everything changed the day after the deal. Everything changed for me at Jonathan's funeral. I swear to you on us that from that moment it became less about the money and more about the people surrounding it. I know I screwed up. I've done things I never thought myself capable of. It scares me; the doing and the ease with which they were done. But I'm sorry. Beyond words I'm sorry. So please don't walk away from me. Not now. Not ever. You're the only and best friend I've ever known."

She smiled. He couldn't imagine why, but she smiled and took his hand. He knew at that moment they were partners forever. Her love was a gift too great for a man so low and he knew he'd be called to pay the piper at some point. He wondered about the price, then didn't. Any price would be worth the paying.

CHAPTER 37

Grimis, Jonathan, and Amber huddled at the far end of a massive oak table. The coliseum was filled with the deafening whispers of the masses it contained. All words concerned themselves with the thoughts of the man behind the curtain. What would he say? What would he do? What form of justice could suit a fallen titan?

"What's taking so long?" asked Jonathan.

"Geez, give the guy a break," said Amber. "He's only trying to make the most important decision of all time. Heck, Grimis takes longer to order lunch at a hot dog stand."

Grimis hugged her around the waist. "That's why I love you. So witty."

"Seriously, guys, what do you think he'll say?"

"Don't know," said Grimis. "Could go either way."

"Yeah. The Boss is one of the sweetest men I've ever known, but there's history between those two that none of us can quite comprehend. One thing's for sure: he has the power to do whatever he wants. All we can do is trust his actions will be just."

"Would you fry him?" asked Jonathan of Amber.

"I would," said Grimis. "Pompous jerk."

"Oh now, honey, you don't really mean that."

"Sure do. Okay, well, maybe not fry him exactly, but he definitely deserves a little sautéing after all that went on."

"What did he do that was so bad?" asked Jonathan. "I mean, he started everything. Without him there would be no us, so how can we fault him for getting the ball rolling?"

Grimis patted Jonathan's hand like a father before telling his son his mother passed. "You've just touched upon the biggest misconception of all time."

"How do you mean?"

"Earth is. Right?"

"Guess so."

"So is America. Correct?"

"Yeah. What's your point?"

"Well, is George Washington responsible for starting America? Did he up and decide one day to move to the New World and begin a civilization unlike any on Earth?"

"No."

"Right. He may have been a major contributor and designer of the grand scheme, but he was by no means the creator of it all. That America you love so much exists because so many people wanted it that they managed to will it into existence.

The same holds for life. There wasn't one soul creating for the sake of creation. There were infinite souls, searching for a new plane of experience. They brought themselves to the Earth that is as humans. Humans with all the problems and wonders the existence entails. They designed the schools and theaters and laboratories where tired myths were dispelled. It was us. Us from the beginning."

"That's impossible."

"Why, because it goes against the Sunday school crowd? Who do you think gave them their information? Is it really so hard to believe that each person is responsible for his or her actions in the course of life? That there is no predestination, no single lifetime, no one reality, and no limitations brought forth by a puppet ruler who wishes himself the most advanced? That's what happened, you know."

"I don't follow."

Grimis looked at Amber and silently passed the torch.

"What would happen if the president of the United States refused to step down after an eight-year run?" she asked.

"Anarchy, I guess."

"But what if everyone loved him and wanted him to stay?"

"Tough. His leaving is what makes the place so great. It's not about the office or the ruler or the power he wields. The country is about the people. If he stayed he would be acting against that which he sought to nurture."

"So too with the North End, Jonathan."

The couple allowed their friend a few moments to reflect on the weight of the concept presented. Could it be true? Could the figure he saw as almighty be just an advanced version of every human in existence? Maybe, but is that too much to believe and hope for? Is the theory crafted from insane pride and an overindulged sense of self-importance? Jonathan gave careful consideration to the later questions and answered "no" to both.

Perhaps it was time for the constitution to be rewritten. Maybe that which worked for our forefathers failed in the face of current problems. He tried to focus on a single issue, something to bring the theory down to a workable level. He closed his eyes and an image of a musket came to mind. He thought it strange for a moment and then realized its significance.

He understood suddenly that many of the debates in his country, in his world, would never be solved as long as people placed so much weight on past regulations. The issue concerning the right to bear arms, for example, screamed for change. America was built by people who lived on farms and defended their land with weapons kept as close as car keys. How can we dare remove something so vital to our existence? How can we take away from people that which they might use to defend themselves against those who wish them harm? How do you take the fight from the farmer?

The answer seemed so simple when examined without passion. Weapons must be removed because they were no longer simple muskets owned by decent Puritan family men. They were armor-piercing automatics stolen by children, fired for drugs.

"I understand now," said Jonathan. "I understand and I believe in the words."

"Why?" asked Amber. "What do you see?"

"That our constitution should have been written in pencil to remind us it is a living, breathing document. Laws, rules, and those who are called to enforce them change when change is needed. So too with the guides. Whether kings on Earth or gods afterwards. If they are not willing to step down and become part of the society they profess to love, then they are not worth the praise sought."

"You got it, Jonathan. You finally got it."

A rumbling in the crowd told the threesome that the Boss was making his way to the bench. They turned and watched him enter the court.

"Good evening, friends," said the Boss. "We are here to witness the sentencing of the former ruler of the North End."

Many cheered, but he hushed them. Clearly this was not to be looked on as a day for celebration. It was a solemn occasion in his eyes. Victory, yes, but at the expense of a friend. He couldn't be happy, despite the prize.

"Bring him in."

The Big Guy looked smaller than any could have imagined. He draped in a rough brown garment that hung from his shoulders like a poncho and came to rest just above his bare ankles.

He wore a hopeless expression—not fear or sadness, but the void that comes from knowing all power over one's destiny has been stripped away. He was a broken stallion slowly coming to the realization that the days of roaming free about the plain were at an end. It was cages now; cages and trainers trotting him about in circles for their amusement. He watched the ground, unable to muster even the strength to look at his adversary's feet. He simply knelt and waited, counting his breath and the endless eyes upon him. So many. Too many. How had he forgotten these souls? Why didn't he reach out to them as friends? So many regrets danced through his mind. So many reasons for his reign to end. The Boss was right to conquer him. It should have been done long ago.

"Rise and hear your fate."

The Big Guy slowly worked his hobbled body vertical.

"Look at me. I wish to see your face when I hand down the decision."

Grimis had never seen the Boss so harsh of voice or stern of glance. Maybe this treatment was deserved after all. He looked at Jonathan, who was watching intently, mouth open, eyes wider than a 747.

"Old friend, I will not belabor my point with winded words and rhetoric," the Boss said. "The judgment was an easy one and it shall be revealed quickly. What has been done is known to all, but mostly it is known to us two. Your sins are great. Sins against me, against humanity, against yourself. There is only one punishment that would suit the crimes committed."

The Boss stepped down from his platform and walked to his fallen foe. He placed his hand on his shoulder. Then, slowly, as if he'd forgotten how, he knelt and embraced him tightly, as best friends do.

"Rise and join us as the equal you are. Honor us with your presence on our elected council. Help us to make all life— After-Earth and before—Eden again. I stand before all that are and swear that my older brother is forgiven. He is forgiven because there is no sin in being human. No sin to try and fail."

The Big Guy dropped his jaw, amazed at the wisdom of his younger sibling. "I missed you," he said through tears.

"And I you."

They turned to the masses before them and raised each other's hand in victory. The crowd erupted in glorious cheers. They praised no god that day. They praised the divine power that is humanity, a power they all had and could learn to use in time.

* * *

Long after the crowd had dispersed, Jonathan sat in silence. Amber noticed him in thought and met him with a gentle arm about the shoulder. He knew who she was without turning and melted into her caring arms.

"Do you think I'll ever be forgiven?" he asked.

"I wish I could comfort you with easy words, but it isn't up to me."

"I just wish I could tell him that I love him, that he wasn't the worst father. Things happened for so many reasons. It's never the fault of one man or one day—I see that now. Blaming him was the easiest way to deal with the hardship. Funny, we all put so much pressure on the fathers we are lucky to have at all. Maybe I should have worried about being a better son."

"Take heart, Jonathan. Good happens. Maybe not when we expect it to, or when it seems we need it most, but it does happen eventually. You have to believe that good comes in the end."

"Why? Why should I believe in fairy tales?"

"Because you write them. You are the author of your life story and if you refuse to allow it to end until you are most happy, you will live on forever. You will live to learn and grow and seek happiness that the former you never thought possible. Be the better son, Jonathan. That is the only realistic penance. Be who you wish you had been. Not for you or guilt or an urgent need to right a wrong. Be the better son because you long for the endless journey that is life."

Jonathan smiled at her wisdom. She was a marvel through and through.

"Quite a shock about the Boss, huh?" asked Jonathan.

"What do you mean?"

"Him being the Big Guy's kid brother."

"Yeah."

"Did you know?"

"No. No one knew. Maybe Grimis, but I doubt even him. We all have brothers, Jonathan. Grimis is as much your brother as I am your sister. That's what gives us our strength."

Jonathan sat for a long time after she left. He was thinking of siblings yet to be found and journeys yet to begin.

CHAPTER 38

Visiting hours were long gone by the time Sam and his bride-to-be reached the hospital. A grim-looking orderly shrugged off Samantha's sad eyes and looked towards her companion. Sam knew the type. All it took was a wink and five spot to coax him into altering hospital policy. For a moment Sam thought himself cool. Then he didn't. If he could work such wonders, imagine how easily MacLoughlin could gain access. A chill stretched itself across his spine. What if they were too late? What if the deed had already been done? He pictured MacLoughlin standing over his father, smiling at his handiwork. The image bred anger and the emotion engulfed the man. He grabbed Samantha by the arm and darted towards the elevator.

Both Sides of Broken

He tapped the button ferociously, but the aging contraption moved no faster for the pressing. They grew impatient and made for the stairs. Four flights to his father's floor. Hearts pumping, feet flying over two and three steps at a time. They burst through the door breathless, he more than she. They pressed on, running the length of the hall to room 347.

They almost collapsed upon entry, but the sight seen was a good one and it lifted their spirits. The old man was looking worse for wear, but he was holding on, still stubborn. MacLoughlin had yet to arrive.

"Let me call this in," she said.

"And what, tell them you think some mystical creature is going to kill my dad? How would you explain it? What would you say?"

"Let's at least get that orderly up here."

"And get him hurt too?"

"Well, we have to do something."

"We will. We'll sit here until he shows."

"Then what?"

Sam shook his head. "I haven't figured that out yet, but I'm sure it will be brilliant."

"Better be," said MacLoughlin, as he entered the room.

Sam turned to face him, fists clenched.

"Relax, Samuel. I'm not here for you. The game takes me to the man in the bed. His time has come and I am here to collect."

"Can't let you do that."

"Excuse me? Did you say you *can't*?"

"That's right."

MacLoughlin grinned at the little man's bravado, brought

341

up his stick. His eyes were colder than the stone floor.

"I'm afraid you've forgotten our last encounter, Samuel. You know I can kill you if you stand in my way."

Samantha looked at her man, trying to guess what had happened between them. Sam's faced fixed on his adversary. It offered no clues.

"I'm not here to fight you, MacLoughlin." He pulled a packet from his coat and tossed it to the menacing figure.

"A hundred grand. Count it if you want, but it's all there. Take it and leave us alone."

"I told you before. That can't happen."

"Why the hell not? We played and lost. I'm willing to accept that. I'm giving you the cash and letting you walk, paid in full. Just forget the murder. Forget your rules."

"I was playing for a soul and I won your father's. The money is nothing to me. It was never about the rules, or the game. It's about the sin you committed. It's turned on you, Samuel, and now you have to face it."

"What?"

"You've gotten all you've wished for and now you want to alter the contract. You want your past erased. You want the girl and the money and a ticket out of the life you knew. But you're no longer willing to dip your hands in blood to get them. You don't want the guilt to get in the way of the future you've designed. That's your sin. You've no remorse. Only self-interest and ambition exist within you."

"Bullshit. You've no idea what I've been going through, how I've changed."

Sam took his girl's hand and rubbed it nervously. "I've found something real, someone who means more than any of this."

MacLoughlin stroked his chin. He knew Sam's words were sincere, but words were no longer enough. Too many people hide behind dialogue. Too many people lost too much via lack of action. He required more convincing and so he stared on.

"Take it," said Sam. "Take it all. I'll sign over the money, the garage, whatever you want. Just leave us together and let my father live."

"No. That's too easy and you know it."

"What then?"

"Your life."

Samantha pulled her gun, but he cracked her across the arm before she could utter a threat. She dropped to her knees.

"You fuck!" screamed Sam. "What's the matter with you?"

MacLoughlin picked up the weapon and pointed it at Samantha.

"I don't like being shot."

He stuffed the piece in his coat and dropped his stick to Samantha's shoulder.

"Very good, little one, but we're in different leagues, you and I. Now, I need a body. Whose shall it be? Decide quickly or I'll take three. I'll give you a moment." MacLoughlin ripped the phone from the wall and stepped out of the room.

Samantha began to cry. Sam went over and hugged her tightly. The impossible was before them. There was so much to say and no time to speak. His kissed her softly, his lips telling her that he'd love her for all time, his eyes explaining how he deserved the fate.

He called for MacLoughlin, not wanting him to have the pleasure of interrupting.

"I'm ready," said Sam.

He stood before his executioner with eyes closed and hands dangling loosely at his sides. He was amazed by how calm he felt. It was as though destiny had come and pointed the way home. It wasn't the road he'd chosen. He wanted the long one. He wanted to travel with Samantha for as long as she'd let him. But he was a nothing, so he stood and waited for eternal darkness to fall.

"So it shall be your death then?" asked MacLoughlin. "Funny, the last Holiday." He drew the stick back for the kill, inhaled deeply, and began the descent.

"No!" screamed Samantha.

Sam opened his eyes at the sound and instinctively threw up his hands to form an X. The stick landed hard, shattering both arms. But for once Sam focused not on the pain, but the love. He kicked his assailant in the groin and watched him topple to the ground.

"Run," said Sam. "Get help."

Samantha did as instructed. He cursed MacLoughlin, kicking his face with each word until thick blood soaked his scalp.

"You fuck. You miserable son-of-a-bitch. This is my life. Mine. Not yours or God's or my father's. It's mine. Mine to live."

Sam stepped away from the body. He hadn't killed him, but he had come close. MacLoughlin's breathing was shallow and he wasn't moving. Sam looked at his broken body, only now beginning to feel the pain in his arms. He started to pace like caged beast.

"Kill me? Fuck you and your stupid rules. Who are you to

judge? My life, my rights."

Sam raised a foot to kick him again, but hesitated. His fire gave way to tears.

"Who are you to judge? Who is anyone?"

"No one," said MacLoughlin calmly.

He rose quickly as if free from injury. He waved a hand through his hair and the redness was removed.

"How the . . . ?"

"Give me your hands."

MacLoughlin ran his palm over Sam's arms and he was healed. Sam turned his arms, unable to believe the miracle witnessed.

"Are you?"

"Hardly," said MacLoughlin.

"Then how? I mean why?"

"Your sin is forgiven, for you have finally forgiven yourself."

"I don't get it. I didn't face death. I cheated. I tried to kill you. How is that remorse? How is that anything?"

"Did you not hear your own words? After all those years of wishing yourself into the abyss, you finally chose to fight. You chose to grow. You accepted responsibility for the life you made. Before this day you existed, but you never lived. Live, Samuel. Show the world how well you can live."

MacLoughlin walked to Sam's father and kissed him on the forehead. He turned to Sam, smiled knowingly, and vanished.

A moment later, Samantha walked in alone.

"What happened?" asked Sam.

"I don't know. I left the room and the pain in my hand went away. I wanted to find help, but I couldn't move. I just stood outside the door and listened."

"So you know?"

"Yes. God, it sort of changes your views on things, doesn't it?"

"Sure does. So what now? How do we start living as the people we can truly be?"

Samantha kissed him gently. "There's a chaplain downstairs. How about we throw him some business and figure it out together?"

CHAPTER 39

Time was kind to Earthlings past. Three After-Earths blended peacefully into one. The Boss and the Big Guy discovered the goodness within each other. And all people, no matter their previous locale, were given the chance and encouragement to achieve the impossible. Eden had returned, only this time it wasn't a fairy tale.

Jonathan sat with his friends around a huge oak table. Marvin and Marge to his left; Amber and Grimis to his right; new brothers and sisters dotting chairs as far as the eye could see. It was a family reunion of startling proportions.

The Boss sat at the head with his brother. He held a gavel he didn't need and tapped it to the table more for symbolism than anything else.

"Thank you all for coming. We've accomplished a great deal together, and I'm proud to have served as your guide these years."

The table exploded in cheers, all eyes but Amber's focused forward. She beamed at her husband, holding his hand to her heart. She had never told him, but the man with the gavel gave her the courage to propose. She was grateful and would love him always for the happiness that their conversation had convinced her she deserved. Jonathan turned and smiled at the soul mates. It may have taken them centuries to find each other, but it was clear from their expressions that the finding was worth the wait.

"As you know," said the Boss, "I'm going off to work on some new things, things I've always wanted to try. I've nominated Grimis to be the new guide. The ballot counters inform me that you concur. I salute your good judgment, for he is a fine soul."

The Boss motioned for Grimis to stand. He did and the crowd applauded. The Boss waved Grimis to his chair. The two men exchanged smiles. He had made the right choice. There was a time, however, when Grimis had dreaded the occasion. He knew a lot about the After-Earth, but could never think himself as smooth or collected as his uncle. He felt it beyond his abilities. He was disorganized and haphazard. The self-doubt almost caused him to decline the nomination, but his bride convinced him otherwise. She explained that the position was not a ruling one. It wasn't a government office or a legal title. All he had to do was live as he always had. Live, learn, and seek new skills. Lead by heartfelt example.

She told him the job was similar that of a sensei in a martial arts class. His experience awarded him the role. Yet, as it is in the arts, even the oldest of masters is really only the head student. Knowledge is passed, not top down, but from person to person regardless of time in rank. He would be called upon to answer questions regarding form and balance, but little else. Most would find their way by watching and teaching and learning. He smiled at her analogy, for it was as true as her love. He was already gaining insight from others. With the pressure off, he accepted.

"Before I pass the torch," said the Boss, "I'd like to take a moment to open the floor to old business. Are there any outstanding concerns or issues?"

Amber patted Jonathan's hand. "Go on," she said.

Jonathan rubbed his palms on his pants and slowly stood. Every eye shifted to him. The weight of their glances made him feel weak at the knees.

"I would like to reopen the Earth pass issue."

The Boss whispered the story to his brother. He nodded and the two looked at Jonathan.

"Please go on."

"I feel that I've learned a lot and am ready for the journey."

"You do?" asked the Big Guy. "You seem to have forgotten the policies set forth by the council. This case has been heard by the two After-Earths past, has it not?"

"Yes," said Jonathan. "But so much has changed since that time. Everything is new."

"All but the facts of the case."

"Easy, brother," said the Boss. "I'm inclined to agree with Jonathan. He has done much for the After-Earth. We owe a great deal to him, for without his stubbornness we might not

349

have come together. I think he should be granted the pass."

"I disagree. Mistakes are made so that we may learn from them. They are not made to be fixed via special powers."

Jonathan scanned the countless faces for support, but few knew of what they spoke.

"I'm sorry," said the Boss. "I'm afraid that since the case is older than the system presiding over it, we have little choice but to dismiss it from the records. There is no one left with experience enough to break the tie."

"I wouldn't say that," said MacLoughlin, appearing out of thin air.

He startled all but the boys at the head of the table.

"How are you, Uncle?" asked the Boss.

"Fine. And you? Looking good, I see."

"Yes, yes. My brother and I have reconciled."

"It's about time."

MacLoughlin looked at Jonathan and watched his fear turn to intrigue. How could it be that this man was here in the After-Earth? Could he have died and learned so much so fast? Why hadn't he seen him before this day? Countless questions filled his mind.

"Still trying to settle up with your old man?" asked MacLoughlin.

"Is he . . . ?"

"Depends on when you go back."

"You mean you'll let me?"

"Nothing's for the letting, Jonathan."

MacLoughlin pulled an unopened deck of cards from his coat and went about his ritual. When the cards were spread on the table he motioned Jonathan over.

"It seems we have another draw."

"Yeah."

"So pick a card, my friend. Take the pressure off yourself. Let chance judge you and decide where you will go. Pick a card, and I'll do the same."

Jonathan looked at his friends, but they seemed to be made of stone. He hated having to decide. Who was he to cast judgment on himself? Who was he to allow the impossible to happen? Wasn't he just a man; a stupid, selfish little man who deserved no place at the table?

"No!" screamed Jonathan, as he pushed the cards to the floor. "I won't let this happen again. I will not play your games any longer."

He turned towards MacLoughlin, snatched up his stick, and snapped it in two over his knee.

"No more. I decide where I go and what I learn. I choose to right my wrongs. And I choose to forgive myself. I'm going to Earth, pass or no."

MacLoughlin looked at the men at the head of the table and smiled. "You were right about him," he said. "You were right all along."

MacLoughlin mended his stick with a clap and walked to Jonathan. He hugged him tightly and whispered words of admiration in his ear.

"Have a good trip, my friend. You've more than earned it. Oh yes, and remember to take that brother of yours. Brothers belong together."

Jonathan walked to the door, excited at the thought of saving his father. He paused slightly, produced a clipboard from the air, and tossed it to Grimis.

"Hold down the fort while I'm gone."

Grimis smiled at the man he had discovered, then watched him vanish. "Will do, my friend," he murmured. "Will do."

* * *

Jonathan and Windy appeared at the entrance to the hospital. They passed the busy nursing staff and climbed four flights to their father's room. They were about to enter when a familiar voice surprised them. They paused to eavesdrop.

"This is Samantha, Dad. We're getting married. I sorry you and Mom couldn't meet her. She's a helluva girl. I know you'd love her. Almost as stubborn as you."

He tried to laugh, but the redness about his eyes was too much for him. He needed to say something before he went about his new life. He needed to say it in front of his bride-to-be.

The brothers crept closer and watched Sam stroke his father's head.

"I'm sorry, Dad. I'm sorry for wanting to hurt you and for forcing my brothers to think the same. I'm sorry for chasing money I didn't deserve, for blaming you. I'm so damn sorry."

Sam cried. For the first time since boyhood, he cried and meant the tears.

The brothers entered as spirits might and called to him. He turned, unafraid, almost expecting their arrival. He held Samantha close and introduced them. She was startled at first, but so much had happened that night. Little seemed impossible anymore.

"How have you been, Sam?" asked Jonathan.

"Better. Not all the way yet, but I'm getting there. What about you?"

"It's been quite a ride, I can tell you that much. But don't fear it. Just be thankful that you found your way and can go about . . ."

"Living?" Sam guessed.

"Yeah."

"That's what MacLoughlin said."

"He's quite a character."

Sam looked at Windy and felt a pain in his chest.

"I'm sorry. I really thought you wanted me to."

"I know," said Windy. "Maybe I did. I would have passed anyway. You just helped me along, as always. There's nothing to forgive."

Samantha hugged each in turn, then gave them a moment alone. The boys gathered around their father and spoke of happy times. There were more than they had realized. Amazing what an open heart can recall.

"We've decided to turn off the machines," said Sam. "It turns out it was easier than we thought. It'll be done before the week is out."

"So all this was for nothing?" asked Windy.

"I wouldn't say that," said Sam. "Look how far the oversight took us."

"True."

"What about the money?" asked Jonathan.

"Nothing has changed. I'll keep my share and donate the rest."

"To who?"

"Does it matter?"

"No, I guess it doesn't. Good move, Sam. I'm proud of you."

The brothers talked for an hour or so. High school, first dates, Mom's Sunday spaghetti sauce. They discovered a lot of things about the family they had. And though they missed it, they knew that someday, in some corner of the After-Earth, they'd be reunited. The warm thought guided Jonathan and Windy back to their rightful home.

EPILOGUE

Two Years Later

Sam stood staring through a slowly spinning mobile at a framed photo of him and his brothers. They were kids of about eight, dressed for Halloween. Windy a cowboy, Jonathan a Yankee, Sam a magician. He smiled at his boyish grin. Even then, it seemed, devious thoughts had roamed through his mind.

To the left of the photo hung the yellowed scrap of paper he'd received at Jonathan's wake. He remembered the old woman's face when he'd carelessly crumpled it and stuffed it in his pants without a glance. He was sorry for the frown he'd caused. If only she could see the poem in the frame he'd chosen. She'd be happy to know that he'd read it a hundred times and the truth of it meant the world to him.

Sam read the title in a whisper and repeated it in his mind like a mantra: "Family Is."

He looked down at his sleeping son and smiled. What an amazing concept for a child to grasp.

"You had some set of uncles, Jonny," said Sam to his son. "Some set."

Samantha entered and pushed her full belly against her husband's back. She covered his eyes and playfully pecked him on the cheek.

"I've got news," she said.

"The doctor?"

"Yup."

"Well, what'd he say?"

"You'll never guess."

"What?"

"Twins."

"You're kidding?"

"Nope."

"My God."

"There's more."

"What?"

"Guess."

"Come on."

"Boys."

"Really?"

"Yup."

"I can't believe it," he said.

"I know. Spooky, huh? Is someone trying to tell us something or what?"

"Maybe they are."

"So maybe we should listen this time around."

"How do you mean?"

"I mean picking names won't be a problem."

"Not . . ."

"Yes. What else could we choose?"

"But . . . Sam and Windy?"

"I think it's a great idea."

"Talk about your second chances."

He rubbed her belly and said hello to his unborn sons. Fear approached: mistakes past, unlucky namesakes, sins and regrets and failures beyond measure. Then he looked into her eyes and the fear ran like a puppy from the thunder.

There would be mistakes and sins, for sure, but they'd be little ones.

Family is.

About the Author

Tim Toterhi is a blue-jeans kind of guy. He likes rainy nights, top down days, and sipping good wine with cool people. He believes in soul mates, sad songs, and learning through the lifetimes. He lives in North Carolina with his wife, Melissa and daughter, Vienna. He is currently working on his fifth novel. To learn more, visit www.timtoterhi.com.

Fiction by Tim Toterhi

Lunches With Larry

God and a nuclear fuel broker meet in a sports bar to discuss women, work, and other life mysteries... What sounds like the start of a classic political joke, is actually the beginning of a thought-provoking philosophical adventure. Set against the scandalous decline of the  largest, privately-held business empire in the nuclear brokerage industry, Lunches With Larry follows a young, romantically-challenged, business misfit on his crusade to find true love, lasting friendship, and the answer to the oldest of questions.

If you've ever felt confused, lost or all alone in a world you can't quite figure out; if you've ever thrown up your hands in frustration and shouted, "I just don't understand anything anymore," pull up chair, settle in with a spot of tea, and have a look. You may find something you've never lost and loose something you've never needed.

Two Minutes Too Late

We've all been there – missed the boat, missed the point, missed the chance at that something or someone special now long gone. We ache for a do over knowing full well if the wish were

granted it would forever change the person we've become. Two Minutes Two Late is a collection of stories detailing the missteps of a hapless romantic. From career blunders and criminal exploits to dating debacles to goodbyes unsaid, it reminds us that while follies happen the future is unwritten and ours to explore.

The Amazing and Somewhat Sarcastic Tad
This is a largely ridiculous coming of age adventure book set in the 1980's. It's sure to make you chuckle and aggravate any idly standing authority figures. That said it's pretty whacky so I apologize in advance for any counseling you may require after reading this work.

So here's the gist: Six Florida-based buddies struggle to maintain their youthful idealism as they travel to New York to stop a local mob boss from blackmailing their friend. During their quest they are guided by a talking tree; a partially invisible spirit-like substance; a hyper-galactic, Bee-ben-bobble playing number stealer; the evil corporate Zukes, and a semi-superhero called Barley Man. After navigating a series of moral dilemmas they stand ready to fight for life, love, and a big bucket of cash.

A special note for "old" people:
Sometimes parents forget to take their children seriously. Whether it be their emotional stability, their ideas on spirituality, or even something as simple as their tastes in music; somehow, some way, many kids get the feeling that

you're just shrugging them off. Sad really. Perhaps we should enhance the dialogue. After all, kids have so much to say, and so much to ask.

So chill out already. Sure the book contains some off-color humor and a few whacky philosophies, but hey look on the bright side, your kid is literate. Way to go parent people! Besides, how badly can it warp their brains? I think the Internet has that covered. Loosen the reigns. Let them dream a little. Who knows, you might decide to join them.

Nonfiction by Tim Toterhi

Defend Yourself: Developing a Personal Safety Strategy

Note: Fifty percent of the author's profits resulting from the sale of Defend Yourself will be donated to RAINN. (www.rainn.org)

While most books in this category limit themselves to citing statistical data, describing case histories, or displaying various self-defense techniques, Defend Yourself! covers the entire issue in a clear, concise, workbook format. Instead of simply skimming chapters, the reader is encouraged to actively participate in the exercises within each lesson.

The book describes the most up-to-date prevention, empowerment, communication, and self-defense methods. In addition, the physical techniques are complemented by an in-depth analysis of potential attackers including a description of each offender type and the various modus operandi employed.

Each lesson concludes with a summary of the main points and a series of questions and exercises that will assist the reader in developing a Personal Safety Strategy. In addition, the Afterward contains a follow-up plan to help the reader keep her skills current. This is critical because a safety strategy is only useful if it is consistently used and continuously improved.

Stay safe and if you are in an abusive relationship, seek help. It's out there. You're stronger than you think!